"In this outstanding novel, Ed Davis takes a deep, dark look at the sometimes fatal wounds that separate parent from child, husband from wife, and body from soul. In setting hard-core religion against hard-core rock & roll, he demonstrates that the line between death and redemption can be a fine one, indeed. I loved this book."

Clint McCown, author of *The Member-Guest*, *War Memorials*, *The Weatherman*, and *Haints*

"Is Israel Jones a nearly mythic figure come to redeem us? Sure. But he's also a fellow who respects an art form born of anger and woe and desperate times. His story obliges us to look back even as we drift farther and farther from the promises we once upon a time made.

I love this book, not least for the zillion writers and religious thinkers I find in it, among them Dickens, Melville, Jonathan Edwards, Increase Mather, Jimmy Swaggart, and Walker Percy. The plot is straight out of *On the Road* with the same moral risk and ambiguities and the prose is rich."

Lee K. Abbott, author of *Dreams of Distant Lives*, *Strangers in Paradise*, and *Love is the Crooked Thing*

"*The Psalms of Israel Jones* is a raucous yet spiritual journey where religion and rock 'n' roll duke it out in the hearts and minds of a father and son trying to find new identities, or to reclaim the identities they've lost. You might think you know how religion and rock n' roll are connected, but Ed Davis tells a unique story here that's going to spin those connections into their own funky dance full of moves you've never seen before. It's a rollicking read with a great big heart."

Jim Daniels, author of *Eight Mile High* and *Birth Marks*

"From the opening power chord to the feedback echoes that keep crashing through the mind after the last sentence, this novel is a rock testament to the power of music and the Word. Tight as a spring coiled to release and generous as an open hand, this is a book for fathers and sons, lovers, losers, doubters and believers–in short, for us all."

Valerie Nieman, author of *Blood Clay* and *Fidelities*

"An excellent, lively read."

William J. Cobb, author of *The Bird Saviors* and
The Lousy Adult

"If you've ever wondered how the transport of searching, Bob Dylan-esque rock and roll differs or is similar to what religion aspires to, this novel of healing through faith and music is for you. It's also at heart a raw and absorbing father-son combat. Just imagine Abraham as the lead singer of an edgy Appalachian band and Isaac the admiring, angry, terrified son, with his very own knife, standing in the wings."

Allan Appel, author of *High Holiday Sutra* and
The Hebrew Tutor of Bel Air

"*The Psalms of Israel Jones* takes us on a wild ride—from snake handling holy rollers in a West Virginia chapel, to sleazy roadhouses in Ohio, Kentucky, and North Carolina, pursued by Furies, a self-destructive tribe of Israel's fans. A particularly American blend of religion and rock & roll infuses the book with lyricism and rage on the road to the protagonist's salvation."

Deborah Clearman, author of *Todos Santos*

"*The Psalms of Israel Jones* travels to the universal intersection of personal and cultural legacy, both of which have wounds that fester up through the blood of offspring. Music and performance become rituals of redemption for father, son, and a host of interesting, flawed, and interconnected characters that illuminate the deepest sense of human conflict in juxtaposition to the urgent desire for a Heavenly boon."

J. Frederick Arment, author of *Backbeat: A Novel of Physics*,
The Elements of Peace, and *The Economics of Peace*

"This tightly woven novel, full of surprising reversals and sudden drops into new layers of understanding, carries the passions of Appalachia in its bones."

Susan Streeter Carpenter is the author of *Riders on the Storm*

"Reading Ed Davis's elegant prose is a little like listening to a Bob Dylan album: it's nearly impossible to choose a favorite line. Between the tears and the laughs is a moving story of two men seeking to understand the world and to be understood themselves. That's the heart of songwriting, and storytelling. With *The Psalms of Israel Jones*, Davis contributes to this greater understanding of ourselves and our world with a masterpiece that hits all the right notes."

Sheila M. Trask, *ForeWord Reviews*

THE PSALMS
OF ISRAEL JONES

A NOVEL

ED DAVIS

VANDALIA PRESS
MORGANTOWN
2014

Vandalia Press / An imprint of West Virginia University Press

Copyright 2014 Ed Davis

First edition published 2014 by Vandalia Press

21 20 19 18 17 16 15 14   1 2 3 4 5 6 7 8 9

ISBN:

PB: 978-1-940425-13-9

EPUB: 978-1-940425-14-6

PDF: 978-1-940425-15-3

Library of Congress Cataloging-in-Publication Data:

Davis, Ed, 1951-

The psalms of Israel Jones : a novel / Ed Davis.

   pages   cm

ISBN 978-1-940425-13-9 (paperback) -- ISBN 978-1-940425-14-6 (epub) --
ISBN 978-1-940425-15-3 (pdf)

1. Fathers and sons--Fiction. 2. Rock musicians--Fiction. 3. Cults--Fiction.

4. Clergy--Fiction. 5. Reconciliation--Fiction. 6. Redemption--Fiction.

7. Psychological fiction. 8. Domestic fiction. I. Title.

PS3604.A956853P73 2014

813'.6--dc23

2014020732

Cover design by Michel Vrana / Black Eye Design.

Cover illustration by Nick Craine.

Book design and art direction by Than Saffel / WVU Press.

For Viki:
My best, most loving reader

"A song is like a dream, and you try to make it come true. They're like strange countries that you have to enter."

—Bob Dylan, *Chronicles*

"Rock and roll is . . . like wind, rain, fire—it's elemental. . . . Rock and roll is fire, man, FIRE."

—David Briggs, from
Shakey: Neil Young's Biography

"He that findeth his life shall lose it: and he that loseth his life for my sake shall find it."

—Matthew 10:39

Chapter One

I STAND MESMERIZED BY the cacophony of sound and color. The room, as large as a dancehall, is alive with blazing neon and electric guitar. At first I think we've stepped inside a roadhouse circa 1958 with a rockabilly band in full swing, until I see the hand-lettered sign at the front: *No bad langage. No woman in pants. No long hair.*

We aren't in a rowdy nightclub where a pimply-faced Jerry Lee is wailing; we are in church: Whitechapel Church of Lindsey, West Virginia, to be exact, and it's 2005. But before I can fully savor the first flush of recognition, I see, lifted high above the whirlwind crowd, shimmering obscenely like a naked breast at communion, a tight coil. The sound I make is thankfully absorbed into the din surrounding me. A man holds a large snake in his palm.

No need to fear being forced to the front where the serpents are. I know, according to the documentary I'd seen in seminary, that there are many other snakes, that they are kept in wooden cages with chicken wire up front until the right moment, when the Holy Spirit dictates. I also know they use rattlers or, failing that, copperheads; that before us lies a great mystery as old as time, as universal as pain; and that it does not require my belief to work its wonders. When someone pats my arm, I turn and see Murphy sitting in the back pew against the wall. Dad sits beside him, his gnarled hands loosely clasped before him, the veritable picture of unhip humility.

What in the world are a rock legend, his lapsed-pastor son, and his alcoholic manager seeking here? But it will do no good to ask. My father doesn't answer questions; he takes hostages.

"We'll just watch," Murphy shouts near my ear.

I sit down and face forward. I've gone from a crowded, diesel-reeking bus to a snake-handling church in under an hour. Am I rolling toward Nineveh or heading back inside the whale's belly? (The latter, I figure, strangely calm.)

The music, I now see, pours from the hands of a teenaged boy sitting on an ancient tube amplifier that once might've belonged to Chuck Berry. The kid's old Les Paul sounds good as he fingers non-stop lead riffs. No chords, no discernible melody, just continuous sound. I have to laugh. Maybe that's all he knows. But it is enough, along with the tambourine, flailed by a tight-permed, grey-haired grandmother moving in rhythm (not dancing, no!) with the others up near the front.

Every now and then the sea of bodies parts, and I glimpse a man holding a snake on his palms, his sweaty brow furrowed in concentration, and I can't help wondering what he is seeing and feeling. Judging by his closed eyes, sweating forehead, and swaying body, it is the opposite of fear. (And what is that? Love?) He handles the treasure in his hand so gently, making me imagine those coal-seamed hands on his wife or children, hopefully just as tender. Then up fly both arms as he holds his offering aloft. To God? Or to his fellows? "See: I am this moment without sin." To be bitten—and people are, but not as often as you'd think—means taking your eyes off the savior, or worse, some secret sin now bared before all. And the pain of public humiliation probably dulls, even annihilates, the pain of the bite, which a preacher on the video claimed was like a thousand toothaches.

I lapse into a daze that carries some part of me—my soul?—to the front of the church. At the same time I know I'm dreaming, it's intensely real. The walls, the wailing, stomping, suffocating mob surrounding me fall away; even the enveloping night, suffocating, too, in its vile darkness—all fall away and I enter a waking vision . . .

I bend, open my palms, and somehow the serpent is in my hand. I do not clearly see the instant when flesh and scales meld. (The Lord takes care of that—otherwise it could be too terrible to bear.) Once I feel the steely weight of living chain in my hands, obedience is complete. I am the boy with his fingers gritting against strings; the preacher striking the anvil air with his words; the children clapping in their pews; the old woman beating the tambourine against her hip. We are all part and parcel of the same body. For, once my arms are aloft, I look around me at the swirl, see sweat purling on the end of a young man's nose, scent the thickness of menstruating females, hear the roar of blood in my head, though I'm calm as a babe in Mama's arms. The creature in my hands is of God, therefore is God.

As if I've been underwater, my dreaming mind breaks the surface, I'm back inside my body at the rear of the church, my hands are empty, and I hear the words they are singing:

"If you don't want it, give it to me."

Grotesque. Beyond bizarre. Yet somehow as ordinary as any Christian's belief in miracles.

"If you don't want it . . ."

I glance at Murphy, staring straight ahead. Dad's manager tolerates this as he does all of my father's eccentricities; it's an experience, like his boss's awful concerts, to be endured. Back at the motel, after Dad's show later tonight, there'll be time for him to erase visions of snake-waving ecstatics with a quart or so of bourbon before bed. He looks as bored as a kindergartner watching porn.

* * *

Less than two hours ago, I'd met Murphy at the auditorium's back door. It had taken eight hours from New Prestonburg, Ohio, to Charleston, West Virginia, on the bus—and I had the bad luck to sit next to a gum-chewing cell phone addict.

The Whale was parked behind the auditorium. Good thing Murphy prepared me. No longer blue, the retooled Greyhound has been painted dull beige. It mostly fools media, if not fans. If I hadn't been so tense, I would've laughed at the block lettering: *Senior Tours: See American Historical Sites.* I wasn't about to barge on board—it's been my plan, since getting the phone call, to observe unobserved.

Beside the auditorium door my father would soon walk through leaned Gunnar Oesterreich. I grinned at the appearance of the big German kid (now a man) Dad adopted as his personal bodyguard back in '91: a foreign exchange student who'd defected, first, from his sponsoring family, then from his native country, for reasons never clear to me.

Gunnar is Dad's doppelgänger, whose entire spoken word stock consists of one-word sentences: Stop. Come. No. Though he hadn't laid eyes on me in four years, the German nodded solemnly and summoned Murphy to my side within moments.

When the manager emerged from darkness, he was grinning his satanic smile. His olive face looked like the cracked leather of a suitcase that had lain in an attic for decades. As usual, he reeked of alcohol and tobacco.

"Good to see you, Skip. I mean, Reverend."

"You too." I hadn't expected to be glad to see the alcoholic most responsible for my dad's departure from any semblance of reality: Murphy Angus Kelleher—pimp, jester and errand-boy; who provided his boss with so much more than women, drugs, and amusement, who provided him complete freedom from life, period. As an adult, my father hadn't written a check, bought a gift, or shopped for insurance. Murphy was the filter, fence, door, and wall against distractions, enabling him to do all he'd ever wanted to do—or at least all he'd ever done—which was write, record, and sing songs.

Murphy wrung my hand, and his felt warm and rough. "Does he know I'm here?" I said.

He shook his head.

"Is it drugs?"

Another solemn shake. "Since the Bigger One, nada. No drugs." He snorted. "Not even cigarettes."

He smiled, proud daddy of a precocious six-year-old. After Dad's first heart attack in 'or, dubbed the Big One (Dad named everything), until the second, two years later, I figured he'd probably abstained from cigarettes, booze, and various controlled substances for a month or two, then gone right back, exceeding his earlier consumption. Resulting of course in the Bigger One. I'd been AWOL for that one.

"You're kidding."

He stuck out his chest, gripped his tarantula belt buckle with his bricklayer's hands. "I'd know."

"Whatever you say, Murph." Before I knew it, I reached out and squeezed his bicep, my pastorly way of solacing men, and though I recognized it as a mistake—you don't touch men like Murphy unless you want to feel their fangs—the aging alcoholic smiled, the corners of his watery, pickled blue eyes furrowing as his face unfolded a little.

"I'll go get him."

And like that, the journey began.

* * *

The inside of Whitechapel Church is now sweltering with over-heated bodies, a Holy Roller mosh pit from the fifties. While the walls ring with the too-loud-by-half guitar assault, the bodies continue to sway and weave together. Before long, I see a grandmotherly woman, her thick glasses blanking out her eyes, holding two coils above her iron-grey hair squeezed into a tight bun. Her mouth twists as she speaks in a language only her savior knows. I am surprised to find myself unafraid, resigned. Though I am not about to feel that power through my hands, I respect their dire need and, especially in my current godless state, envy their faith.

Leaning forward to see if I can discern anything from my father's face, I see the pew where he sat is empty. Arms folded, Murphy stares into the middle distance and shakes his head. "Guess Boss wants *us* to see this."

I stand up so fast it dizzies me. "Let's go."

And I am out the door, Murphy behind me. Outside, the cold is like a punch in the gut. A nearly full moon appears and disappears among shifting clouds. I am furious with my father. This is the man I remember: the teacher-preacher-prophet-prick who makes it abundantly clear who is the moral meridian, the superior consciousness. Well, screw him. Now I have a few credentials too, even if they aren't anything he will ever acknowledge.

I half expect to find him smoking a joint, even though Murphy said my father had quit drugs. Hands pocketed, Dad stands off a ways staring up the hill toward the graveyard, his back toward us, the grim black coat making him look like a pallbearer.

"Whatever it is you wanted us to see, I think we've seen it," I say, louder than I have to. "As for why—"

When he turns toward us, moonglow illuminates the harsh lines carved on his face. His breath ghosts before him.

"She's buried up yonder, you know," he whispers.

"Who?"

"Mama."

I absorb the word that would be a little odd coming from any over-sixty man's mouth, but is incredible coming from his. I try to keep my eyes and face as empty as his.

Does he want me to feel something so that he doesn't have to? *Sorry, Dad, I never knew your mother. She was dead before I was born.* But even after the roller coaster drive on the road from hell, after snakes and now revelation, I soften in spite of myself. I'm almost ready to say something pastoral when his thin lips curl into the tiniest hint of a smile.

"Daddy too."

When I glance at Murphy, he looks down. The man knew—knew and didn't tell me. What now? Am I supposed to ask questions? *Hey, Dad, did growing up in a snake-handling church lead straight to rock and roll?* Looking back at my father, I see the glimmer of grin is gone. He's back to hollow eyed and sunken cheeked. A great weariness has settled onto my shoulders like an oil-black buzzard. I want to be gone from this place. I've seen one too many cemeteries in the last few years.

"I'm ready, if y'all are," I say.

He strides forward to stand so close I can smell him, musty as an attic. When he whispers again, I feel his breath, though his eyes are shadowed. "You can't forget, though you try."

I turn so quickly I nearly stumble. There's nothing but the sound of our shoes crunching gravel as we descend the hill. The moon has been completely eaten by clouds; I smell the snow that should arrive by morning.

* * *

The December night is black as Beelzebub's basement beyond the foggy glass of Murphy's '85 Cadillac, and it has begun to rain. I can barely make out occasional clapboard houses, some lit with Christmas decorations, far below in the valley.

God's country. Yeah, right. Earlier tonight, we left the lights of the capitol far behind, passing chemical plants, lights ablazing, smokestacks belching. What I mostly look at now is the backs of heads, Murphy's mostly bald but Dad's still as full as it was when he sang on the Mall in Washington for MLK.

I am surprised, sitting in the backseat again, to find my head not reeling from all the curves. But my fury has returned, and it cuts through all other sensory data. Hate burns clean. It focuses the mind like a white-hot brand, like orgasm, like live rock when the band is *on.* Not rote and mechanical posturing but the real thing—not play acting but ritual. Eating the body, not the host.

Or stroking the serpent.

I am grateful for the silence in the too-warm car—and, surprisingly, for the feeling of letting go. Maybe it has something to do with the mess I left behind at Suffering Christ Church of Holy Martyrs. The deacons at Holy Mart have frowned on their pastor's wifelessness for the past year (they shudder at the very hint of the D word). And when my soon-to-be-ex-wife's face appears before me in all her pale beauty, I close my eyes tight.

* * *

A nurse had found me making pastoral rounds on the oncology ward that late March afternoon and quietly whispered, "Your wife's been admitted."

Doctor Peters was waiting in the hall. "Congratulations, Reverend. You're a father."

I shook my head. "But Mim's not due till—"

"Your neighbor brought her in. Come see."

When we reached NICU, he pointed out my daughter's tiny body behind the glass in the isolette beside the other preemies, all three pounds of her.

"All those wires and tubes . . ."

"The incubator, plus she's on a ventilator for now. It won't be easy, Reverend, but we have lots of things we can do that we couldn't five years ago."

And as he began his litany, I began to pray—for her, for me, for us. Was my child's risky entry into the world my fault for not wanting her more?

In the end, medical devices and procedures weren't enough. Without an immune system, Catherine's cold became pneumonia. Mim, pale and weak from the Cesarean, was in NICU with her when our daughter breathed her last. The attending nurse said she was worried *Mim's* breath would fail, so loud were her sobs.

I hear them in dreams, though I wasn't there. In what I could've construed as God's biggest joke on me yet, Catherine passed away on Easter Sunday, and I stood in the pulpit preaching while my wife watched our daughter's breath slow, then stop. Biggest day of the year for a preacher, I'd said the night before when I visited my wife, exhausted from worry and all the blood she'd lost. The congregation would be crushed if I had to get a sub, I said. My sermon was woven around poetry readings and special music from the choir—weeks of practice. My trump (though I never spoke it aloud): God will save our child if I do His bidding. Magical—not Christly—thinking.

So I did the gig—just as Dad would've. I might've left drink behind when I joined AA, but I was still drunk. My rock and roll days in flames and tatters, I'd be Graham, King, and Billy Sunday rolled into one. My baby girl died without her father present.

After the funeral, we never mentioned her again and taught others not to. I'd been reading my dad's mind since I was born; my wife's averted eyes, tight mouth, and turnings-away were later chapters from the same book. We never had sex again. How could we, after the giddy joy of creating a child? She knew that, with my daughter barely clinging to life, I'd chosen my work. Now it's been six years. And eight months.

Six years.

Grief broke open the floodgates, and I eventually wrote Dad, telling him everything: my fear of fatherhood, my rage at having it taken away; the loss of sex, then my wife. But my daughter's death came between his father's death and his first heart attack. He had his own mortality to deal with. He never wrote back. Since I simply could not bear the knowledge that my father didn't say a word about my loss, I decided he never received it, that Murphy must've taken one look at the return address and said Boss doesn't need bad news. While taking Step Nine with my sponsor, I "forgave" him.

* * *

I lapse into a stupor as Murphy's lead foot flings us down mountains, inches from guardrails, one hand off the steering wheel gripping his ubiquitous cigarette. The moon reemerges, and I glimpse the gleaming Kanawha River. I am determined for once in my faithless life to truly put myself into the Lord's hands. Within moments, I quit shaking—whether grace or simply the lack of anything else left to lose, I have no idea. I try praying, with no luck, as usual. For the time being, at least, Purgatory seems to be where I belong.

And then, as if reading my mind, and ever-ready to mock me, Dad is singing, his voice curving around a syncopated melody at once new and old as the stars. It's Curtis Mayfield's "People Get Ready," and, just like that, I'm shot back in time. A song synonymous with sweat-slick summer nights locked in hot, beery embrace on some country back road, in garbage-strewn alley or spidery basement (even once in a church attic). Yet sweetly religious too, like so many pop songs written and sung by former choir girls and boys: Aretha, Gladys, Marvin, Sam. Eyes closed to better take in this naked rendering of a song whose power I'd forgotten—only one song of a million sung to bass and drums, played in bar and brothel, high school gym, on radios of parked cars, forever able to bring me to my knees. Snakes and sex, rock and gospel, guilt and grace.

Dad fills the car with this altar call for the lustful and the lost. Murphy, head wreathed in smoke, casts dark glances at Dad, as if the patient might expire before he can get him to the ER. And though I want to join my father, link my voice to his, I stay silent. God—and Dad—sings some songs only once.

Lord, how I miss the stage sometimes. Miss it in my loins, my hands; feel the drought its absence leaves by the dryness of my tongue, the curl of my right hand's fretting fingers, my pounding pulse greedy to release. Miss pouring gasoline onto the roaring fire. Suddenly I remember what I still carry in the inside breast pocket of this suit my wife made me buy.

Reaching into my pocket, I touch smooth, warm metal and relax. The Lee Oskar Major Diatonic harmonica I played on October 5, 1988, at Shakey's in Athens, Ohio: the last note I'd blown in public. I see the place in rock noir: misted in bar smoke, lead guitar man Danny Kirchner and I swap endless licks on the final song

Subterfuge played together: "Last Gasp of Weary Foes." It had to end—the night, the band, our dream—and it did, the way most rockers' dreams do, not with a bang but a whisper. But some nights we had it, and when we did, we gave it back.

I shake my head vigorously to exorcise these devils. I haven't touched fret nor string in seventeen years, though my Fender, Gibson, and a Gretsch Country Gentleman are buried below Christmas decorations in the parsonage attic.

The song has ended. I smile, looking at the back of my dad's head, watching Murphy sneak glances as if at his mail-order bride just off the train, both of us waiting for another song to top that last one (Dad could do it, if anyone could). It is the endless waiting that comes at that Mother of all Concerts, that nerve-torturing ache for the song that, if it comes, on the right night, at the right moment, might save you or damn you, but will leave you as bloody and raw as the night you were born. But by the time we see the towers of DuPont Chemical rising through the sulfurous steam across the moon-gleaming Kanawha, I know that it won't come tonight, if it ever comes at all.

I drop the harp back into my breast pocket and feel its tiny weight against my heart.

Chapter Two

Only fifteen minutes remain till showtime when Murphy pulls the Caddy up to the Coal Palace's back door. He'd floored it as soon as the gold-domed capitol came into view. Being on time hadn't mattered in the old days. I was pleased to see it did now.

"Put it somewhere near the back of the lot and meet me here in a few." Catching himself, Murphy grinned. "If you don't mind, Reverend."

Walking back in wet snow that hasn't begun to stick yet, I'm shocked to find the parking lot only half full and decide to cruise by and scope out Dad's arriving audience. Nose-ringed, purple-haired, midriff-baring millennials stride right alongside grey-haired, tie-dyed boomers who've come to see the legend before he's gone.

"I thought he was dead," a teenager says to his date as he raises his arms to be frisked by the front door. "So many of them are."

As if there's more than one Israel Jones. My father may be a royal pain in the neck, but he's one of a kind.

"I want you stage left," Murphy says when I find him. "That's where he stands now, never in the middle."

"At his age, he's found a new place to stand?"

His eyes narrow with disapproval. "He's a legend, your father."

"My father's a man."

He turns away so suddenly it feels like a slap.

***

The chant begins: *Is*-reel. *Is*-reel.

I peer around the edge of the stage. Although the lights have come down, I can see a few glows here and there, smell the sweet scent of cannabis rising, sparking a small answering glow in my lower abdomen. I smile in spite of myself. If the congregation of Holy Martyrs could only see their slightly greying pastor, poised on the threshold of forty, hiding in the wings at an Israel Jones concert, my *father's* concert. They think my father is dead; until I received that call, he was.

Reaching into my pocket, I feel the harmonica's warm steel. What would Dad do if I suddenly appeared at his right shoulder, stepped in to share the mic, and ripped off a blues bar to make his teeth ache, blood freeze, and bones shake? It makes me giggle out loud, and I'm glad no one hears. I press the silver talisman between my palms, like Superman squeezing a lump of coal into a diamond. Holding it up to my mouth, I breathe and hear the tiniest faint hum. *Awake, o harp and lyre!* I drop it back into my pocket and shake my head to exorcise the memory of coiled serpents on upturned palms, the electric thrill of that guitar-boy's repeating riff. The devil's music in church, naked and bald as a backseat birth. Imagine that.

I'd finished preaching Wednesday night prayer meeting and returned to the office to find my friend Deacon Henry Owens counting the offering, when the phone rang.

"Holy Martyrs, this is Reverend Thomas Johnson," I said, watching Henry's broad back at the table across from my desk. I heard nothing, or rather the nothing that is tense waiting. But all the tension was on the other end—I was calm, even relaxed. My sermon on Jonah's pride had gone well, Jo had not attended (as she said she wouldn't), and not one of the folks whose hands I shook had looked at me as if I had AIDS. They looked relieved I hadn't confessed to anything.

"May I help you?" I said. The same silence, as if something coiled, waiting to spring. I tried again.

"How may I be of service to you?"

"Your father." Female, throaty and low. Heavy smoker, or someone disguising her voice?

"Are you a doctor?" I asked. One of his women, more likely. Before I could conjure the features of any of Dad's many concubines, she spoke in a rush.

"You'd better go to him. He's going off the deep end."

I laughed bitterly. Henry sat up straighter. "He lives on the deep end. Has there been another incident?" That's what they'd called the first heart attack, before they'd known: a cardiac incident.

The person on the other end seemed to ponder. Henry had resumed counting.

"He's exciting them to violence."

I let that hang in the charged air for a second before answering. "Last I heard he's on tour, doing fine." Anytime I got on the Internet, I always checked out his tour schedule.

"You'd better go to him." A breathy whisper. Was she crying?

I'd leaned back in my desk chair. "May I ask to whom I'm speaking?" Watching his back, I was certain now Henry was waiting too.

"A friend."

That was all. When I hung up, Henry resumed counting. Keeping my eyes averted from the deacon's back, I reached inside my desk and found my father's last birthday card: geese on a lake. The cards had started coming in '01—the year of the Big One, the last time I'd seen him—and had come right on time every year since, signed "Dad" with a PS: Murphy's cell phone number. I waited until Henry was gone before punching in the numbers I thought I'd never use.

"Skipper—I mean Reverend—your daddy's acting mighty weird."

I snorted into the phone, not just because he'd used the nickname I hadn't heard in a couple of decades. "Murphy, my father left weird in the lurch around 1973."

"This is different. You gotta see it to believe it."

See my dad after five years of silence? The palm of my hand gripping the receiver was sweating. "Is he doing anything that would incite violence?"

"No more'n usual."

"Where is he?"

"Charleston, West Virginia. He was s'posed to play the Civic Center, but crowds have thinned lately, and it was moved to the Carson Coal Palace."

I closed my eyes. A dump. In the fifties, it had been the site of grand culture in the heart of the Appalachian coalfields, but when I played there with Subterfuge in the seventies, it already smelled of mildew, the seats torn, their stuffing coming out.

I had hospital visits, prayer meeting, blah, blah, blah. But I had no family to tell good-bye, and I could always get some retired pastor to sub for me. (Plus, it would be good to get out of Dodge and let the Joanna debacle die down.)

"When's the gig?"

"Friday night, eight o'clock." Then he hesitated. "Could you arrive by six?"

My turn to hesitate. Two extra hours to stare at each other in silence? As the word "no" formed on my tongue, he rushed on.

"Boss wants to take a little side trip first. Might be something you want to see."

I knew if I started asking questions, I'd never go. Murphy spoke before I could.

"Six sharp at the back door. Look for the bus."

"It's December, Murph. Don't leave me out there waiting."

"We'll be watching for you."

"All right."

The hand that hung up was shaking.

* * *

The memory of that voice—*exciting them to violence*—makes me shiver, though it's hot behind the footlights. Right now, Dad's flock is going crazy. Four figures lurch onstage, wraiths emerging from darkness to the cheers and whistles of the five hundred or so faithful. Three strap on guitars, and the lone black man, shirtless and wearing shades, settles himself behind drums and thumps the bass three times aggressively as if to scatter bad spirits.

Then comes Dad, shambling, head drooping to disguise his height, arms adangle as if useless, paralyzed at his sides, though he had strength enough once to throw me to the ceiling and catch me until Mom, mouth quivering with fear, made him stop—at least in her presence.

My mother: Emily Sky Kryssokos Johnson Jones.

Sometimes I feel like a motherless child
Sometimes I feel naked and wild.
Sometimes I feel like an inch is a mile
And I'd kill for the glimpse of your smile.

Ignoring the audience has always been Dad's hallmark; he's sometimes gone years without saying a word to them, and tonight is no exception as he takes up his battle axe, the same beat-up old black Gibson acoustic he's played since *This Is Israel* in 1961. (Never play the white Stratocaster first—flagship superstition for a fleet of other ill omens and bad karma evolved over almost a half century of performing). He strums E minor and nods at the lead man beside him, who riffs into "Dead Man's Blues," an instrumental so portentous in its minor chords and half-step build to a roaring descent of distortion that it screams suicidal apocalyptic revolution.

It is going to be some night.

The lead man's screaming strings are a squealing semi's brakes; drums and bass are marching doomsday armies. Dad, biding his time, strums his six-string tenderly, its tiny voice lost in the mix. The tails of the black mourning coat he's worn since the Eternal Tour began in '93 hang like limp, dismal crow's wings. When he turns sideways to the crowd (another signature move) and faces my direction, I see he's wearing a black satin shirt buttoned to the neck and gold lamé gambler's vest: Johnny Cash in Goodwill garb. If he sees me hunkered here, he makes no sign.

Good thing Israel Jones is more original than his clothes. But I know they work for him, keep the darkness on the outside, the disguise he finally settled on after trying on and discarding many over the years—there was even a ghastly John Lennonesque white period. Maybe for a while he thought he was Jay Gatsby: self-made, tragic, and very American. But since the seventies, it was too late to die young and leave a beautiful corpse.

Dad mostly stares at the floor, while the band members, not one older than twenty-seven, go through their motions like accountants, eyes on their axes, timing like clockwork, licks assembly line work, pretending Dad isn't there, avoiding the face of furious fate they know can incinerate them in a second. Finally the instrumental ends in a cymbal-smashing din full of guitar flourishes and feedback fireworks. After the tiniest pause, the lead man strums the opening chords to "Tears Torn from Eternity's Eyes" from *Moses on Mount Sinai*, his best seller from '71, and the audience screams approval. Dad staggers to the mike.

At first I think the vocal is merely muddy, but as I listen, I hear all too clearly that Dad is at his mumbling worst. "Gargling marbles," "growling agony," "dying loon" are some of the more complimentary journalistic descriptions of Dad's singing at its most incredibly incomprehensible—but so far I haven't made out a single word as he rocks side to side, bawling away. And this a gorgeous ballad about Mom, about constant regret, unfulfilled promise: the day a man wakes up and sees he's not the man his wife married, and that he never was nor will be. But there are no words, only howling vowels, bitten-off consonants, high-pitched moans and wails as my father lurches behind the mic like a man raging in a language he doesn't speak.

Then it's over, and the crowd goes nuts, the faces of those standing closest to the stage contorted, like begging lepers. Didn't they hear what I just heard? Blasphemy is the only word for what he did to Mom's song. Sacrilege. Is this what the voice on the phone meant? Has my father finally lost his mind completely and become an even worse self-parody than he's been since the Bigger One?

When the screaming and applause finally fade, there is an awkward break. I crane my neck to see what is happening—tuning, consultation over the set list, sound problem? But the bass, lead, and rhythm men are simply waiting, heads bowed.

Then it begins. At first it seems a kind of hum beginning in Dad's nasal cavity and moving deeper into the throat where it vibrates for a time until, as his mouth opens wider, it becomes an ululation that rises and falls. I feel the vibration around my heart, almost as if I am lying on his chest, as I did a lot, according to Mom, my first year, when he'd stayed home with me following his car accident, when he declared he'd tour no more.

My soul goes cold. A dull knife rakes flesh from my lower spine.

If that were all he'd done, if he'd quickly kicked off the next song, it would've been awful but bearable. Lord knows, I wanted him to get on down that cracked blacktop he'd been on all his life, all my life, just get this gig over, with as little fuss as possible. He'd been on the Eternal Tour so long—through death, divorce, debilitation, estrangement, and collapse, financial and physical—that I'd decided he'd croak out here on the road, right in the middle of it, with all of *them* watching, judging, shaking their heads (how I'd hated them, especially when they'd most viciously compared me to him—what had I expected?). I'd given up years ago thinking I could save him—even after I was saved—finally deciding to let the rabble crucify him, if he didn't crucify himself first. I wondered if he weren't perhaps begging for it now.

My eyes fill as my father utters sounds of a man having his flesh flayed. But as it continues, my scorched nerve endings cool to numbness. My arms hang limp, shorn of all strength. My legs lack the muscle to carry me outside. And as my vision clears, I focus on those standing right in front of the stage. They seem silent penitents prepared for baptism, their loose garments wavering in water.

A lanky, bald boy, at least a head taller than the others, appears to be shaving his cheek, head thrown back, golden hoops dangling from his ear, eyes closed. But as I focus more closely, I see dark trails snaking down his neck and upper chest. He is making quick incisions into his hairless face, blood running like water.

Sound goes first—I'm gasping for air. Then the corners of my vision sear, a photograph in a fireplace, corners curling: I see a bathroom, tubful of blood, and white, white flesh. I fall into blessed darkness.

Chapter Three

I've just gotten to bed when I hear a rap on the door. I hop up and throw on my robe. Looking through the peephole, I see it's Murphy. Taking a deep breath, I open the door.

"You doin' all right, Skip?"

I fold my arms around my robe and nod.

He sighs, glances to his right. "With you passin' out and all, I thought I'd better check."

Coming to, I'd found myself staring into what I thought—hoped—might be God's face. But it turned out to be Gunnar's. He got me out to the bus, where I'd slept through the rest of the show.

"Just exhausted," I say. "That bus ride did me in."

I don't care whether he believes me or not. I know Dad didn't, or he wouldn't have taken a room nearby. After checking in, I tried to pray (nobody home); then I digested a voice mail from Henry Owens ("Deacons are meeting tomorrow night about 'the incident'"). After that, I collapsed.

"Can we talk?"

I usher him in with a flourish. Not till he's inside do I recall my irritation about his failure to tell me the significance of Whitechapel Church. But I squelch it; if I play my cards right, maybe he'll explain what the snakes are about.

He flops down on the unused bed, thrusts his long legs and muddy boots at me, and is already uncapping Jack before I slump into the too-hard desk chair at the little table. Watching his bouncing Adam's apple as the slug goes down, I feel the sudden desire for a drink well up in me like lust. It doesn't happen often, and it never lasts more than a few seconds. I try to get a deep breath, but tightness in my chest stops it halfway. I'm not looking forward to what the man has to say, but it will keep my mind off the deacons' meeting tomorrow.

"So," he said. "What do you think?"

"About what?"

He drops his chin to see me better. "About Boss, *Reverend*."

Not *the* boss. Boss. I hated that: short for god. "He seems in fairly good health," I say.

"Yeah, physically."

His joyless laugh becomes a rattling cough like the kind I sometimes hear from one of the elders during my sermon, giving my spine a mortality check.

"Funniest goddamn thing, but you know how he's always had this thing about the devil? Well, last summer we were playing an outdoor gig in Syracuse, New York—gorgeous blue-as-hell sky, Adirondacks a perfect backdrop—when all of a sudden he jumps back, knocks the bass man on his ass, throws off his axe, and runs offstage. Would probably be running still, if Gunnar hadn't caught him."

"Guitar not properly grounded?" I suggest. "Did the mic shock him?"

"Claims he saw the man, Skip."

I manage a slightly deeper breath this time. "Okay, Murphy, who'd he see?"

"Old Scratch hisself, I reckon." His laugh is as high and giddy as a teenage girl's except for the extra phlegm. When Murphy holds the fifth's mouth to his lips, I have never wanted a drink less.

I imagine Satan's forces aligning, spearpoints glinting in reflected firelight from the surrounding pit. I don't really believe in the devil, or in hell, for that matter—this is not something you admit to a conservative Christian congregation—but I try to still believe in the god I'd found at my first Alcoholics Anonymous meeting in 1990, and He so far has not required my literal belief in hell—or heaven, for that matter. He requires service, compassion, and love. Of the three, I am best at the first and working on the second. As for the third . . . (I get a quick image of my wife Mim before she left me, her mouth drawn in a tight line.)

"And that was the beginning?" I say.

He smacks his lips. "Boss got back up there and finished the show, but by the time he got to the bus, that was it. Went in that little room at the back, and by the time we hit the Big Apple, he came out looking like he does now. Like goddamn Buddha."

"You mean he went in the cave a legend and came out a saint?"

Murphy sprays spit and liquor as the laugh erupts from deep down. The coughing afterward is horrible. When he finally tamps it down, he reaches into his shirt pocket, tweezes out his cigarette pack, and shakes one out. Then he glances up at me with rheumy, bloodshot eyes.

"You mind?"

I shake my head. The manager is a puritan when it comes to any drug besides Old Faithful. Like Dad, his obsessions are focused: booze and betting. He's made—and gambled away—millions of my father's money. "So that's when he started howling, after Syracuse?"

Murphy exhales a long column of blue smoke. He sits up straighter, the bottle sloshing beside him. "Don't say nothing to him about it. You weren't gonna, were you?"

He looks so serious, I laugh. "What would I say? 'Hey, Pop, you might fill an arena again if you actually started singing in a language that your audience—that *you yourself*—can actually understand.'"

"Don't fuck with me, Skip. He's fragile as a doobie in a monsoon right now. I don't know what it would do to him if you made a stink, 'cause he don't know he's doin' it."

"*What?*" I lean forward to see if he's putting me on.

He shakes his head sadly. "It just comes over him, the same way it comes over them snake-wavers. They start off in their right minds, thinkin', 'Now I've got a choice about this. I'm a free man. I don't have to pick up a snake tonight. Maybe a good roll in the hay after this little shindig will do it for me.' Snakes, sex, rock and roll, religion: it's all the same."

"I hate that! If sex and drugs and rock and roll are the same as connecting to God, then religion has about as much relevance as . . . table manners." But I hear that voice—*exciting them to violence*—does Dad really not know?

Murphy grins. "I don't know, when that guitar gets gratin' on the spine, adrenaline starts pumpin' like Cuervo through the bloodstream. Next thing you know—*blooey*—you're holdin' a goddamn snake."

"Or screaming like a banshee in front of thousands—okay, hundreds—come to watch the freak show."

His eyes seem to glow red, making me see something wild, treed in the dark. "Don't ever call your daddy a freak. Maybe some things he does is strange, but he ain't no friggin' freak."

"Then what's up with these kids cutting themselves in front of the stage?"

His face clouds. "We picked 'em up around Knoxville coupla weeks ago, and they been with us ever since. After that first show where they did it, I cornered 'em outside and told 'em we ain't the Grateful goddamn Dead. Boss's music is for adults. Last thing we need's Israelheads sellin' bongs and shit in the parkin' lot."

"But why do they cut themselves? Because of what Dad's doing?"

"It ain't his fault!"

"You don't see a connection with Dad's howling?"

We let it hang in the air. If he says yes, then he'll have to act, defy, defend.

"Murphy, those sounds he makes . . ." I let it lie there between us. His eyes, fully in the light, reveal pupils white as eggs crisscrossed by a million red radii. He nods violently, laces his fingers to contain their trembling. "They're the sounds of someone in a great deal of pain."

"But he ain't—that's the hell of it. In ways, he's the healthiest he's ever been."

"Physically."

He opened his hands. "Well, that's somethin', ain't it?"

He raises the bottle, swallows, sighs, and caps the Jack, lets it fall, sloshing, beside him on the bed. "I know Boss's on the edge of a high cliff. The hell of it is, I can't think of a thing to do to keep him from fallin' off. Can you?"

"Stop the cutters."

"He likes 'em."

"*What?*"

"Calls 'em his Pharisees."

We just stare at each other for a long moment before he speaks again. "Listen, Skip, do you think you could . . . talk to your daddy?"

"Have you lost your mind?"

He starts to argue, then lapses silent. Finally: "Maybe it's enough that you're here."

Nothing's ever enough for my father, I want to yell but don't. I've got another bone to pick. "Why didn't you tell me Dad's parents are buried in the cemetery at Whitechapel Church?"

He throws up his hands. "I didn't know, Skip—swear to God. All the times we been there, we saw snakes, heard testimonies. One time a girl 'bout twelve handled. That's it. I had no more ideal his mama and daddy was buried down there than the man in the moon."

I shake my head.

"I can't blame you if you don't believe me. I've given you a thousand reasons to hate my guts."

It was my turn to sigh. "Murphy—"

"You coming to Cincy?"

"Coliseum?" I remember the old days when Dad and his band of gypsies packed Riverfront.

"McGillicuddy's. Near the university. Seats five hundred."

"He's not on the cliff; he's fallen."

"Bus leaves at nine, if you're interested."

Though his face is impassive, I hear the plea in his voice. A couple of days ago, I'd've never believed it, an old Irishman losing his poker face.

"So who's he with these days?" I say.

He shakes his head.

"Come on. Giving up booze and drugs I can maybe fathom— that's going to keep him alive. But *women*?"

"God's truth."

"You mean, if we burst into his room right now, we wouldn't find him with some razor-blade slut?"

Murphy's stare ignites the haze between us. I've shown him at least a pair of jacks. "He sleeps with me; I mean, in the same room. Ever since it happened." He wags his wasted old muzzle side to side, looks at the wall again before rasping. "All curled up on his side, like a little boy."

I laugh, but it wouldn't convince Sunday schoolers. "Best birth control I've ever heard of."

"Been no paternity suits since the eighties," Murphy says, glaring.

"Dad would've been dead a long time ago without you and Gunnar."

"Damn straight."

"You always took care of him." As much of a drunken con man as Murphy is, his devotion to Dad is real. I've gladly ceded the manager any responsibility I might've been tempted to feel before Dad banished me from the tour and sent me home to Mom in '83. Murphy has given his life—for big bucks, which he's famously squandered in all sorts of schemes from real estate to dot-coms—but isn't bailing, now the bottom seems about to fall out.

While Murphy lights his next cigarette from the stub he's holding, I consider. I do owe him. Taking another breath, I lean forward, as if Dad is on his knees in the hallway at the keyhole, listening.

"Someone called me the same day I called you." I let my breath out. "A woman. She warned me Dad's losing it."

His eyes narrow. "Anybody you know?"

I hear the voice in my head: low, sexy. "I don't think so."

"If she calls again, try and get her to talk, find out her name, where she's at, anything."

"Anybody following him right now?"

He snorts, stands up, and stretches. "When ain't they? Goddamn groupies and hangers-on, maniacs, and wannabes. But no, no hardcore stalkers, not in a long time. He's outlived 'em. They're all in jail or dead. And the young 'uns—well, you saw what *they* do. They don't wanna watch the show; they wanna *be* the show."

Another chill. The room is getting pretty crowded with my dad's complicated audience.

"I care about your daddy. I may be the only one."

I take the hit. Where have I been since the Big One? I walked out of his hospital room and didn't look back.

"What about Gunnar? Does he sleep in the room with you two?" I glance toward the wall.

"Naw, he sleeps on the bus." Patting his pocket, he pulls out a bright green cell phone and pats it. "He's right here, but it's you and me, Reverend, gotta see your daddy through this howlin' thing."

"And how do we do that?" If he doesn't leave soon, I'll collapse.

He draws deeply on his cigarette, exhales slowly. His smile is crafty. Doing something about something is Murphy's territory. He's done a lot to people who wanted to get close to my father, but unless things are radically different these days, he's seldom changed Dad's mind, and it drives him crazy—to drink, I could say, though Murphy always claimed it was in his mama's milk. Indeed—she died of cirrhosis in '84.

"Hell, I don't know what your daddy thinks. All I know for sure is what he does."

"He's gone many times . . . to that church?"

"Not in a long time. Used to go every time we played the Civic Center. Been seven, eight years, though."

"You sure you didn't tell him I was coming?"

"Skip, you know Boss just knows things."

"Clairvoyant? Hardly. He'd've probably quit drugs a lot sooner if he'd seen a heart attack coming. And he surely would've told Gunnar to bar the door if he'd known I was coming."

Murphy finally stands stiffly. He takes a step toward the door, then turns back. "I know you hate me, Thom. But don't hate him."

The air between us flames for a moment, then dies in a hail of sparks. I wave my hand weakly. "You and I have had our ups and downs, but we're on the same side."

"Well, at least you're here."

"Yes, I'm here," I say, my voice the one that gives the call to worship, pronounces the benediction, holds aloft the cup containing grape juice turned to Christ's blood.

He cocks his head. "You may be just in time." Three steps and he is gone. The lock clicks gently.

Exciting them to violence. I wonder.

Chapter Four

The bus ride is excruciating. The band plays poker endlessly and consumes cases and cases of beer—but no cigarettes. Signs are everywhere in Dad's cryptic hand: "Here lies the hide of the last SOB who smoked on this bus." I gaze beyond the rain-webbed glass, hunker lower in my seat behind the driver. I try writing—the idea of doing some journalism hits me (an ecclesiastical *Electric Kool-Aid Acid Test?*)—then reading, but so far the Bible on the seat beside me—the Thompson Chain-Reference Red Letter Edition that Mim got me our first Christmas together—remains unopened. Finally I settle for gawking at rain-ruined cornfields and leafless trees on Route 52 along the river. At least it isn't snowing. A blizzard before Christmas is all we need.

Dad keeps to his little closet of a room in back, ostensibly writing. But there hasn't been an album of new material in six or seven years, just rehashed compilations, an album of traditional tunes from the British Isles, and *Greatest Hits, Volume Ten* and *Eleven*. I try to fathom what it must be like to live decades beyond megapopularity, to stand up and sing those ancient chestnuts to greying masses of people who come not to experience cutting-edge art but to gawk at a legend and be reassured that, if Israel Jones still lives and breathes (more or less), they might be immortal too. I'm a bit jealous, I admit. You have to be an *is* before you can become a *been*, and I was and am neither. I'm the "son of"—a great liability in the music biz.

Tracing the golden letters of my name on the book beside me, I think of Dad's old black Bible with pale drink rings on its cover. It was on the table by his bed the day I stalked out of his hospital room. If the signs are to be believed, my father is still "religious," though not in any conventional sense. He went through his famous Born Again period and dragged his audience with him, kicking, screaming, and stomping out of shows demanding their money back— then shrugged it off when it was all over. The Christly mantle—as well as all those songs he wrote then, two albums' worth, that fueled concerts at which he played not one non-gospel tune—simply disappeared between shows in Birmingham, England, and Tempe, Arizona, in the fall of '93. Back were "Black, Battered Highway" and "Whore of Destiny." And, after word quickly spread, huge multigenerational audiences.

Today I have more personal reasons for not reading Psalms (which I'd read every day till the Phone Call). I've been unable to make contact with Henry Owens, who, on principle, doesn't own a cell phone. Not wanting to bother my friend the retired high school English teacher at home, I've been trying to catch him at the church office when he comes in to help Maxine with the newsletter and bulletin, but so far no luck. It was great to hear my secretary's voice.

"I think there are unofficial deacons' meetings going on, Reverend Johnson. Henry had just walked in yesterday when Kenny Branch took him off somewhere. Very hush-hush. They're not talking to me." Max laughed her smoker's laugh. "For some strange reason."

Deacon Branch knows Maxine and I are tight. Despite my fears, I smile. Allegedly Max was a pistol in high school, driving teachers wild with skirts that had to be measured every morning in the principal's office. Voted "Most Likely to Follow in Janis Joplin's Footsteps" (she fronted a local band beginning in ninth grade), she made the dean's list every term at the local community college and shocked everyone by staying in New Pres and working for a *church*. Of all those judging my soul right now, Maxine is the only one I don't mind. I'd seen her through her heartbreak with Barry Diggs, the first man to court her in thirty-five years, and with whom, if she'd married, she'd've never spent a happy day. I know a nonrecovering alcoholic when I see one.

I ask her to tell Henry I called.

"And if I have any uh-oh feelings—"

"Then don't hesitate to let me know."

"Okeydokey."

I am toying with the idea of calling some of the other deacons, but better to let sleeping dogs (I hope) lie. I trust Henry to be the voice of reason in my absence. He's never let me down. I'm trying not to worry.

"Hey, Reverend, mind if I set down?"

Startled out of my reverie, I stare up slack-jawed into the face of the wavy-blond-haired rhythm guitarist.

"Please do."

"Shit, I'm sorry," he says, reaching down to hand me the Thompson. "Oh, damn, pardon my French." He puts his hand over his mouth like a kid caught cussing in church.

"Don't sweat it. I'm not that kind of reverend." *What kind are you?* I wonder, not for the first time, *who doesn't believe in hell or the devil, who isn't totally sure there's an afterlife, and who hasn't been able to pray*—not really—*in months.*

He sits gingerly, as if my Bible were still there, and his butt might wrinkle Genesis. "What basically are you, then?" Sweet sincerity ripples in waves around him. I remember what it was like being on this bus when I was seventeen, tough as a nut outside, all mama's boy mush within, but mostly just stoned.

"I guess I accept the world on the world's terms," I say.

He looks puzzled. "Is that Catholic?"

"AA."

He glances away, out the opposite window. I don't blame him. Before I found the fellowship, the last thing in the world I wanted was somebody preaching that crap.

He lifts his beer to his lips. "You mind?"

"It's a long way to Cincinnati."

"We've never played there. I mean, *I've* never played there. I've only been with Boss for a year."

"A great equal-opportunity employer, isn't he?" I say before I think better of it. "Union-scale pay, health insurance, disability, retirement with stock options." His look of bewilderment almost softens me.

"Actually, Reverend, he's paying me cash. See, I'm sort of on probation, on account, mostly, of the last guitar player who Boss had to fire. Nathan would, like, come late to gigs and stuff." Blondie shakes his head as if he's described a heretic. "You just can't believe somebody'd do that, would you, working for, you know, a man like your father?"

"Beyond belief," I reply. Irony is probably a language as lost on the kid as Urdu. He's part of Dad's endlessly self-renewing fountain of youth: pluck kids loaded with talent from their mama's breast to come make you sound/look young again. Let them do all the heavy lifting while you prowl the stage looking legendary. And howl. But I find myself warming to the boy, against my better judgment. (Maybe he'll come in handy, I think, the angel on my shoulder shaking his head at my cynicism.)

"I'm Thom," I say, offering him a hand.

"Patrick." He offers me five damp fingers.

"By the way," he says, "Nice suit. What kind?"

"Brooks Brothers. It's my preacher uniform." Mim insisted I buy the thing, a navy wool blend—good for weddings as well as funerals, she'd said—way out of my price range ten years ago when I got the call to Holy Mart.

"Yeah, but why're you wearing it now, since this ain't exactly a church?"

I mime astonishment. "You don't think it's right for a rock tour?"

The kid actually blushes. "Well, I mean, you know . . ."

"I'm kidding, Pat. I'm used to being treated as different. I walk into a sickroom or a wake and the laughing stops. *He's* here. Time to get holy."

"I'm sorry, Rev."

"I like it sometimes. Makes me different." From *him*, I don't say. "But you guys"—I waved my hand to include everyone—"don't make me feel different, because you're still doing what you did before I got here."

"That's for damn—dern—sure." He casts a glance over his shoulder, but the only sound now is the slow slap of cards.

"So what's it like, this gig?" I ask genially, now we've bonded.

"Oh man, I love playing with someone you never know what they're gonna do. I mean, Boss never does a song the same way twice. It could even be in a different key, with a totally new rhythm, new chords, verses where choruses used to be, and—"

"Screeches and moans for lyrics."

He nods. "Boss can be a tad bit weird at times," he says quietly.

The kid must think this part of the bus might be bugged (Dad wasn't beyond that in the bad old days), or, God forbid, that Boss's boy will rat him out. "But that's just who he is. Y'know, your dad is still original as all get-out. He's a force of the universe."

I take the deepest breath I can get, which isn't deep enough, because my mind careens into a tirade. *So you don't mind playing behind a has-been rock star whose heart could explode at any moment; who's jerked his loyal fans around throughout his career by baiting them with lyrics that could mean this, could mean that, in the end probably don't mean anything; the same legend who's berated his audiences to get a life, think for themselves, or blow their brains out at concerts where the front row paid a hundred and fifty bucks a head; a man who walked out on his fragile wife and five-year-old son in order to live free as the wind and sow his seed across five continents, leaving at least a score of children and bereft mothers without alimony in his wake?*

I've had too much caffeine; my hands are shaking. I haven't surrendered to self-pity like this since I told Dad off at a rest stop outside Albuquerque in '83, when I quit the Eternal Tour forever (or so I'd thought). As I sink back into the Naugahyde cushion, I regret including the lovely wife—my doomed mom—in my tirade. I'm glad I didn't berate this boy beside me, who only did what I'd done at his age: fallen in love with the world's most seductive quasi religion.

"Look," I say, reaching out to squeeze his arm, "Dad's not God."

His eyebrows lift. "I'll say. He can be pretty naughty."

I almost fall off my seat. *"Naughty?"*

"I mean I really like the way he's working these wacko kids who show up to cut themselves and sh—stuff. Heck, maybe they'll even git neckid tonight."

I look back out the window. We are apparently still on the outskirts of hell, the huge cones of a nuke plant passing us beside blasted burnt fields some farmer recently torched.

"Your daddy teach you to play?" he asks.

I try for Murphy's grin. "How did you know?"

"Oh, *man*"—he punched my arm hard—"I got the Subs' album. Great sh—stuff. Bet you learned everything you needed to know right at the foot of the master."

I can't tell him the truth—not in the face of that wide-open, innocent grin of his. After all, God has already tweaked me good for going off about Dad's other sins, even if only inside my head.

"He was a mighty tough taskmaster, Patrick."

His eyes glaze. *Oh, please, please,* they say, *toss me some nugget from the treasure trove of His Legendariness.*

"I can tell," he says, "from your CD!"

I cringe. After the drubbing it took from the pens of the critics, comparing me to *HIM* mercilessly, I trashed every copy I'd owned. "Well, I tried to play a little harmonica—"

"Tried! On 'Wounded Knees' you sounded better'n Delbert Mc-Clinton. And you bent notes better'n Howlin' Wolf on 'Trial and Terror.' A lot better'n you played guitar." He hangs his head for a second. "Sorry, man. I mean, in my opinion."

"It's all right. The almighty arbiters of taste at *Rolling Stone* totally agree with you. But my father didn't."

"'Course not. He seen you as a rival. Y'know, the son trying to knock off the old man. He prob'ly didn't take lightly to that."

This time I hardly feel Patrick's shy fist strike my sleeve.

"Man, you were hardheaded to keep on going after that."

He looks so earnest it banishes my anger and shame. For an instant, I hear myself drawing and blowing like the bellows of hell at the back of the bus on the corroded old Hohner I'd found beneath a seat, squeezing, bending, uselessly striving to make music out of air and failing so miserably that *somebody* had to intervene. Somebody like my dad.

"You know, Boss don't hardly blow harp no more."

"What?"

The boy shakes his head sadly. "Maybe he don't have the wind anymore."

I'm shocked I hadn't noticed, but I've been distracted by all the other sounds he's making onstage.

"Anyhow, that's how I come to hear your CD—mandatory listening." He giggles. "Swear to God, that's what he said, 'Mandatory,' you know, in the voice of God. Like those NFL guys have to watch all that film of other teams, we have to listen to your CD." He laughs full-tilt this time. "Glad you only made one!"

I feel light-headed. Dad *liked* my playing! Unbelievable. The boy beside me waxed silent for several seconds. "Maybe *you're* why he quit playing the harp."

"Yeah, right."

"You don't think your dad's proud of you, man? All right, then, explain something."

And before I could implore him not to do whatever shameful act he was about to commit, he was up and gone. Within a few card-slaps he was back, laying a huge binder on top of my Bible. He flopped down, grinning.

"Discovered this one day in the middle of a stack of *Playboys* when I was bored outta my frickin' mind. G'wan. See what your dad thought about you."

I get a quick Polaroid of Mom, twin braids flopping beside her face, urging me to open presents. Birthday, Christmas, she always loved to watch me. But where was Dad when that happened? He's not in the picture at all. I take a big breath and open the book. The first one, black and white, shows me holding the black Stratocaster I got on my tenth birthday. Mom laughs in the background; she said she'd made him wait a decade to give me such a gift, to make sure it was right. For others, a BB gun, perhaps a real .22, or a bike, or even a two-wheeler. For me, my first electric (I'd had a half-sized acoustic since I was old enough to walk). In the photo, I am watching my short, thick fingers fret. Memory jabs me again: I recall Dad behind the camera, and he is smiling.

"Guess that's you as Clapton, Rev."

Patrick's chuckle brings me back. And though I've seen enough, I dutifully thumb through the book, marveling where and how Dad obtained a particular shot—me in the talent show, at my first band's first paid gig, rehearsing with Subterfuge in the studio, on tour at small clubs, me singing, wailing on the harp, smoking, drinking whiskey, grinning goofily, never sober after that first birthday photo. Where'd Dad get all these? He was never there. My mother surely found, saved, clipped, and sent them all to him. He probably had one of his backup sluts assemble the whole shebang for him. At last I close the book with relief, knowing I'll never open it again, knowing it's drawn blood. Before I think better of it, I speak.

"The first time he heard me play harp, he screamed at me. The second time he slapped me so hard my ears rang. And the third time, he ripped it out of my mouth—nearly took out an incisor—and threw it out the bus window."

The bus explodes with laughter. I glance up to see the driver in the rearview lower his guilty eyes and tighten his quivering mouth. They've been listening! Of course: they probably couldn't wait to see my reaction to Boss's ode to nostalgia they've had flung in their faces forever. *Philistines.* Shame flashes.

As my eyes blur, I return to the first page. I need to see the three of us sitting around that oak table where Mom would soon serve up chocolate cake with white icing, my favorite. Dad would pick up a book, and I'd pretend to be lead-picking. (He didn't buy me an amp for another six months. "Why hear bad *loud*?" he said behind his newspaper.)

"Maybe you should set in with us sometime, Thom."

His grin might be sincere or might be a smirk. Humbled by the band's laughter, I'm not inclined to ask. I let my hand drift up to my chest where the harp lies in my shirt pocket, warm as a pistol, behind the cigarette-pack-sized New Testament above my heart.

"Well, nice talking to you, Rev. I'd better put this back in the stack or your old man might kill me."

He removes the binder, uncovering my Bible, the white pages with so much black type a counterpoint to the images I've just seen. The words blur, become notes, and I feel like sleeping for a very long time.

* * *

I never see Dad the whole day. As soon as we pull up to the bar—at least it's in Clifton, near the university—and de-bus, Murphy meets me. He's driven the Caddy behind us, probably smoking sixteen million cigarettes and going through at least a fifth of Jack. He claps me on the back, paying no mind to my tipsy bus-mates staggering to the pavement. It's gotten warmer, isn't even drizzling anymore.

"Let's get some grub before the gig, Skip." By now, I think I can detect the manager's mood by what he calls me. Thom is let's-pretend-to-be-peers. Reverend is ain't-no-way-you're-a-real-preacher, and Skip means he wants to extol wisdom to the kid.

"No load-in to supervise?" I stall, not relishing an hour with the enemy.

"We rent local sound. Way less expensive."

"Sound check?"

He wags his head sadly. "Standards've slipped."

"What about . . . ?" I jerk my thumb backward.

"Boss'll read until the gig starts."

"Psalms?"

"Psalms're for morning. Romans, Corinthians, Ephesians, evening stuff."

I lift my eyebrows. "He used to be mostly Old Testament."

"Boss says Paul's the Christian with the most balls. Come on, Reverend. I know a great Eye-talian place up the block."

At the word Italian, my wife materializes, my wife whom I left behind—or I *thought* I'd left behind—with everything else in New Pres. She now stares at me from across the street inside the tinted glass window of Deep Brew Sea Coffeehouse and Fine Wine Emporium. She nods solemnly, her chin resting on her palm. Her violet lips mime *what were you thinking?* Her eyes spill. I sag against a parking meter.

Murphy has returned to collect me. "Come on, Thom. I don't bite much."

"That's a laugh." Turning, I see him flash his gold tooth. When I look back across the street, she's of course gone.

* * *

By the time we get back to McGillicuddy's around nine, the place is packed. The opener is finishing his set—a local guy, Murphy told me over dinner, who worships Dad and begged to play first.

"Bet he don't think it's such a great idea now," Murphy says, lighting the tenth cigarette he'd smoked since leaving the bus, "opening for a legend."

As we stand in the aisle, the kid finishes an intense acoustic version of "It's Alright, Ma (I'm Only Bleeding)," and the huddled masses begin screaming, "Is-reel, Is-reel." "Tough audience," I shout near Murphy's ear.

"Just drunker'n hell. They'd already let 'em in before the bus docked, so they've been drinkin' for hours. Bar gigs ain't for pussies. But your daddy eats 'em like candy. Likes 'em loose, he says, 'wide open and ready to receive.'"

Has this audience heard him howl or seen the cutters? I wonder but don't ask. Snakes, raving drunks, blood: all in a week's work for Dad.

"You want a table?" Murphy hollers. "I could call the bouncers to knock some heads and get you front and center if you want." He cracks his knuckles.

At dinner he dropped the bombshell on me that Gunnar is gone, "prob'ly on a plane to Berlin as we speak." Last night, the bodyguard told Dad that his mother back in Germany apparently needs emergency surgery if she's to outlast pancreatic cancer another month. "Damnedest thing you ever saw, Skip. They swapped about five sentences of Tonto-talk, Boss had me write a check for ten grand— severance pay, he said—and the Kraut took off—boom, gone—back to Deutschland."

When I suggest replacing Gunnar, Murphy bristles. "I took care o' Boss before the Kraut, and I can take care of 'im now." I bite my tongue before saying how seriously things seem to've gotten out of hand.

* * *

The stage doesn't have wings, so Murphy gets me a stool at the rear in the corner. In the darkness, out of the spots, I'll look like a guitar tech.

"Don't make any sudden movements," he drawls close to my ear. "Don't want Boss confusing you with the Dark 'Un."

I give him my most ministerially disapproving stare.

"Getcha some soda water or somethin' before I get the hell out of here?"

"You're not staying?"

He keeps his gaze level. "Legend ain't good enough. Gotta be the Messiah now. I ain't watchin' it."

I think about reminding him Dad is alone without Gunnar nearby, but I know he'd just grin and say: "But *you're* here, Skip." Besides, I'm distracted by the Messiah comment. Earlier at dinner he'd said the same thing. I'd put down my knife and fork.

"Dad said that he's God?"

Murphy shrugged, lit a cigarette even though he had hardly touched his linguine. "Not exactly. Said something like it was God speaking through him when he does that thing he does."

I didn't remind him that he had claimed earlier that Dad doesn't know he's doing it. "My father, as you know, has never been one to avoid the outrageous, especially if media are lurking."

"Huh-uh. He told me this shit one night before beddy-bye, all seriousness just before he zonked out."

"So he never actually said he's God, but that God speaks through him?"

"Same difference. Still loony."

Then he drifted into an extended rundown on the glaring flaws of the band, personal as well as professional, and I wasn't too surprised to learn that Patrick Stiles, the wavy-haired one with whom I'd schmoozed earlier, had mega-women woes and a crazy mother who, Murphy swore, must've screwed her own son every day till he was twelve, and who occasionally showed up at shows, sending the guitarist into cold sweats.

"Boss has to play all the rhythm guitar when Patrick's mom shows up, if there's to be any. And guess what?" His biggest grin before he smashed his spent cigarette into his half-eaten potato gnocchi. "He's gotten real good."

"I thought you never listened," I said, chewing with decreasing pleasure.

"I said I don't watch. 'Course I listen. Gotta know what the hell the product is I'm marketing."

I was more than ready to leave when Murphy signaled for the check.

* * *

Now I can no longer hear my own thoughts. All I can hear are shouts of *Is-reel* above the banging of beer bottles on tabletops and stomping feet, the noise rocking my bones. I am comforted that Murphy isn't too far away, maybe outside in the alley, listening through a headset, or somewhere above us in the light booth, or hovering over the sound man, suggesting a bit more monitor so Boss can hear how bad he sounds and shape the hell up. Brutus won't stray too far from his Caesar.

The poor kid caught in the spotlight in front of me can't do anything to suit the mob. They're about a chorus away from stoning him when he finally shambles off. I wonder if the Razorblades have gotten in—a perfect venue for them, since they can get up close and personal, but also one where the consequences of their antics could be more costly. At a private club, they can be bounced onto their bleeding ears rather than escorted out the door. On the other hand, they might be tolerated, even enjoyed (I shudder). I'm not going to be ambushed tonight. I am ready. I will allow myself to see only my mother's porcelain face above the porcelain tub. Though I will it away, the melody comes:

Sometimes I feel like your bath has gone cold
Sometimes I feel you're a million years old
Sometimes I feel like your body's been sold
And you're soaked to the bone in your blood.

Suddenly, I am itching to ease off my stool, unpocket my harp, palm that bullet, and squall, smash bricks and mortar to bits with spears of sound, glittering riffs, howling growls. My palms are sweating, my throat constricts, and I am right back where I'd left off at the bitter end of the eighties. Finally, the band comes out. As before, Dad comes last, and the place goes nuts when, after strapping on his Gibson, he lifts his right hand in silent consecration.

I confess my pride. I scream inside: *You'd better love this man who's given you not just his nervous system but* HIS SOUL. *You'd better appreciate it.* But they don't. They can't. Imprisoned in vanity and sin, they project their needs onto their hero to save themselves. But a hero—and my Dad isn't one—can't save you; only Christ can. Oh, I can be righteous when I get going. And I am in tip-top Moses-on-the-mountain mode. Before "Dead Man's Blues" is twelve bars down the road, the Bleeding Boy and Girl Scouts materialize from their corner and stand shimmying before the stage. Reflexively, I pat my pocketful of Psalms right next to the harp. I've foresworn my need to ignite a crowd—but my father? He must know he's the flame beneath tinder. I want these infidels gone, these last gasps of Sodom and Gomorrah. I've reached my own razor's edge, staring into the pit.

Dad is singing now, actually enunciating. And the young ones—vampirish in their chopped, spiky green and purple and blond hair, nose rings and tattoos, vapors and veils—prance and sway, the spotlights illuminating faces agog with ecstasy. All they lack are serpents. Is my father, in truth, inspired by them? Does he even *see* them?

The song ends, and the place erupts like gunfire. I find myself wishing it *were* gunfire, scourging this iniquitous den, myself included, myself especially. Maybe God has put me here to judge, and in His holy name I am judging myself chief among sinners, for I know the names of my sins and commit them anyway. These children are guilty only of forgetting.

After that first song, I lapse into a nearly catatonic state. Dad can be a master of pacing when he pays attention, and tonight he is actually stage-managing, slowing things down with several quiet, acoustic songs—some of the most beautiful from his early days— and, amazingly, he calms the den of lions. The crowd is still rowdy, but not frenzied and ravenous. He threw them a bloody bone, then backed off. The razor rabble drop to the floor, beneath the lights, sunk back into the ooze from which they sprang, awaiting their time to rise again.

Dad is downright mellow, and though the crowd clearly wants blood, they get flesh instead. Dad mixes it up, including upbeat country rockers and sweet ballads. By the time he rasps that they'll take a short break, I'm feeling pretty upbeat. Has he decided to maintain some semblance of sanity after all? I think Murphy has it wrong; Dad knows what he is doing, or is conscious of what he is doing, as conscious as he ever is of doing anything. But *why*? Is he fanning the flames only in order to consume himself? I tear myself away from that thought. Surely he doesn't need to take down his audience—or the most devoted, demented part of it—with him when he goes. *Surely.*

* * *

CHAPTER FOUR   45

Dad shuffles offstage while the band heads to the bar to refuel. *Why don't you just ask him, for a change, what he thinks he's doing?* Before I can talk myself out of it, I decide to try to catch him before he cloisters himself. He's a couple car lengths away and about to take the first step up onto the bus when I holler.

"Can I ask you something?"

He turns, leans his body into the streetlight's glare. His face, ageless now in the hard glow, holds an innocent curiosity, reminding me of Patrick earlier.

He shields his eyes. "That you, son?"

I stand half-shadowed, paralyzed. "Yes, it's me." A heartbeat, distant siren, cars hissing past. I step closer, but not wanting to be too close, I yell across the distance between us. "Do you know what you're doing?" I'm being so ambiguous, I could kick myself.

His chin drops to his chest for a moment before he looks back up, stares straight at me. "It ain't up to me," he finally says.

Something stops me before I say, *Of course it is.*

Thrusting his hands into his pockets, he lowers his head, as if to dodge a blow or a bullet, then steps inside. The door whisks shut.

* * *

When Dad slouches back onstage, I've whipped myself into a frenzy of guilty self-loathing for not telling the legend exactly what I think. *You could stop this now,* I should've hollered, *before somebody gets hurt.* But at the last moment, I lapsed back into little Skipper, the good boy neither seen nor heard. I can only pray I'll have another chance.

From the first song, "Stripped, Whipped, and Hungover in the Waco County Jail," I know—this set, he will take no prisoners.

He blazes through one rocker after another, even covering the Stones' "Hang Fire" and Neil Young's "Like a Hurricane," driving the audience into a frenzy. Strangely, the cutters remain seated on the floor, only occasionally rising to shake a fist, wiggle a bare belly, or sway. Maybe they're zoned out on downers? Maybe the management has spoken to them about public displays of blood?

At last Dad seems to be winding down, as he launches into a lush, lovely arrangement of "The Garden," ostensibly about a fighter in Madison Square Garden, but suggesting Gethsemane with the lines, "I prayed, let me go/even though the willing sacrifice must believe what he cannot see." After the seventh verse, he steps away from the mic to become the diminutive boy folksinger he'd been four decades ago, just a voice, a guitar, and tongue afire. When he unstraps the Gibson, the crowd, thinking the show over, begins to stomp and scream. His back stiffens as his head rolls back on his shoulders, his greying blond mane alabaster in the white spot.

The cry shakes him. His arms come up, tremble, and fall back to his sides while a longer, high moan seizes him, and he begins to move. His legs pump and his heels click on the wood as he does some sort of jittery jig, out of the spotlight now. I can't imagine what his face looks like. The bleeders—I've dubbed them the Furies—are on their feet now, crowded at the edge where I can't clearly see, even though I stand too, staring from my darkness. Then it comes, like an animal with its belly slit, the sound a coyote makes after chewing off its leg in a steel trap, the scream of Jesus when the first nail struck bone.

The spotlight finds them swaying before him. A beautiful latte-colored girl stands a mere twelve or so feet away from my father, her hand outstretched. Though blood gleams like new silver beneath the eyes of the tall, bare-chested boy beside her, the girl's face, chest, and arms are smooth and unmarked. She reaches slim, trembling fingers into the spotlight's glare. They curl, beckon, and importune.

Arms lifted, eyes closed, Dad opens his mouth, head lolling back on his neck, and begins the same tuneless, painful wail I'd heard last night in Charleston. I cover my ears. Then, to my amazement, the girl enters the spot's harsh glow. Dad's arm stretches toward her, where she stands, perfectly still, as small and fragile as a child. His fingers are white as bone; and though I've never seen my father implore anyone, anywhere, for any reason—his fingers tremble and beckon. Time stops. No one moves, no one breathes.

Stepping closer, she reaches toward him and their fingertips touch—I would laugh at such a mirroring of Michelangelo's Sistine Chapel ceiling—Adam touching God—if the scene weren't so holy and inevitable, so ready to erupt in flames. My heart skitters off track for a couple of beats; then, finding its rhythm, it picks up steam, heads uphill, smoke pouring.

It's over in a second; she moves back before someone intrudes to protect the legend, for legends must be protected, always, from intimacy. But that protector isn't me. My own arm is outstretched—not to defend, I realize, but to take some of what's being offered, if there's any left. As the girl melds back into the crowd and time resumes, my arm falls limply to my side. My fingers uncurl, empty.

Chapter Five

I read the article to Murphy at breakfast, and it is a blessing I ate an hour before. I still might throw up.

"'... traveling tent revival, concluding with Jones's altar call, during which the latest generation of Israelites bathe themselves in the new century's version of sixties-style flower power. The Dead had their stoned-out disciples; the latest flavor-of-the-month bands have their head-bashing, teeth-gnashing mosh pits that leave their legions bloodied by combat, but you've never seen anything like this—unspeakably intimate, as, inches from their messiah, an arm's reach away, they fuse their souls with his, and, in so doing, create the ultimate bond between rock prophet and audience. And did I mention they shed their blood for him, nicking themselves till blood drizzles vampirishly down their faces? Absolutely thrilling to watch, as it must be ecstasy to participate in, everything burned away by love.'"

There is more, but my throat is closing. I glance at Murphy, hunched over his plate as he attacks runny egg yolks, a long-ashed cigarette in the hand wielding his fork. Thank God the article doesn't specifically mention the girl and my father touching. For some reason I can't bear it today. My dreams were full of them, and I awoke sweating.

"Burned away by *hate*, more like it," he mutters, and it startles me. Last night I'd been ready to believe my father is as capable of inciting his new disciples to love as to violence, but doubt has settled in again—and jealousy that that girl got a piece of him, the piece I want.

Murphy snorts. "But, nah—these kids love him. What's more, that article will fan the flames. There'll be even more of 'em Saturday night at the coliseum in Louisville, you wait and see." He lowers his eyes, returns to murdering his food, smoke curling around his head. "Best publicity money can't buy. We need it, Skip."

I should've known his take would be about the bottom line. Mine is fear. At some point, touching fingers won't be enough. Their hunger will eventually demand more, a lot more. Though it must be over eighty degrees in Betty Jean's Home Cuisine, I shiver. Despite an hour of attempted prayer last night following the show, and another wasted hour this morning, I am having trouble keeping my mind off Henry's message last night about the deacons' meeting. At least it took my mind off the Deep Brew woman I thought I'd glimpsed before the show, off of Mim.

"So." I fold the paper, playing with the thought of putting it under Dad's door—he prefers, of course, to dine alone in his room, Murphy told me, on dry cereal and soy milk. "I'll bet the coliseum's management will be less tolerant of bleeding teenagers."

"Nah. Easier to get lost in the crowd once you're in." Turning toward the grimy window, Murphy lights a new cigarette from his last one. As I watch, it takes five seconds for his vibrating fingers to make the two ends meet. The sickly sweet scent of bourbon lingers above the table, and I realize the man hasn't yet imbibed enough to tamp down his shakes. After all I'd so far seen—my dad declining into some sort of veggie demagogue, his stature sinking as his audience shrinks and he consciously or unconsciously encourages kids to bleed before him by channeling the sounds of all the demons of hell—the sight of his manager, a man well past sixty, his ugly muzzle grey and egg-dotted, trying to make the ends of two cigarettes meet, makes me the sickest I've so far been. I have to look away. A dirty brown dog is sniffing at a McDonald's bag in the parking lot.

"Your dad wants you to meet him outside at ten thirty," he says as I stand. "Wants you to take him somedamnwhere. Alone." He gulps down his coffee and closes his eyes, holding the cup with both hands, his ancient face—so like that of a ferret or coon—wreathed in smoke. He waves his arm, dangling keys on a chain with a green rabbit's foot. "Caddy's out front."

"You're letting me drive your car?" I can't stifle a grin.

He squints hard, probably not seeing me too clearly. The bourbon has kicked in.

"What Boss wants, Boss gets, right?"

Then I walk away, leaving him with the check too.

* * *

At 10:29, Dad appears in the lobby. Looking up from the Psalm I am reading—*For God alone my soul waits in silence*—I can't believe my eyes. He is wearing a grey pinstriped suit with a neon-red tie. Even though the pants bag at his boots and the arms are too long, my father looks as dapper as a circa-1931 banker come to foreclose on some poor devil's farm.

"It's Murphy's," he mutters. "Do I look like a total fool?"

I suppress a grin. Never in my life have I seen my father in a real suit. "You could almost pass as a civilian."

He's already shambling toward the door, and his gait reminds me of the car wreck he had just before I was born, his "brush with mortality," as the media reported, which had, according to the wise rock sages, more to do with his subsequent five-year exile than having a kid. As always, they were wrong. But they were right that the only lasting legacy of the accident was a slight limp. He is in the Caddy, passenger side, by the time I get my Bible zipped shut and join him.

I turn toward him. "Where to?"

He stares straight ahead. "Church."

I let the word hover like Murphy's ubiquitous smoke, the scent of which rises up inside the car, making my eyes water and throat burn.

"Any particular one?"

"Got directions." Reaching inside his breast pocket, he pulls out a white sheet and hands it to me.

"Snakes?"

Staring ahead in silence, he doesn't answer.

* * *

I drive in silence, past cud-chewing cows, hardscrabble farms, watching pockets of fog rise up every now and then. A heavy cloud cover prevents any sunlight from ungreying the landscape, and it's gotten colder, but there's no snow, nor even rain, in the forecast. Henry Owens's rotund visage appears in my mind. After breakfast, I'd returned to the room, retrieved my phone, and found a new message. The deacons had asked Ron Jenkins, thirty-two year-old assistant pastor from Guiding Light Baptist, to preach in my absence. Furthermore, they were granting me a sabbatical, no period specified, during which I should feel free to pursue my "own interests."

Then the bomb:

"And they want to interview Joanna Strickland, to get her point of view on the . . . incident."

The shoe fell, slapped the black pavement. "But, Reverend, I talked them into letting me do it. It will be just she and I, getting the facts straight."

My mouth was ashes. They were firing me without firing me and plotting an inquisition behind my back. I pressed down on my legs to keep them from shaking.

For I know my transgressions, and my sin is ever before me.

I had successfully resisted the urge to call Maxine and get the scoop. Not yet. Now I let off the gas, pull hard to the right as we round a sharp turn. Peeking, I see Dad's face remains impassive, staring straight ahead. I sigh. Why hasn't Henry's little coup cheered me? Of all the ways they can perform an inquisition, this will be the best for me. Henry is the only advocate I have left at Holy Mart (Maxine's a great ear, but she's powerless). The retired high school English teacher is modest, humble, fair, and tolerant. Conservative, yes (a staunch Republican, I suspect), but he will listen to Jo—and he'll get the truth. Even if they don't believe him, even if they make my "freedom to pursue other interests" permanent, can't I live with that, knowing I've had a fair hearing? Still . . .

Coming to, I see the lone beam of sunlight cut through the cloud and enflame the frosted field on my left, burnishing the dead brown grass.

Ron Jenkins: the name sounds familiar, but . . . now I remember. I heard him pray at a revival once. Tall, blond-crew-cutted, with a pockmarked face, he'd looked as gawky as a third-string basketball player till he'd opened his mouth and displayed the most beautiful baritone I'd ever heard. And the prayer, simple as a child's before bedtime, had moved me. But can he preach like he prays? I doubt it and immediately feel a sword in my gut. *Judge not lest ye be judged.*

I lift my hand at the cow staring at me through the fence. "God be with you," I say aloud. Blushing, I look at Dad.

CHAPTER FIVE   53

"B'lieve this might be it on the right." He points.

I pull into the gravel parking lot at the sign bearing, as the map said it would, the white dove with the stars and stripes in its mouth (the flag added since 9/11, the mapmaker added helpfully).

Broad Branch Church. Services 11:00 a.m.

It is two minutes till eleven. I look at Dad. "Methodist? Presbyterian?"

"Tony's singing."

"Tony *Romeo?*"

Dad nods, grim and pale in his too-big suit. If I didn't know better, I'd say he looks afraid, but Israel Jones never, ever shows fear. He always strides straight into the storm, whether playing raucous rock to a crowd expecting a folksinger with an acoustic guitar strumming ballads, or facing down a mother-to-be suing him for all he's worth. Dad seems, though, finally afraid of something: a little white clapboard church in the wilds of Kentucky, probably without snakes, even. I feel nearly jovial. This is my element. "Then let's go hear Tony sing."

At last he opens the door and gets out.

* * *

An elderly gentleman in a plaid polyester jacket and baggy pants points us to seats on the aisle of the second pew from the rear. Though a few heads turn, I see not a single look of recognition. It stuns me for a second, makes me a little resentful even, that Israel Jones, sinner par excellence, can travel incognito among the anointed of rural religious America. We squeeze ourselves in beside a family with four stair-step children, scrubbed and glowing, all good health and innocence. I smile at the father, who is sporting an open-collared shirt and red suspenders, a brown, curly beard, and blue eyes. He nods and returns his eyes to the front. I am totally at home.

Up front, the elderly pastor, bald, thin, wearing glasses so thick I can barely see eyes behind them, raises his hand in welcome, prays, then sits between two huge poinsettias while the choir rises. All hangs suspended, heaven and earth, waiting. To my left I hear outside the whinny of a red-bellied woodpecker against the foreground of clothes rustling and throat clearing I used to know so well—the lovely-awful anticipatory moment before I stand to walk the three paces to the pulpit and find out whether God will fill my mouth, mind, and heart one more time. Before the edifice crumbled between me and Mim, me and God. Glancing at Dad, I see sweat on his upper lip and receive a quick image of him shuffling out from backstage as he's done ten thousand times to take his place and let music possess him.

"'Even if no salvation should come, I want to be worthy of it every moment.'"

When I read Dad quoting Kafka in *Rolling Stone* after the Big One, I'd seen stars, I'd been so mad. How dare he? It took me back to when Dad began to preach at his concerts after recording a batch of bizarre gospel songs, embarrassing not only himself. When the media called for a comment, I refused. Looking at him now, sitting beside me so frail, I feel heat rise in my cheeks. Why had I assumed his religion was phony? Well, maybe because he'd gone on drinking and "dating" his female singers, at least one of whom turned up pregnant before the Born Again tour was over. I'd taken my dad's conversion as seriously as I did Manson's belief the Beatles talked to him in code.

I squeeze eyes shut, and the heat rises higher till my neck burns. Who am I to know my father's heart? When I open them again, a smiling black man stands towering over the pulpit, dressed in a stunning gold suit that hugs his running back's body like a second skin. Tony Romeo, the only kid Dad ever fired himself (he hated that—but when Tony'd shown up the night after Murphy had fired him, jumped onstage, and started singing with the backup girls, Dad knew the kid would have to hear it from him). Now here is that same Tony, whom Dad had discovered in his own motel room with a hypo sticking out of his arm, nearly dead on a smack highball, whom Dad himself drove to the ER at 4:00 a.m. The only "boy" (what Dad always called him while everyone, even Murphy, cringed) Dad ever indulged to the extent of firing him personally.

The glowing bronze man spreads his arms, pauses three seconds to make certain every eye has him in its crosshairs, every breath is held, cough contained, and then begins to sing.

> *When men revile me, hissing behind hands,*
> *When feet stumble and I tread desert lands,*
> *When I am left with dregs of days*
> *Ashes and blackness, burnt churches, blazing grace . . .*

I shiver, though the radiators along the walls steam. The song's imagery so stark—not your typical hymn. Glancing around, I see all faces are upturned and expectant.

> *I'd known only lightning since my youth,*
> *But longed for the thunder of Mt. Sinai's truth.*
> *Beneath blaring eyes of my father's stone gaze,*
> *My mirage melted, left me terrible grace.*

"My Father's Land"—Dad's song, the one, according to *Rolling Stone*, he always sang last at the Born Again shows. His "altar call," those brilliant pundits dubbed it. I sneak another peek at Dad. Now he sits at attention, eyes alight with the fire he usually reserves for the media, the piercing intensity that loves to pillory fools, put on the pretentiously hip, and blast the righteous out of the water, the look he reserves for those who despoil the temple.

I could not fathom when earthly fathers turned to ash,
When mothers gnashed their teeth
And turned deaf ears to their sons.
Then sanctuary seized my heart like a hand,
I passed, eyes bleeding, into my father's land.

Two heartbeats, then, rising like wind, the choir comes in behind Tony:

My father's land, so vicious with love,
Runs knee-deep with martyrs' blood.
It scourges men with searing blade.
My father's land is the tender brush
Of a babe's lash 'gainst bitter cheek.
I will seek the one who never left me,
Though Him I often sought to flee.
I will seize silver fingers,
And in my life be twice as blessed
As someone who sought only peace and rest.

Tony bows his head. It's over. During his prayer, my mind wanders . . .

* * *

"Give me that!"
Dad tore the joint Tony had passed me two seconds ago out of my mouth, threw it to the pavement, and ground it with his bootheel.

"The hell you think you're doing?"

I'd just smiled, high enough not to care, hoping he'd hit me in front of the musicians. He'd just finished sound check inside the arena, and things must've gone badly. He was in a foul mood.

"Being you." I would've never said it sober—or if we'd been alone. But it was my first month on the tour, and every cell in my miserable, seventeen-year-old, zit-riddled, hormone-raging body missed my mom. Plus, we had an audience. I guess I thought it was cute.

His eyes cut toward the big man beside me. "You give him this?"

"It was going around."

"Not to him." My father's head turned, a cannon on its turret, locking on targets. Most were studying the pavement.

Then he was on Tony like a seizure. It took all of them to pull Dad off, and though it hadn't lasted five seconds, Tony, when he got up, was bleeding from his mouth, nose, and a cut above his eye. Not one roadie spoke to me the rest of the tour. I scored my dope off groupies from then on.

* * *

I come to sometime during the final hymn. If there was a sermon, offertory, communion, or altar call, I missed them. Afterward, I want to go right to the front of the church and greet Tony, but by the time I return the hymnal to its rack on the back of the pew and turn back, Dad is halfway to the door.

* * *

Outside, we wait beside the Caddy. I hope Tony saw us—how can you miss a legend in a too-large suit? The sun stays hidden behind grim December clouds. No stranger to Dad's silences, I watch the parishioners depart, conscious that I am coveting the ancient pastor's simple congregation. His doesn't require the high maintenance my finicky bunch does. At Holy Mart, there seem as many conflicting beliefs about the smallest things—from the brand of grape juice used at communion to Jesus's likely hair color—as there are bodies in my congregation. But I also know I'd never be accepted here—too liberal, though I'm only about three degrees to the left of Jimmy Carter.

"Sorry about your daughter."

I'm stunned dumb for five seconds. "You got my letter?"

Dad nods, looks at his feet. "Miriam all right now?"

I stand up straighter, my back stiff not only from sitting on the pew but the blow he just dealt me. "She's devastated."

"Helluva thing, losing a kid. You'll try again?"

I'm suddenly having an out-of-body, where I'm one of the parishioners watching this touching father-and-son tableau from a few paces off: the older man with his look of grave concern, the son's gaping jaw, eyes like he's looking at his own spilled guts. The younger man speaks; he has to say something, or there's no scene.

"I don't have any idea, Dad, because right now—"

"You better call her. She's too good a woman to lose, Miriam."

Actually, I'm about to say, *I have no clue where she is.* But before I can speak, Tony strides up, gold suit glinting in the stingy light. Six steps away, the big black man's eyes lock onto Dad's. I am certain he hasn't seen me at all (it's possible I've been revised out of the scene); or, if he has, doesn't recognize me as the punk kid who shared a joint with him once.

"Israel."

Then he's clasping my father to his broad chest, eyes closed, rocking him gently, Joseph embracing his long-lost Jacob. And, shock of shocks, Dad is letting him, his long fingers clutching the big man's golden armor, eyes cast downward. If I thought I'd been envious of the pastor, that hardly prepares me for the sudden burst of envy that begins in my belly and embers up into my throat. There is nowhere I can gaze into the departing sea of worshippers without seeing my pitiful image in the mirror of their eyes.

Poor man. Hasn't he ever seen Christians hug? Not Christians, I want to scream. Men with a past they can't ignore/redeem simply by dressing up in suits and pretending songs meant for drug-and-booze-drenched rock concerts are appropriate for church. Righteous? You bet.

At last the two saints part, and Tony stands looking my father up and down.

"Thank you so much for coming, Boss."

"It's 'rage,' Tony," Dad says. "'Blazing rage,' not grace."

"My, my, you look fine." Tony turns to me and winks. "Doesn't he wear this suit well?"

"It's 'in my *death* be twice as blessed,' not '*life*,'" Dad says more loudly.

Now the big black man claps his gaze back on his former employer. The smile stays in place, but his mouth tightens.

"I know, Israel. But I couldn't very well sing 'death' to these folks on a fine morning like this, could I?"

"Saint Paul did. Die to live."

Tony holds the gaze five seconds longer, seeming to search for something in those eyes that have yielded me little enough in the last four decades. *Good luck, Tony.* The big man finally turns to me.

"I'm Anthony Romeo," he says, thrusting a huge hand with a diamond ring at me. We shake.

"I'm Thom, Tony. The son. Remember?"

Tony's mouth gapes open. "Skipper?"

"The song was incredible."

"It is," he says, glancing at Dad as if about to be struck. "Those words were forged in the suffering spirit's fire."

"Then get 'em right next time, boy." Dad opens the car door and gets in.

Tony is smiling so hard his facial muscles must be screaming. His eyes are full.

"Thanks so much for inviting us," I say softly. "It means a lot to him, it really does."

He nods, unsmiling now, reaches inside his breast pocket to produce a card that I take. I expect it to say minister, healer, choir director. What it says is attorney-at-law.

"Call me, Skipper, if you ever need me."

He turns and is gone. I know how he feels. *Fired again.*

Chapter Six

Monday morning, Dad approaches me in the lobby where I'm reading the flyer that Maxine laid on my desk a few weeks back. Men's retreat. **TRANSFORMING THE SELF THROUGH NATURAL ALCHEMY**. The font is NASCAR masculine. Below the bold graphic of a sword crossed with a rose appear credentials for three hands-on spirit mentors (shrinks with PhDs and clinical psychology degrees, one in music therapy, whatever that is). Exactly the kind of thing Dad pilloried following his born-again period in songs like "Mourning for Skin" and "Emotionally Incested by Jesters Macabre."

He walks over and stands behind me, reading over my shoulder. I await the derisive snort that used to occur on the bus every time I screwed up the nerve to ask him for something. It doesn't come. Instead, he flops down in the chair across from me.

"You know, a retreat's just what you and me need."

"Yeah?" I say, pretending to take the bait. "Why is that?"

"Good chance to get away from all these distractions, put things in perspective. Get reacquainted. We got six days off. Wanna go?"

His face is rigid as stone. I become cagey too. "Dad, somehow I don't think you're the type to sit on the floor in half lotus while some guru in a white robe tells you—"

"Look at 'em—no robes, just beards and PhDs." He hooks a thumb behind him. "Best thing, *he* won't come."

Incredible. My father seems in earnest. In the old days, I'd've known a punch line loomed, with me the butt of the joke. But there's no one around to laugh at the hapless kid. Stalling, I hold the paper between us and read aloud:

"'Workshop will take place in simple rustic setting away from the world. No phones, pagers, laptops, iPods, or iPads allowed. We need a dozen good men who want to reconnect with their inner lives in a supportive, natural environment. Preregistration required. All major credit cards accepted.'"

I figure he'll lampoon that last sentence, so I offer my best smirk to get the ball rolling. "I suspect they'll take cash too."

He shakes his head. "Aren't you listening? 'Connecting in a natural environment.' We'll be out in the woods. Man, I could use some fresh air."

"*You're* not listening, Dad. Connecting with their *inner lives*. Men might cry before it's over. Might be some break*downs* before there are break*throughs*."

He plucks the flyer from my hand and pretends to study it, brow furrowed, lips pursed. I'm still hoping for the punch line when he looks up suddenly. "You afraid, son?"

It takes every ounce of pastoral restraint to keep my face impassive, though he's thrown down the gauntlet, and he knows it. *Time to see who's the most spiritually evolved.* My voice is barely controlled when I answer.

"Spiritual transformation is what I do for a living, remember?"

Now he's wearing his most irritating gotcha grin. "Me too, son. Maybe they can teach us old dogs some new tricks. If not"—he tosses over his shoulder an invisible rabbit pulled from a hypothetical hat—"we can say we tried. Let's go, what do you say?"

I wait for the tiny fissures to betray his face and voice. Does he think he can win a test of spirit, or is he just yanking my chain?

"You like vegetarian food?" I say, stalling.

"I'll manage," he says brightly. "You?"

"My favorite."

"Then I'll pick up the tab, son. Call it an early Christmas present."

"It's in the middle of the week," I say. "Nobody's going to come."

He shrugs. "They will, if it's important to 'em. But it don't matter. *We'll* be there."

It's time to call his bluff. "Okay. I'm ready for some harmonic convergence if you are."

He lurches to his feet. "It's settled then. We'll leave after lunch."

"Wait a minute. It says preregistration required."

"They'll take us."

"But where is it?" I shout at his retreating back. California, I hope. Taos, New Mexico. *New York City, for God's sake.*

"Twenty miles northeast of Louisville. We'll take the Caddy."

* * *

Temps are in the fifties, and we're encased in a steady downpour. We've been on I-75 for only a few minutes when the first waves rise into my stomach. What are we doing? I know enough from AA to know what could go down at this gig. When the talk turns to feelings, Dad will clam up, storm out, or, worse, crucify everyone there. But wait, I tell myself—that's my old dad; and the only reason *he* would go to a men's retreat would be to mock. I cringe so hard my jaw aches. Dad and Murphy, in their prime, were Kings of Pain. Like evil twins, they twisted the words of anyone with enough guts to engage them in dialogue, much less debate. I'd even seen them turn, like cruel playground punks, on Jodie the Roadie, a wide-open-faced kid with red hair, freckles, and rotten teeth, who had less than half an oar in the water.

"Them ears," Murphy'd say as if Jodie weren't present and blushing to the tips of his elephantine lobes. The kid worshiped the ground my dad puked on. "And that breath." He downed a half tumbler of bourbon. "Knock a buzzard off a green and red shit wagon."

"In the middle of hell," Dad agreed.

"On All Saints' Eve."

And they'd roar, Jodie joining them nervously, till, stifling his strangling cigarette cough, Murphy would punch the boy's arm. "We're talking about *you*, ree-tard."

Then Dad would punch Murphy. "Don't suffer fools, Jodie. Tell this man he's a fool."

Grinning, blushing the color of a tomato, eyes on the floor, he'd mutter, "F-f-f-fool."

Then they'd stroke and pat Jodie as if he weren't the dog they'd just kicked. I hated them with a passion not unlike religious ardor at such moments, though I noticed I could never just get up and leave. It was too much of a relief to sit there and think *it's not me*.

When the semi behind me honks, I snap out of my trance and see I'm doing forty-five. When I floor the accelerator, the Caddy springs forward like a crazed groupie. I look at Dad out of the corner of my eye. Since this morning when he'd proposed this little getaway, I've been on red alert. I still think he might be setting me up, seeing if maybe he can unpastor me. (Maybe *that* was what the snakes were all about: show the boy what *true* religion is all about.) He'd done to me the same thing he'd done to Jodie. Many times.

"Boy wants to play guitar," my father said backstage one day after sound check. I'd had a couple of months to recover from his flinging my harmonica out the window.

"Really?" Murphy smiled, showing his fangs. "Let's hear 'im."

"Says he wants a lesson."

"Well, give 'im one." Though their eyes never met, I felt panicky inside that in-between space I'd inhabited ever since I'd joined the tour—one minute, I'd be with my dad, we'd be getting along; then, suddenly, I was stranded on the other side of a wide, gaping gorge.

"Well," Dad drawled, "these things are strings." He ran his thumb across them. "These are chords." He barred up and down the neck with his index finger.

"There's the hole." Murphy pointed.

"And this is the . . . plectrum." Dad held the pick under my nose so that I smelled his nicotined fingers. My chest was starting to hurt from holding my breath. He sounded mad. What had I done? I was seventeen and a half. I didn't know shit. Just when sweat rolled down my sides, he struck the strings so hard, I couldn't believe he didn't break them all.

"End of lesson. Now you know as much as Neil Young."

And they almost fell off their folding chairs laughing. I slunk off, wondering why they hated me.

* * *

Dad snores, his mouth slack, and I find myself unable to work up the old anger at him. I *was* a spoiled momma's boy, tagging along after him on the tour, needy as any moony-eyed pubescent girl. And no doubt I had driven him crazy with my harmonica "playing" and begging him to teach me guitar. So why aren't I pleased he seems to want us together now?

Maybe Murphy is right: he wants me to witness. And now it's just the two of us. I smile to remember how indignant Murphy had looked when he'd seen us off.

"Retreat?" he hollered after glancing at the flyer. "Fuck retreat. I say full goddamn steam ahead, damn the torpedoes."

Dad held out his hand.

Murphy made some horrible spitting sound, got the car keys out, slammed them into Dad's palm, then turned on his heel and stomped off. "Be at the coliseum by five on Sunday, or you can find another manager."

Dad's face was blank. But it isn't now while he sleeps. He's dreaming—a look of fear makes his mouth tighten, before he releases a sigh that becomes a word: *quiche.* Is he already imagining the vegetarian delights awaiting us at the retreat? The next time I hear it more clearly: "Keesha."

I have to smile. Apparently there *is* a woman Murphy doesn't know about.

I take the next exit.

* * *

The first sign that there might be trouble occurs when we take Buck Road, which quickly turns to gravel. Though the rain's finally ceased, huge puddles are everywhere. I slow way down and say, "Good thing Murphy isn't here to see his precious paint job damaged."

Dad grunts. We'd begun to descend ever since leaving the highway. Now we enter a heavily treed area. I'm just beginning to relax when, coming over a rise, I see water and hit the brakes.

"Creek's in the road," Dad says, his longest sentence so far. "Drive on through."

I glimpse a guy standing on the other side of the water wearing a bright red baseball cap, glasses, and a neat goatee.

"Sure," I say, "and you can buy Murphy a new transmission."

"It's fine," the guy yells, waving. "Parking's over here."

"We come this far," Dad mutters. "We ain't going back."

Easing down the bank, I enter the stream. Shallower than it looks, the clear water doesn't even come to the tops of the tires. Still I grimace, imagining Murphy's apoplectic face if he'd seen it. But for once Dad and I are off his manager's—off the world's—radar. I find myself unable to conjure a single face of anyone in my congregation. Except Joanna Strickland's. *I need you*, she mouths soundlessly. As it dissipates, her image reveals the Deep Brew woman in Cincy that I'd mistaken for Mim, pondering, scrutinizing me, chin in hand. Her cheeks glisten.

* * *

The lodge is one long room with separate kitchen, dining room, and living room with roaring fireplace and dorms in the rear. We are late, but expected, so I know Dad at least called and preregistered, though I wonder what name he gave. Arnold Rickenbacker is a favorite alias, but he likes Devlin L. Baxter a lot too.

"I'm Dan Kress," the baseball-capped, grey-goateed guy says.

"Hello," I say, returning his firm handshake. "One of our therapists?"

"Facilitators," he replies quickly.

Aha. No shrinks and nutcases, only facilitators and facilitated. Fine by me.

"I'm Thom Johnson." It feels good not to put Reverend in front of it—weird but good.

"And your friend?" He says, turning and engulfing Dad's dangling hand between both of his. I could swear the word *friend* is in quotations. Is he on to us already?

"Raphael Lordstrum," Dad rasps, "but you can call me Rafe."

Dan's blue eyes glitter in the firelight. "A pleasure, Rafe." He seems to mean it.

"We'll be getting started after dinner. My colleagues are helping in the kitchen. Come on, and I'll introduce you."

Following our guide, I see shadowy forms occupying chairs and couches pulled up around the fire. *Contact. Communication.* I grin. Dad's in big trouble.

Al Marks is the music guy, and Fred Loftus is the other therapist. And dinner is wonderful, marred only by the forced amiability of all us first-timers with no idea what to expect. I scarf down the stuffed mushrooms, rice pilaf, spinach quiche, and white-chocolate cheesecake and am shocked to see that Dad does too. By the time we park ourselves by the fire facing Dan, Al, and Fred, I feel almost high. Though I did not choose this little soiree, it's growing on me. Dad, though, seems in full body armor; he's gone from grunting to sullen silence. Incredibly, I don't think a single man knows who he is. I figure that'll change soon.

"Welcome, men." It's Al, the youngest of our leaders, bushy-black-bearded with a shit-eating grin. I figure him for a touchy-feely professor who has all the girls in his class swooning and the boys pissed. "How about a round of applause for Mickey and Howard, who prepared that fine meal."

Both men's bald pates blush as we hoot and clap, and I think of Adrian Baldridge, Holy Mart's choir director, who lives with a man no one sees except on the nights of special programs. The congregation knows in their bones who and what Adrian is but denies it entry into their consciousness (much less their conscience). If he doesn't admit it, they don't have to, and the charade can go on. In private, Adrian has told me how much of his soul it has cost him.

During intros over dinner, I learn that most of the men are patients of the two shrinks. Still, I don't feel like an outsider, even with my dad, Godfather of all Outlaws, in tow. To most, it probably looks like we just rode together. In appearance, I'm my mother's son, short and dark rather than tall and blonde.

Al stands before the fire, hands pocketed, grinning away. "Now. If you wanna play, you gotta pay. Each of you is gonna give a three-minute introduction of himself. Right here, where I'm standing." He grins. "And I don't mean *up to* three minutes. You gotta use the whole time. So no sitting down till Dan here"—Dan holds up his pocket watch—"gives you the sign. And I need an answer to the question, 'What are you doing here?'" He pauses to look us over. "Okay, now, no bullshit."

Then he takes three steps and flops down beside Mickey and Howard on the couch. Something in me settles. I flick a quick glance at Dad; he stares straight ahead. I wonder if he still thinks he can handle this.

"I'll start."

A tall and thin guy, thirty-fiveish with a head of brown, curly hair, makes his way to the fiery little stage-circle Al has abandoned.

"I'm Chris Strand. I'm a high school gym and science teacher, married, three kids." His eyes dart like squirrels, cut toward Dan, then back. He is as pale as the coffee mug I hold. "And I'm a sex addict." He gazes just above our heads. "I knew I needed help when I began to have dreams. Of my female students." He swallows hard. "I love kids—they're my life. And I want to keep teaching them. That's why I'm here."

He looks right at Dan, left at Al. Sweat beads on his high forehead. Dad's stare would melt sheet metal, vaporize concrete. *Please let him sit down*, I telepath Al.

"Well, nothing has happened—I mean, almost nothing. But lately when I touch a girl—you know: helping them off the trampoline or something—I wonder if I'll let go." He pauses to wipe his forehead. The top log on the pile hisses like a hundred devils sucking souls to perdition. "I wonder if I'll touch her breast, and for that second before I let go of her hand or shoulder, I see the whole scene as officers handcuff me and lead me away. Then I wake up and my whole life, my family falls down around me like a house of cards."

He looks right at me. I can't even blink.

"And I hear myself say, 'It's worth it.'" He swipes at his eyes, pauses a second before continuing. "Time's not up? Okay. I'm getting better—at least . . . you know, I've been seeing Dan three—no, four—years now, once a week. I don't touch anybody anymore if I can help it. Not even my wife, most of the time."

His grin allows us to laugh. God knows we need it. It feels like an AA meeting on speed.

"I . . . I don't touch my daughter—Mindy's four—though I used to change her diaper, bathe her." He seems to gather himself. "I don't trust myself. Not yet. Maybe someday." He mumbles the last word. "But today I—"

"Time!" Dan shouts, raising his arm.

Air leaves my lungs in a rush. How long have I held my breath? But when I look at Dad at the opposite corner of the oval, I cease breathing again. He is looking off somewhere into the middle distance. I'd give a lot to know what he is seeing. The fire keeps on crackling, consuming, fierce and simmering. I panic a little for the first time. I sit back and manage to keep my eyes off my father.

* * *

Finally it's down to Dad and me. I know better than to ever follow Israel Jones, so I say the Serenity Prayer, stand up, and move to the front.

"My name is Thomas Peter Johnson." I pause two heartbeats.

"And I'm an alcoholic"—a spate of laughter—"and the pastor of Suffering Christ Church of Holy Martyrs in New Prestonburg, Ohio." A log crashes behind me, and when the room brightens, their faces glow with interest, even eagerness. I feel light-headed, nearly giddy. "Worse, I'm accused of being involved with a young woman in my congregation."

Now I have their full attention. So far I haven't looked at Dad—thank God he's on the end.

"That's what my deacons suspect. True, I'm separated from my wife and have been celibate for six years. But I will not take advantage of a twenty-eight-year-old to meet my needs." My gut quiets. It feels like giving a lead to a group of alkies, and my old sponsor Gus Wetherford, dead these last five years, always said, "Coming clean is for *you*, Reverend, not for them." Poised at the edge, I decide I can tell these men anything, anything at all—I close my eyes, step forward, and meet the air.

"I love Joanna Strickland like the daughter I never had. She's a very mature twenty-eight, but the need she fulfills, or fulfilled—I'm on sabbatical now—for me was, *is*, spiritual."

The floor rises, and I nearly lose my footing. I meant to say intellectual.

"We have a lot in common—the same literature, music, heroes—Thomas Merton, Dostoyevsky, Rilke, and Neil Young"—*don't look at Dad!*—"and we're both aliens within my congregation, in this little southeastern Ohio Appalachian town. Somehow she's lived in this tiny burg all her life and grown up with a mind like a sponge and a soul as wide-open as St. Francis's. If I'm in love with her—and I vehemently deny it"—I have them grinning now—"it's with her soul."

I stop. By now, if this were an AA meeting, some old-timer would holler "Keep comin' back," everyone would laugh, and I could get on with how I stumbled into treatment and got sober. But these fourteen men are waiting for the whole truth. My chest is light, my knees weak, and I am totally present. I can't look at my father, although I know perfectly well I am talking straight to him.

"She's an extremely plain person, ordinary looking in every way, but, to me, very beautiful. Like me, she walks into a room and becomes wallpaper. Brown hair and eyes, short, thin. But when Joanna Strickland opens her mouth, out come the most amazing things. Mozart, Goethe, Van Gogh, Rickie Lee Jones, Bessie Smith, Virginia Woolf. More passion than my entire grey congregation, God bless them—and their greyness brings everything she is into stark relief."

They wait in the dark—the fire has died down a bit—so patiently.

"Jo is married to a man who is—forgive me—belligerently ignorant. She came to me about a year ago, swore me to secrecy, and begged me to save her marriage. Joanna needs a million things—emotionally, intellectually, spiritually—that her husband can't provide. But she's told me more than once that not one of those things is worth harming a single hair on her kids' precious towheads. And, knowing that, I still let those evenings continue. I don't want to believe it was my own loneliness; my wife left me—she'd been gone a month when we first started. I convinced myself I was right to encourage Jo to leave her husband someday. Some weeks we met every night until ten, eleven o'clock, even once till midnight while her husband waited at home, kids in bed, counting hours the way he counts the money she spends on every household item."

Surely time is up, but there is no signal.

"But our relationship apparently hasn't remained completely in the study. Twice, Jo came to the parsonage—I'm all alone since my wife left a year ago—after her husband humiliated her. Someone saw her. Now, quite frankly, I don't know if I have a congregation to go home to. I've been cut loose." My anger boils up, and with it, self-righteousness. "But I intend to fight—"

"Time," Dan hollers, and the room tilts as I stumble back to my seat, accepting the hand of the man beside me, or I would've fallen. But there is no time to get my bearings. Dad is shambling up to the fireplace. My hands sweat, and all moisture evaporates from my mouth.

Dad's eyes are fierce. I figure he's mighty pissed at us sniveling crybabies who need thrashing, every single one of us. But he smiles and spreads his hands.

"I haven't been entirely honest with you. My name is not Rafael. No, and I'm not no steeplejack, as I told y'all at dinner. The truth is my name is Lucious Riley—and I'm a pilgrim." He lifts his eyes to the ceiling, and all eyes follow as if his biography's inscribed there. I relax for the first time since we crossed the water. Thank God he isn't going to tell the truth (though, I confess, two-fifths of me wants him to).

"I been a drifter all my life, and a seeker. Traveling salesman, itinerant actor, a carnie, a barker, even a thief. Until I decided to quit." He has their attention, the old scam-master. He jerks a thumb at the center of his chest. "But recently the old blood-thumper started tellin' me stuff—at first, stuff I didn't like, like slow down, quit doin' this or that. I ignored it for awhile, but as some of you probably know, you can't let your engine go without getting its oil changed but for only so long. So I changed. Next thing you know, I got all brand-new blood." When he smacks his palm with his fist, every man jumps. "Took some doin' to convince doctors, but, y'know, pay 'em enough and you can get anything you want. So let's see . . ." Eyes back on the ceiling as he counts on his gnarly fingers. "'Bout this time last year I got me a set of transfusions, yessir, got me some SAE approved, guaranteed for a hundred thou or more. And I'm a new man!"

Everyone sits rigidly, watching the cobra rise from its basket. Dan just watches his watch, which I swear I can hear ticking like a bomb.

"So my problem," Dad continues, "became metaphysical. What do I do with all-new fluid coursin' through these formerly sludge-crusted old tubes?" He waits. Not a rustle, but the embering fire seethes, purrs, hums. "I let it rebuild me from inside. I thought it would. I hoped it would, that, like the Nile flooding out the Fertile Crescent, a new civilization would be reborn inside this dry, dyin' desert of a dude you see before you. And slowly, so painfully, in little fits and starts, stuff started happenin'. Some days I needed to choke it, seems like, to get the durn thing goin', but then, oh, maybe five months after, my river rose, crested, and a warm, gentle flood spread all through me."

His arms rise before him, hover, splayed fingers rippling the air, arms widening apart as the men around me imagine the river spreading horizon to horizon. His arms drop as if shot. "Then I knew I had to hit the road, share the source, seek the Fountain of Truth, share the joy, try out the new me, born again from within this time—with the blood of a Zen Buddhist monk, a washed-up magician, and a postmodern poet (once laureate of a great southern state), making my engine whisper Gregorian chant, along with incantation.

"So how can I do that, 'xactly? Well, as a God-fearin' man, I hoped religion would have the answer. I've read the Good Book all my life, and it makes me crazy a lot of the time, confuses me, makes me mad, even sad. But one thing's for sure. You can't escape two facts. One, judgment. And two, parenthood. Even God had a son."

When he looks straight at me, I stare right back. The last thing I want him to see in that instant of contact is that I give one shit what he thinks of me.

CHAPTER SIX

"And any man with a son knows the sacrifice the Lord made to send His boy down here to be tortured and misbelieved. So if God could go through that—and, folks, the book says we're made in His image, so He must suffer too—then I must go through it too." He takes a deep breath. "I've come here not to try and be God. Believe me, I've been there"—now they laugh for real—"but to—"

"Time!"

Dad bookends his palms, chest-high, bows slowly from the waist, eyes closed, then slips back to his seat. Take it from one who's seen a thousand Israel Jones performances, both on- and offstage: on a ten-point scale, this was an eight and a half.

"Good job, men." Al stands, no longer his smiley self, looking a little shaken. After Dad, maybe they'll rethink the three-minute intros next time. "Now we're all introduced, I think you've earned a break. Fred's got the coffee made in the kitchen. Might be some leftover cheesecake in there as well. Back in ten, all right? All right."

It's a good five seconds before the muscles in my lower back unclench and let me rise on legs wobbly as stilts. Blindly, I make my way to the kitchen. If I ever needed bourbon on the rocks, now is the time, but if there isn't a big crowd, I'll settle for a stiff shot of caffeine. Blessedly, there is no line before the coffeepot.

My right hand shakes as I hold a mug, lifting the carafe with my left, aware of someone standing right behind me. After setting down the pot, I turn, and there's my father, grinning.

"Didn't preacher school beat the need for young snatch out of you?"

That fast, I am seventeen, looking for a rock to hide under. Instead I pick up a stick. "They beat a lot of things out of me, but I've got *you* to thank for the young snatch."

He speaks so low I barely catch it. "Spirit's willin', son, but flesh is weak."

I open my mouth, but, praise God, I'll never know what venom I would've spat, for he turns and walks back into the main room. Lifting the mug to sip, I notice my hands strangely no longer shake, and it's the vilest brew I ever tasted.

Chapter Seven

Everyone waits before the fire, though the silence this time is far from awkward; it's the foxhole feeling of being under serious siege for a long time and emerging bloodied but alive, relieved, and surprised. I feel Joanna leaking back into my brain, no doubt a palliative to recent events. Her image is followed by Mim's, from which I look away. Dan, sitting in half lotus and facing us, raises one hand.

"Now we talk." His eyes laser right and left. "Quakers sit in silence till they sense the spirit urging. We can too. Take your time." He lowers his hand.

So we sit while the fire argues with itself, the high-pitched sputtering hiss refuting a low, flapping moan. *This is crap*, the orange-tipped flames insist. *You don't know that for sure*, the baritone bellows from beneath; *so shut up*.

Dan clears his throat. "Issues, problems, manifestos, jeremiads? Anything's welcome."

"Even anger?"

"Especially anger." Dan looks right at me, eyes bright as ice. I maintain eye contact, but peripherally I'm looking for my old man. It'd be just like him to leave before the showdown.

"Who're you mad at?"

"My father," I hear myself say. The floor yawns wide for a moment, and I feel the sucking darkness, imagine how long the fall could be.

"Come sit here."

I rise, stride over, and kneel beside him.

"Take my hands," he says.

His are warm against my frozen flesh. He and I become the only two people in the room.

"Squeeze," he says. "Show me how much it hurts."

I squeeze hard, worrying I might break bones.

"What do you want to say to me?"

I stare.

"I'm your father," he says.

I'm positive now that he knows exactly who me and my "friend" are. His eyes wait for me to speak.

"You killed my mother." I wait to feel Dad's eyes flay my back. Nothing. "You took me away from her, but I made it back, and that's when you—" My throat clogs.

"Squeeze."

I grip Dan's fingers till I know I must be fusing bone. His face remains impassive.

"Go on, Thom."

I shake my head.

"Go on. I'm right here."

His eyes sparkle. A slight smile. I take a breath.

"She asked me a million questions about you, but I wouldn't tell her a thing. Then she . . ." My vision reddens as if a filter has come between my lens and the light.

"Thomas?"

When I take another deep breath, it spreads upward from the bottom of my lungs to my heart. I feel the muscle pounding, steady, strong. Clamping my eyes closed, I focus on her black hair, high cheekbones, and the tiny radii at the corner of her mouth. She'd gotten so puffy with weight the last year of her life. The image wavers, fades, her face blurring into first Joanna's, then Mim's. I feel the first glimmer of panic.

"Thomas, what happened?"

My mind becomes a pinpoint of light, gradually expanding like a spotlight on a stage.

"She draws a bath, lights candles. The curtains shiver in the breeze—it's June, a storm is coming. I'm sitting in front of the TV, stoned."

"What's going on in the bathroom?"

"I don't know." The room is shrinking. I'm tired, I want to sleep.

"*Squeeze harder*. What do you see?"

I weigh tons, can hardly keep my head up. "Nothing."

"The bathroom," he suggests softly. "Do you go in?"

"It's open—because it's so hot . . ." I feel humidity on my arms. "One hand hangs over the side of the tub, the blood and water up to her chin." I hold tighter, keep my eyes clamped shut so I can't see him. "The bastard killed her."

Someone whishes across the floor. When I open my eyes, I see the couch cushion—blue burlap—positioned between us. Dan's voice is soft, nearly a whisper.

"When I take my hands away, you will strike him. Here." He pats the cushion.

Wax drizzles down the tub's porcelain sides. The curtains waver.

"*Now.*"

* * *

Hours later, I come fully awake, and for a few moments I'm lost in the dark again before remembering where I am. A bed. A cabin. Men's retreat. Then I hear the trebly tinkling. At first I think it's the wind chimes on the front porch. Straining, I lift my head from the pillow of the top bunk where I lie. Above the sound of snoring men, I hear the unmistakable sound of fingerpicking, the top two strings counterpointed by a complementary bass line with its own rhythm.

"Always two lines going at the same time," Dad told me during one of his rare lessons. Listening and watching my dad's hands, I absorbed the give and take between treble and bass, the bass descending the scale like a glugging downhill stream; the treble, insistent as salmon against the current, ascending, falling back, rising again.

I lie back and marvel at the journey so far. Snakes, blades, confession, squeezing fingers, striking blows, and now Dad playing for me in the dark. Oh, yes—he is calling me, as surely as Tom Sawyer yowling beneath Huck's window. And I know he is saying one thing.

Enough bullshit. Time to be gone from this place.

Well, screw him. I'm not through here. In fact, I've just begun.

* * *

A quarter moon illuminates the enclosed porch enough for me to make him out, crouched on a chaise lounge. I sit in the deck chair to his left. With big plops of water falling from the surrounding trees, it feels like early spring, though there's no thrumming from frogs' throats. He begins to strum minor chords with a nice bass lick thrown in every now and then. Was he in the room a few hours ago when I killed him? Or was he down by the creek communing with whatever power Israel Jones calls God?

I will not ask.

He sings, almost a whisper, raising hair on my neck: "O, time does give, time takes a-wa-ay, and time stands still for some."

It's the first of my songs I ever showed him! Where'd he get it?

(Then I recalled singing it, drunk, in the studio and insisting it go on the Subs' CD as an unlisted bonus track.) I'd gathered every scrap of my courage and knocked on the door of his room at the back of the bus. Just the two of us, he'd listened, nodded, and not said a word. Now one eye gleams in moon glow.

> Time stands still for those who live
> as if today, they'll die.
> I will not cry to meet the man
> who's come to take me home.

Amazing. They are not the words of a seventeen-year-old, even one such as I was, starved for a pat on the head. I'd listened to all of Dad's records, tapes, then CDs; he loved old Scottish and Irish ballads with their murders, suicides, faithless husbands, and insane wives. Though he began playing electric rock in the midsixties, his soul was always in the seventeenth century. All a song needed, he said, was simple words sung to three chords about the great mysteries: love, sex, and death. And I'd chosen death for my first song!

> My wife is dead, my fields are spent,
> My children fled and gone.
> As sun lies down to die at last,
> I'll howl like hate at time.

I grimace. At *time*. I wasn't able to say *God*. In Dad's road-ravaged voice, my pitiful attempt at balladry doesn't sound half bad. He stops picking and stares at me.

"Shrink's lucky he didn't get his face broke. You ripped that pillow to shreds, son."

So he had witnessed it. In my mind's eye, I see feathers floating right before I stood up and started shouting with the men. Soon after, we all sat back down, and the long litany of woes began, as man after man voiced his grievances, my mind a huge blank sky. I don't even remember going to bed. Now Dad hunkers forward so I can see his face.

"I never knew you found your momma." It's like a blade beneath my rib cage. "In that bathtub."

"Why should you know? What good would it do you?"

"It's all right to hate me."

It's a wonder the sound I make—a cross between a bark and a laugh—doesn't awaken everyone. "Gee, thanks, Dad. I feel a lot better now."

"But it was her choice. You know that, don't you?"

My hands around his throat will do the job; it will take mere moments.

"You don't think," I say, "you played a role in her . . . choice?"

"Ever'thing did. Me, you, the weather, what she ate that day, what she drank, it all added up: oppressive, temptin'. But to blame somebody's takin' their life on one thing, one person . . . Nobody's that important to somebody else."

I clench one fist inside the other. "I think she loved you that much."

He laces his fingers atop his old axe, looks at me, and glances at his hands. "Son, that's hate, not love."

I shake my head. "She may have been a child in a woman's body, but she knew what love was."

"Love was junk to her. She was mainlinin' me 'fore I left."

There is no need for me to speak; I said it all in the other room two hours ago. He and I both know I won't kill him, not now, maybe not ever. Not that many sons kill their fathers, all told, and probably none of them without some regret.

He stands with difficulty.

"Better get some sleep," he says. Then he lays the Gibson back in its beat-to-hell coffin case, turns, and swipes my shoulder, leaving a trace of burn. I soon hear his bare feet shuffling down the hall. Opening my fist, I watch imaginary feathers fall.

Chapter Eight

I wake more slowly this time, as a flute trills outside the door. They told us at dinner that Al would play to summon us to breakfast, where there'd be no talking whatsoever. "To make you mindful," he'd said.

Others snore on—or at least pretend to—while I don jeans and T-shirt. Outside my room, I see the fireplace already ablaze in the dark room and remember, as if in a dream, the night before: staring into Dan's eyes before the hearth, Dad bathed in moonlight, hunkered in the dark.

I hustle toward the dining room. Two others sit, eating, eyes on their food. As I take the seat between them, I feel, for a moment, shy and awkward. Have I done something to be ashamed of? I truly don't know.

A plate is delivered before me, an explosion of color: golden yolks mingle with orange-yellow peppers, green zucchini, and white flecks of tofu. Surrounding the vegetarian delight are white grapes, orange slices, melon. Closing my eyes, I inhale the sweet-salty tang, feel the warmth rising like breath before me, the sound of Al's flute growing softer as he moves through the lodge. But I am not at peace. Flickering at my mind's corners are Joanna, Henry Owens, Ronald Jenkins, the church, the voice on the phone. Then Mim's face overlays the others, and I close my eyes till the wave of pain passes. What is this about? Does it take beating the hell out of my father to bring my wife (*ex*-wife?) closer? One pain triggering another?

Glancing at my watch, I see it's thirty minutes till we reconvene: a window of downtime, and I need every second. I eat quickly, hardly tasting the food, and leave.

* * *

Outside it's cold but not frigid, thrilling my blood. When Dad and I trekked up from the grassy area where we parked yesterday, I noticed a path winding on up the hillside. Now, leaving the lodge behind, I strike that well-carved path. My breath hovers like liquid lace as I crest the hill to see more cabins. Panting, I make out several buildings much smaller than the lodge, half visible in the swirling mist. In various states of disrepair, they look no longer used, though it's easy to imagine families mingling on the commons playing touch football, throwing Frisbees, cooking hot dogs on fire pits, a couple of collies barking as toddlers roll on the grass. I look back down the hill toward our lodge, lost in the fog, except its roof, which looks remarkably intact, though last night we'd done our utmost to raise it.

I approach a dock at which an old mossy canoe is tied. Fog above the little pond hovers like clouds seen from a plane, thick as cotton insulation. After seating myself on the edge, I penetrate the dark-greenish, algae-glossed surface and stare clear-eyed into the water right below the dock. Surely life teems here—snakes, frogs, and fish—but I see nothing but darkness: no sudden, flashing movement, no swirl of plant life, nothing.

I let my gaze go within—a common pattern of my life. By my tenth birthday or so, I'd learned that the only safe place lay inside Fort Thom. Solid steel surrounded my soul. Only God got in.

Till now.

A cardinal rasps sharply overhead, the water clears, and it's as if I'm staring into a crystal ball. It's breakfast, the week after Easter, and Mim is finally home from the hospital. Doctors, grief counselors, social workers, parishioners, and well-wishers: they're all gone, at last, and it's just us. It's Sunday again, and I'm contemplating the sermon I'm about to deliver, something about Jacob and Joseph's reconciliation, when Jacob rejoined the son he thought he'd lost forever—hardly relevant to what had just transpired in our lives, mine and Mim's.

Both of us seem to have somehow survived the first shock after losing a child and are trying to tiptoe into the next phase in silence, alone. Once home, Mim refused to take it easy, refused all human contact, and resumed her duties—even devised new ones—with a fury unlike any I'd seen. That Sunday morning she sets the plate before me, a Greek omelet, with four orange slices placed at the edge of her grandmother's china plate, as if an elegant presentation might be useful for mourning.

The buds at the back of my tongue ache like raw nerves, and I bend forward, above my plate. "Are you praying?" she says behind me, alarmed. I shake my head. Soon I walk to the church alone and tell how Jacob fell upon his son's neck and wept. Afterward, I shake hands, smile, walk home, and think, *oh, it was about the restoration of a lost child, and I just lost my daughter.* Everybody but me probably got it. But they didn't, not all of it: Joseph was a son. And he reconciled with his father.

Son, that's hate, not love.

It makes me mad all over that he's right. For all my mother's beauty, her great capacity—or at least need—for love, she was too weak for the world. Of course dying was her choice. Of course she was needy; no one had ever given her anything. With lawyer parents who had too much fun saving the radicals, plus a drama queen for an older sister (who hated Hugh Palmer Johnson as soon she laid eyes on him), she'd married at eighteen, emotionally a seventh-grader. Could Dad, or anyone, have saved her?

And the even bigger question for me: did I likewise force Mim's choice? Were we Johnson men like that? Rescue, then abandon, leave 'em to die? Somehow it all led back to that mystery woman's voice:

He's exciting them to violence. Now is my father forcing others to make *his* decision for him? If so, it's as cowardly as abandonment. So what if he's right about my mother making her choice? He still needs to accept the responsibility for making his.

And I feel pretty sure that, although Dad didn't actually call me himself, he arranged it. He wanted me on the tour, to witness, to *see*, so he can confess and be forgiven.

Something—a frog?—leaps into the water, and I come to suddenly. So clear before, the water now churns with mud. Can I know my father's motives? I hardly know my own. A clang brings me back: the old dinner bell outside the kitchen calling us to group session. I rise and move stiffly back down the bank.

* * *

Men gather silently before the fire, some on the chairs and couches, some on the floor, lying on their backs or stomachs. Music blares from a boom box at the back of the room, one of those New Agey piano and flute CDs that goes on and on without getting anywhere. I plop down on the couch, avoiding eye contact, feeling oddly guilty for going off alone. I don't see Dad. Still in bed? (What is it like without Mother Murphy to get him up? At first it gladdens my heart to know Dad has spent perhaps a restless night; then I feel ashamed. He needs all the rest he can get.)

Somebody clicks off the music. David, the youngest man in attendance, stands facing us, his mouth askew.

"The man in the black coat fell down by the johns. Might be a heart attack."

* * *

I find myself rushing down the mud-slippery hill, the fog wet on my face. I practically fall on him, sitting in the middle of the path, the Gibson beside him.

"Dad?"

When his head turns, I see his eyes are open. He lifts one hand and waves, his lips moving slightly. I kneel and look at him hard. He clearly can't see me, nor can he speak.

"Is he okay?" David asks behind me, panting.

I point toward the guitar. "Find the case and put it away." I get one hand around Dad's waist and, with the other clutching his arm, lift him to his feet, bending my knees to save my back. "And bring it down to the cars."

Then Dan is there beside me, helping hold Dad up. "Would you drive the Caddy?" I say. "Where's the closest ER?"

"About twelve miles. Fred can follow in his truck."

I nod and begin the trek down the hill, placing one foot, then the other, stepping sideways when it steepens, Dad's weight sagging onto me. Dan precedes me a few paces, looking back over his shoulder every few seconds. Does he think he'll catch us if I fall? We'll roll ass over elbows right down to the creek. Imagining that disaster, I step more carefully, practically carrying Dad. "Please, God," I moan aloud. Dan looks back, stops, alarm in his eyes.

"Keep going," I holler.

He does, and somehow we get down the bank. "Keys're in my left pocket." I'm not about to let go of Dad till the door is open.

"I'll be right behind you," another voice says. It's Fred, opening the door to his SUV.

Now Dan has the Caddy's door open, and we get Dad, limp as a drunk, onto the seat, with his head on my shoulder. David arrives, and I'm aware of him placing the guitar case onto the floor behind the driver. Though I'm trying not to look too directly at Dad, a glance shows me how pale he is. I expect his face to be purple, blood-engorged—or worse. He stares ahead sightlessly. I look up into Dan's blue eyes.

"He's my father," I rasp.

Dan nods and grips my shoulder with the same fingers I tried so hard to crush yesterday. "I know."

* * *

The trip to the hospital is a blur of images, colors, and smells from my childhood: new-mown hay, concrete after rain, creek water after flood (Dad took me fishing once, and we sat in a tiny boat not speaking for hours; I thought he was furious with me, and when, on the verge of tears, I finally asked him, he laughed and let me drink beer).

Then a longer reverie, the Era of Good Feeling, before I was five: Mom shuffling around making herbal tea, and Dad sitting there strumming the Gibson. Sunday summer lunchtime with corn-yellow sunshine streaming in. "Sing with me," he sometimes asked her, but she'd shake her head without turning around, and he'd wink solemnly at me, toying with leftover bread crusts on my plate. It used to make him smile when I'd try to close one eye and wink back, never quite successful but trying to please him. He'd throw back his head and laugh, and I'd laugh too, knowing somewhere in my four-year-old soul that making Daddy laugh was my job, one of the absolute best things in the world, second only to making your momma smile (very hard, but I never stopped trying). But today he isn't smiling.

My father and his young son (myself) both sit at the table, suffused in light, but she hovers, as always, a bird too restless to light.

"Was the morning good?" She refills my glass with lemonade, though I've already had too much to drink and need to pee.

My father just stares at her, hard. He'd pretty much given up smiling by this time too. He had plenty not to smile about. Though he hadn't been onstage in two years, people kept showing up, coming into our yard, peering in the windows, even climbing onto the roof one night. As the sun hits him full in the face, my dad looks too old to be not even thirty yet.

"It was all right." Folding his arms, he follows her with his eyes, already halfway lasers, though there is still something else there. Hope?

My father's body is rigid when he says, "What are you asking? Why don't you just say it?"

She isn't looking at him. She is kneeling next to me, singing, "In the pines, in the pines, where the sun never shines . . ." Her voice is silver thread in the stunning gold light.

Now he's on his feet, running his hand back and forth through his long blond hair. I haven't seen him do that in a long time. It always means trouble. Mom speaks.

"Honey, I was just asking, that's all. I was afraid he'd be bored."

He stops at the window. When he turns, his face has changed. "Why don't you say you think I'll hurt him?"

I feel tears coming. One time he grabbed her arm till she cried out. I begged him not to hurt her. And now he is about to do it again. And we had such fun in the pines. I built a village of pinecones, needles, and sticks, saw a squirrel fall from a high branch, and watched three big birds soar. He wrote a new song. About me.

She doesn't look up at him, cleaning up the jelly I'd dropped with her napkin. "Hugh, it's just . . . I couldn't take it if—"

"*You* couldn't take it. Like *I* could."

I know he'll grab her arm now, pull her to her feet. Watching from up in my corner, I feel my own tears start to come. Lemonade, peanut butter and butter sandwiches, apples, light. Let them walk on the roof. When Dad told him to come down, the boy had acted nice. Dad said if he'd had a gun that night, he'd've shot him.

My father's face, so red and wild when he turns around, begins to change. The biggest change is the eyes. They go blank. He can't see us anymore. He's already gone.

Six months later, we went on the road looking for him in Mom's car. It wasn't till I was nineteen, about a month before she died, that my beautiful mother finally told me what had happened to her in Baltimore, inside an arena's back door. By this time, most of the money was gone. After the divorce settlement, Mom gave generously to pet charities, but when pleas became relentless, she'd entrusted her parents, then their attorney, to manage her millions. It was hard to say who'd squandered more: the agent, a former lobbyist, with his "administrative" costs and bad investments; or the Kryssokoses and their doomed political causes. We were surviving on savings and a few real estate investments. She'd long ago sold the mansion Dad built for her and let everyone but the cook and driver go. She sat across from me on the couch eating Ben & Jerry's right out of the container, chasing it with wine. "I was raped, Tommy . . . by a roadie."

I put down the Stratocaster I'd been playing. "Why do you make this shit up?" I said in my snottiest, spoiled voice, "So I'll hate him?"

Impervious to sarcasm from the years with my dad, she placed the empty ice cream box down on the coffee table and carefully wiped her mouth corners with a linen napkin. "So you'll know the truth. You waited in the car, while I went in the back door of the arena to look for your father. You were only six."

"Okay," I said, "you were raped. When are you going to get over it?" I was so sick of her True Confessions when she was drunk. Plus, I felt guilty. I'd always known something horrible happened that day behind that door. Why didn't I do something? Such a wimp.

She gulped from her wineglass before answering. "You never get over it."

"So you'll eat and drink yourself to death." That's what she wanted: never to get over it, to die of it, over and over. The day I found her in that bathtub of blood, when I saw she'd finally, really done it, my stomach fluttered for a single second with relief. Before the sky fell.

Now thunderheads are gathering again.

* * *

They take my father right in, the receptionist's eyes widening as she sees the name I write with the rest of his history. I know better than to write Hugh Palmer Johnson, if I want him given the best care possible. I do.

Two nurses appear with a wheelchair and help him into it, while I look on. Dad's socks gather around his ankles above muddy boots like a homeless man's. I stand there in the middle of the floor until Dan leads me to a seat in the waiting area. Fred has brought in Dad's guitar. Sitting in its own chair in the small ER waiting room, it looks like another patient.

"Coffee, Thomas?"

When I look up into Dan's glacier-blue eyes that see everything and judge nothing, I wish God were that way, that *I* were that way. I want to hug Dan, grasp his hand, pour my bottomless angst into his ear, but at that moment God dumps the load on me, and I wonder if I might cry. All I can do is shake my head.

Dan turns to his fellow therapist. "Three coffees."

After Fred disappears, Dan sits beside me. At last I glue a few of the major pieces of myself back into some semblance of a human being. I think of the countless times I've been in Dan's seat, waiting the requisite number of heartbeats till I go into my pastoral shtick. Thank God the man hasn't patted my back or shoulder, which is what I would've done. I realize grief likes silence. Grief likes messy and wants to sit in its own excrement. Dan let me. For about three minutes.

"I have a son," he says at last, "a lot like you."

I don't want to hear this, but Dan has earned the right to speak to the bereft (I'm feeling like Dad won't leave the hospital alive).

"I mean he *looks* like you: older than he really is. You know . . . hair."

"Yeah." I finger my growing bald spot, as large as the bottom of a beer can. "Used to be so important."

"Peacock feathers."

We both laugh. For the first time since David ran into the lodge shouting, I feel the gears inside my chest shift smoothly into fifth, and I'm finally cruising.

"What's he do, your son?"

Dan wags his head and grins. "Damnedest thing. Four years of college, one of grad school, and he's a projectionist."

"Projectionist?" I imagine a guy with X-ray vision, hurling his consciousness through walls and buildings, into others. Like Dad does his listeners.

"Works at one of those art houses that show films—in San Diego."

"Fellini and Kurosawa?"

"Woody Allen and Michael Moore."

"Ah."

"He doesn't make a living at it. I supplement him; hell, I carry him. I don't know why. He always loved movies, I mean *loved* them. From the first time he saw *Star Wars* at twelve, he was never the same. Others lived inside them for two hours, then got out into sunshine and went back to math homework, soccer, and girls. Not Oliver. He stayed in the dark, y'know?"

I know. Rock and roll devoured Dad when he saw Buddy Holly live. According to Dad, the torch passed to him sitting on the front row without a word's being spoken. Within a month, Holly was dead. Out of his ashes rose the new messiah.

Dan sighs. "Ollie's happy. He makes dreams visible for others."

"You like him?"

"I love my son."

"But do you also like him, as in admire . . . appreciate?"

He frowns. "Tolerate, maybe."

I punch his arm lightly. It pleases me to find a dad who's all right with a total geek for a son. "His mom?"

Bigger sigh. "We're divorced. She lives in Ireland most of the year. When she's not in Palm Springs or Tahoe."

"Entertainment business?"

"Fancies herself a poet—convinces others she is too. And a healer and a prophet and New Age sage."

"Sounds a little like your line."

His face registers disdain, but for only a moment. "I'm sure people think they're helped by Sarah. The placebo effect is indeed powerful."

"But she's no mother."

"No time for it."

"And *your* dad . . . ?"

Before Dan can answer, I become aware of a presence and look up to find a curly headed, smiling young man wearing a doctor's white smock.

"Mister Johnson? I'm Dr. Stokes, and I have news of your father."

The boy's manner, unless he completely lacks empathy, says my father is yet among the living. "Was it another heart attack?"

He sits on the other side of me, still smiling. Will he be smiling when he tells me that Dad's heart finally burst?

"No. He's having a transient ischemic attack."

I look at Dan, who shrugs. The doctor I'm beginning to think of as the Child Prodigy continues to smile, nodding and lacing his fingers. "It's an episode that lasts a few hours, usually less than twenty-four. Happens when there's a temporary loss of blood flow to the brain."

"But . . . he acted like he couldn't see me, and he couldn't speak, could barely walk."

"Exactly. It's as if a veil comes down." He pats my arm just as I would, were our roles reversed.

"You're sure it's not a heart attack?" I can't seem to let go of it.

"TIAs last anywhere from a few minutes to twenty-four hours. Then they're over."

Understanding is finally catching up: my father apparently isn't going to die.

When the Prodigy removes his hand from my arm, I can still feel it. "They're caused either when a clot forms in a blood vessel inside the brain, or when it travels from some other part of the body. When it hits"—he rams his fist against his palm—"BAM, you're down."

"So it's not . . . ?"

"No. We'll keep him overnight and run a scan, just to make sure." He stands up. "Do you think you might ask your dad before he leaves to sign this for me?" Reaching into his pocket, he pulls out *Greatest Hits, Volume Eight*. On the CD's cover, Dad glooms out from the shadows of an abandoned train station, coattails flapping in the fan-created breeze.

"If you'll tell me how to get him off the road," I say, "and keep him off."

"And put a legend out to pasture?" He laughs, and I see how his patients probably force themselves to get better to earn that smile. He glances at his watch.

"Can I see him?" I ask.

"Very soon. The nurse will page you."

I'll confess: for one point three seconds, I wish that my father had died and the whole thing was over, but before I can work up a full head of guilt about it, I feel a tap on my shoulder and turn to see Dan holding two coffees. Fred stands behind him, looking impatient.

"If things are under control . . . ," Fred suggests.

"If you'd like us to stay around awhile longer . . . ," Dan quickly interjects.

I take Dan's hand between both of mine. "You've been so kind to us. I'll keep you in my prayers, that is, if you don't mind."

He grins. "Couldn't do any harm. Your luggage?"

I glance back to the chair. The guitar case is still patiently waiting. For a single second I feel like I've let my eyes wander away from a child entrusted to my care. Dad's known that axe longer than he's known me.

"Just give it to Goodwill."

"All right then. Auf Weidersehen." Fred, I notice, is already out the door. Dan takes a couple of steps, then comes back. "I should probably keep my mouth shut."

I wait, flexing my hands.

He stares down the corridor, considering how honest he should be.

"Thomas, give your old man a break, okay?"

I nod.

He turns away, waves, walks through the doorway and is gone. As soon as the automatic doors whisk shut, it hits me: I'm alone. In a hospital. With my father, who apparently is going to live.

Chapter Nine

I delay making the calls for as long as I can. There is something highly personal, even intimate, about Dad's care resting in my hands—of course it's mainly the doctors' hands—but for some reason I am enjoying being "the family." After about an hour, though, I recognize the feeling for the illusion it is and decide to go public and make a few calls. I find a tiny alcove near the restrooms out of traffic where I won't have to shout.

"Stay right where you are till I get there," Murphy rasps. "I'll find a goddamn car somedamnwhere, drive the goddamn Whale down there if I have to."

Gauging his stress level from his language, I know the man's at about a nine. I take a shallow breath. "I'm sorry to bother you, Murph, but do you have a number for that cardiologist who treated Dad?"

"Wait one goddamn minute."

Thankfully he gives me the cell phone number of Dr. Carlo Fritzius at Mt. Zion Hospital in Boston, without reminding me I'd know it if I truly gave a damn about my father.

The doctor is a bit breathless. "You know your father's my best patient," he says with perfect Boston diction, "following my program to the letter." He pauses. "Well, except for exercise."

"Program?" My neck hairs prickle. The only heart program I know anything about is AA.

"The Fritzius Plan for Wholly Healing the Holy Heart Entirely, FPWHHHE, or Fipwhee, as some of my patients call it."

"Sounds like a cult." Then I catch myself. "I'm a clergyman, doctor, so forgive my mind for wandering where it automatically will."

"It does sound religious. And, though not denominational, it is, in a very real sense, a *spiritual* program. Doctors want to *snip snip snip*. Nothing against my colleagues, the cardiac surgeons, but snipping—and angioplasty and all the rest—should be saved for only desperate cases. All others must learn how to love."

"Love?" It's sounding more like AA all the time.

"The heart isn't merely the symbol of love. It is the organ that best processes all the emotions we feel. So meditation—even prayer, if a patient is religiously inclined, as your father is—that, and my special diet, is the heart of the program, pun intended. Last I heard from Israel, which was, oh, a couple of months ago, he was doing fine, eating only Holy Heart foods and praying—I mean, meditating—regularly, and avoiding the Six Sinful Sisters."

"Sinful Sisters?" I glance around to see if the woman entering the ladies' room has heard, but she's preoccupied with her toddler.

"Alcohol, caffeine, nicotine, resentments, unconfessed secrets, and unresolved relationships."

My mind freezes on the last item. Am I part of Dad's Fipwhee? "Dr. Fritzius, aren't you leaving anything to God?"

"Au contraire, Reverend. My program, if effective, delivers this owner of a lonely heart right to God's door. As a matter of fact, where are you right now?" I see his eyes twinkling a thousand miles away.

I explain, repeating Dr. Stokes's diagnosis. Dr. Fritzius is quiet for so long I wonder if he's still there.

"If Dr. Stokes is right, the CAT scan will be negative. But what he didn't tell you is what can follow a ministroke."

I stand up straighter. "My dad had a *stroke*?" A few minutes ago, it was an "episode."

"Sorry, Reverend, I don't mean to frighten you unnecessarily or second-guess Dr. Stokes, who will no doubt explain—"

"Please be straight with me."

He pauses. "Sometimes TIAs are warnings."

Down, up, down again. I feel as dizzy as Dad looked with his uncomprehending eyes. "Please, doctor . . ."

"Sometimes the Full Monty comes next."

"A flat-out stroke, you mean."

Silence. I remember my wife's Aunt Florence. Mim had described Flo as her wildest relative, who was always telling risqué stories and smoking like a chimney, playing pinochle, and drinking half beers ("You can't get drunk on only half a beer!") at family gatherings. We'd visited her at the home days after her stroke, when she'd sat drooling in her wheelchair, staring out of sightless eyes, occasionally groaning while Mim chattered until she couldn't speak for weeping. We'd never gone back.

"Tests will help, Thomas. They might show—"

"Thank you, so much, Dr. Fritzius, and God bless you."

"And you."

All my limbs are weak. We are in the river, water to our necks, and it's rising.

In my hand, the phone feels so light, the thread connecting me to my former life so flimsy. With a hollow heart, I trudge down the corridor to see Dad.

* * *

He's sitting up, staring straight ahead.

"Hey, Dad." I park the Gibson in the middle of the floor so he can see it. He starts, so lost in thought he apparently didn't hear me enter.

"They told me I'll be sprung in the morning," he says.

"Depending on the tests," I reply.

"Nope. Got gigs Saturday and Sunday, right down the road."

I fling his gaze back at him, best I can. It makes me sick when people yes-man my father. This time it might be fatal, and even though I am trying to keep it a secret from myself, I know Dad can't get to the end of the road he seeks till he gets back *on* the road. I've been changed by seeing him down, arm waving pitifully, hair in his face, all his hard edges filed smooth.

He claps his gaze back on the wall, while I sit in the same hard vinyl chair that's in all hospital rooms. "Look, Dad, I had a nice chat with Dr. Fritzius in Boston." When he turns back, I grin. "I know some of your secrets now."

His face turns to stone. "Like what?"

"Like what you've been doing at the back of the bus." Closing my eyes for a second, I fold my hands prayerfully, heart-high. "And I know about the Six Sinful Sisters."

He glares. "Nobody can know about that."

"Dad. Nobody cares."

"I do." Eyes back on the wall. And I figure that's that: order given without question. Just when I decide he's dismissed me, he turns slowly back, wearing an entirely different face—one I don't recognize.

"So now you understand?"

"Yes," I hear myself say. "Now I understand."

He finally takes his eyes off me, to stare at the wall. "No, you don't."

"Try me," I say.

His eyes close, and he's silent so long I wonder if he's sleeping. Then he raises his right hand, the fingers gripping an imaginary pencil. "I can't write."

"An hour ago you couldn't even see."

He glances at the guitar case, then away, closing his eyes.

"I don't mean just today. Words won't come." He opens his eyes. They stare lifelessly, empty, transparent blue. "Nothing."

I shrug. "It'll pass. How long?"

He looks straight at me. The urine-yellow smell of fear is instantly present. "Three years."

"Since you last wrote a song?"

"Ever since the Bigger One."

I let it soak in. My dad is by far living his healthiest lifestyle (except for exercise), but has apparently lost the thing he lives for. No wonder he howls.

"It'll come back," I say. Then, before I can stop myself, I take that grasping hand and squeeze it. "Have you prayed?"

He nods.

"Here, drink." I release his hand and bring the straw of his drinking glass to his lips, just as a nurse enters. He sips and turns his head away. "I'll be outside," I say, standing, "if you need anything." He nods, face closed. As I reach the door, he speaks.

"Thom."

I turn.

"Get it out of here."

I step forward, grab the guitar case, and flee.

* * *

Down the hall, in the lounge area, there's not a soul around. I collapse onto the couch, weight sinking like an anchor into ooze.

I want to escape by sleeping, but soon I'm in a dialogue with myself.

Your dad knows what he's doing.

That's giving him way too much credit.

He always gets what he wants.

Nobody *always* gets what he wants.

Most of the time he gets what he wants when he wants it.

That makes him God?

Makes him fully human, whole.

And we lesser mortals aren't. Whole.

When you're mad, you don't see Israel Jones.

I don't want to see Israel Jones; I want to see my father.

Same guy.

I don't think so.

Could be they're merging.

If he has a plan, it's in the ditch now.

He'll be up and running in no time.

He may not make one more show.

He's like a cockroach, runs on air and light.

What if I don't believe the legend stuff?

Don't wait till he's dead.

My father is a very flawed human. Not God.

Maybe he's both.

No. Only one was ever both.

Silence. I fold my arms and wait, but the debate seems over for now.

* * *

So maybe Dad has—or had—a plan. He got me on the tour somehow (though I'm still convinced he wasn't the one who called me). He wants to show me what he's been through, what he suffers on a daily basis, where he's going. Why? So his conscience is clean before he dies? (And there's still the snakes. Melodrama?)

I stiffen for a moment, then sink back into the couch's plastic cushion. Most people would figure my dad's life would be more dramatic, more mysterious, noble, and mythic. At the heart of legend—like evil—is there only the banal: empty theater?

This time I don't need a debating partner. My father's life, my own life, is not banal. Mundane, consumed by minutiae and much ado, but holy too. I close my eyes and wait to be contradicted.

Nothing.

Before I decide not to, I pull out my phone and punch numbers.

"Good morning, Maxine. I was wondering if there were any calls for me."

Her voice lowers. "Mrs. Strickland called yesterday." I see my secretary peering over her glasses, scouting for deacons. "Three times."

My heart races. I can't speak.

"I finally told her that you were out of town and might be gone for a while. Was that okay?"

"How did she sound?"

"Upset."

I wonder how much Max intuits. She seldom attends services, but probably knows more about Holy Mart's issues and inner workings than 95 percent of the congregation.

"Reverend, I heard Henry Owens leave her a message, so I know what's going on. Also, Perry Mason's been hanging around. Is he trying to pull off a coup in your absence?"

I would've laughed if things hadn't been so serious. She's never liked lawyer-deacon Ken Branch, her old schoolmate. "No, I don't think things have gone that far. But just in case, let's keep Ken out of the armory."

"Do you want me to give that woman your cell phone number?"

"I'll call her as soon as things settle down a bit."

"And how are things, if I'm not being nosy?"

"Oh, fine. Busy."

Okay, don't tell your trusted friend and ally, the pause on the other end said. But I just didn't have the energy.

"Well, take good care of yourself, Reverend."

"You too, Max."

Disconnected, I consider. Jo calling the church is too dangerous for both of us right now. But I don't know what to say. I mean, I know what I *should* say: we'll never speak or see each other again. But the wind goes out of that sail before I punch in the last digit of her number. I decide I'm not ready. I drop the phone back into my pocket.

* * *

Hours later, I've reread Job and half of Psalms, dozing to piped-in Christmas carols. I decide if I don't move my legs, I'll never walk again. Limping down the hall, I hear the ding of the elevator, then look up to see a scarecrow figure lurching toward me. In the light pouring through the window, the man looks like a newly released death camp detainee, his skin sickly yellow. When he takes off the dark glasses to reveal bloodshot eyes, I know him.

"Hey, Murph."

He stops, waits for me to get to him, apparently studying a painting of deer drinking from a mountain stream.

"Put the guitar down," he mutters. He still hasn't directly looked at me.

"I'm not stealing it, okay? He told me to—"

"Put it down." When he finally looks at me, his lizard-lidded eyes spit blood. "Now."

I don't know what it is about my having the guitar, but his tone puts me on red alert. I feel like I'm back on the bus, and he just caught me bothering the driver, sitting or standing in the wrong place. And Murphy is my jailer. Dad is too chickenshit to fire musicians or discipline his son; that's what he pays this man to do. The memory dissipates, leaves me calm. Dad's confession three hours ago let me in. Plus, I supported him down the hill, let him lay his head on my shoulder all the way here. I belong. Murphy's a manager.

When he swings at me, I step back fast, and his fist strikes empty air. Then, before I know what's happened, I'm staring into his wide-open, rheumy brown eyes, smelling his terrible breath.

"Skipper . . . *leggo.*"

I release him quickly and step back. The fingers that gripped his turkey-wattled flesh are tingling. His eyes on me are still full of fear.

"You're not as fast as you used to be," I say.

"No, you got faster." He looks like some grim new species coaxed from a cave beneath the earth, never meant to be seen in the light. Not dangerous but comic, pitiable.

"I think I heard something pop." Hunching his right shoulder, he rotates his head. I stand ready for him to come at me again. I will never let him best me again, ever. His punishments were usually a slap across the cheek rather than a real ass kicking, but that was worse, performed before smirking musicians, roadies, and drivers. I was a baby, a mascot, "the one brat Boss'll own up to," Richie Hammer, a sadistic, obese, and brilliant bass player, had once said, making me hate not Richie but my father for bringing me along at all.

"So." Murphy finally seems fairly certain his neck isn't broken and stops hunching. "I trust you with him, and within twenty-four hours, he's had—what?—the Biggest One?" He points a crooked finger at me. "On your watch, Reverend!"

I fold my arms and shake my head. "He fell down, had sort of an episode, that's all." This is family business. Dad's diagnosis is my cross to bear, not his, at least for now.

Murphy's mouth gapes open again, and I look past him at a male nurse jockeying an elderly gentleman in a Yankees cap in a wheel-chair.

"I don't need to tell you that your daddy don't fall down just every day."

"Murph, he's had two heart attacks, and he'd've probably had another now except for the program."

He cocks his head.

"Fipweed or whatever it's called. I talked to Dr. Fritzius, his car-diologist."

"Program?"

"You live and sleep with him, and you don't know?"

His slack-jawed mouth and watery, burned-out eyes say he doesn't. Now I pity him. After filling him in on what Dr. Fritzius told me, I watch the ruin of a man stand there wagging his grizzled head sadly. The news that Dad has a program and hasn't informed him hurts worse than Boss taking his Caddy and leaving with his no-good son at the wheel rather than himself.

"Goddamn, Skip. What's next—sex change?" He rubs his face, wanting, I know, a cigarette.

"Also, he says he doesn't want *them* to know how he lives now."

"Them?"

"Musicians, drivers, fans, media . . ." I trail off. Too late I realize what I've done.

"Of course. Managers too."

He gazes at his spotted, septuagenarian's hands, trembling ever so slightly. I wonder if he's ever gone this long without a drink or smoke. And though I open my mouth to protest, I know the damage is done. Boss betrayed him; and, worse, the son knew the truth first. Sons come and go, but managers are forever—or so he's assumed. (Me too.) But now neither of those things seems clear: either that I will go "home" (wherever that is, and leave Dad), or that Murphy will remain through to the end (when and wherever that might be). Things feel muddy. I decide to stall.

"He's awake." I point back down the hall. "In 212. And you know how he loves hospitals."

He snaps to attention, back at the helm. "I'll take him this." He snatches up Dad's axe as if it's the grail. "Sumbitch'll probably write two albums' worth o' songs before he's released."

That's another secret I plan to keep. Nothing like *the* secret, though, that my dad may have a new type of time bomb ticking inside him. (*Stroke.* The word itself sounds like the swath of the reaper's scythe.) I stagger away, looking for a couch, a chair, anywhere to crash for a while and decide to go forward or go back, or whether it makes any difference at all. I know I need to pray, even though I feel less like seeking God than any time since Charleston. Suddenly I know whose voice, other than God's, might help.

* * *

I'm back beside the restrooms, crunched into the corner facing the wall. During the first ring, my heart begins to hammer as if I am the one having the Biggest One. Would *he* answer? By the fifth ring, I realize I am sweating. Then soft, tentative, as if across an ocean:

"Yes?"

"Hello, Joanna."

A deathly pause. "Where are you?"

The day brightens.

"At a hospital in Kentucky . . . with my father."

"Another heart attack?"

I imagine her taut, thin lips, wavy lines on her forehead. It's been my mission for the past year to erase them.

"No, just an episode. He fainted and fell down." What possible benefit can there be to telling her the whole truth?

"Praise God," she breathes, then lapses silent, gathering herself. "Mr. Owens came by last night."

"He told me he would."

"He asked some odd questions." Her voice becomes muffled as if she put her hand over the receiver. I imagine little Kayla and Kylie staring up at her with wide-open faces while Mommy talks to . . . ? Not her minister—I haven't been that in a while, not really; I'd confessed my doubts to her early on; she'd stripped my beliefs down to basics, the first person since seminary with whom I couldn't maintain the pretense of believing it *all*. Maybe because she'd let me know so soon she'd lost her easy Jesus along with everything else in her world when her husband had revealed himself to be a bully. Now she's speaking very softly.

"His inquiries were all very properly phrased: 'The pastoral counseling relationship lasted for what duration? Also, it dealt only with domestic relationships between you and your husband, correct?'"

I cringe. No matter how gentle interrogation is, it's still interrogation.

"I'm sorry, Jo. It's me they want, not you. And Henry Owens is the best I could hope for. I believe, that is, I pray that he'll be as fair to me as he's always been."

The longest pause yet. She's crying, though struggling to conceal it. Finally:

"He asked whether I knew if you intended to get back together with your wife. Whether I'd considered the appearance of what I was doing by meeting you at all hours—how's that for discreet?—and how the appearance could affect my children and marriage." Now her voice shreds. "He left me, Thom. Dennis is gone."

Yessss, I mentally hoot.

"And he . . . he took the kids."

The world tilts, then stops. Good thing I'm leaning against a wall. Closing my eyes, I hear Jo telling me what her husband had once told her. *All's a kid needs is the Bible. And if God told me to sacrifice one of them, like Abraham was told, I'd do it in a second.* And he would, she'd confessed, weeping, for God spoke regularly to her husband, saying he wanted the family to have twelve children, like Jacob, representing the twelve tribes.

"I don't matter anymore," she whispers. I shudder, imagining her in that empty house. "You and I can never see each other again. It's the only way to get them back."

Since leaving, I've known it was over between us; that's why I hadn't called—to avoid hearing her say it. Now it hurt like hell. But it is time, past time, to think only of her.

"I will carry your petition to God as long as I have breath," I say.

Her weeping is violent now, approaching hysteria.

"If there's a God," I say, "He'd better not let these children be hurt."

She is absolutely right to hang up on such an idle threat.

Chapter Ten

Watching my father, I wonder what goes on in his mind, his soul. Here we are at Tammany's, a foul Kentucky roadhouse reeking of body odor and beer because the coliseum in Louisville sold only one-tenth of its tickets and the show was "moved" here. And while Murphy had a cow—I thought *he* would have the Biggest One—Dad waited till the manager had fully cursed everyone involved. Then he shrugged.

"Long as it wasn't canceled. We can't have cancellations, that's all."

The band complained. Part of the proceeds from a club's admission charge is small potatoes compared to ticket proceeds from an arena show. I saw the look that Wendell Delp, lead guitar, passed to Javier Hayes, the drummer. Somebody better watch the boss's back. Since both Murphy and my father seem oblivious, I, reluctant Ishmael, am elected by default to look out for both mutiny and white whale sightings.

If the last show was raucous, tonight's is a powder keg. The Furies must've been first in line to swap their arena tickets. I imagine them camped on the sidewalk, grimy, pale, seamed, and scabbed faces joyous while one of them beats a conga, the girls sway suggestively, and someone else panhandles. In my fevered brain, it makes me shudder, despite the room's heat—I feel certain Tammany's management is breaking fire codes to honor all six hundred tickets sold. Something will happen tonight, something bad.

And Dad seems more than ready to light the fuse. After "Dead Man," he wanders into "Mississippi Malaise," sure to incite this crowd with lyrics about lynchings and worse. Just typical Israel of the early seventies, material that endeared him to white liberals before Dad hired a band loud enough to obscure the words and attract Gen Xers and now millennials, the new crop of twenty-somethings who came of age in 2000. Gone are the days of seated shouters and raised lighters. This crowd loves to mosh and thrash and raise unholy hell. By the second song the Furies are out of their chairs and writhing practically naked before the stage.

"Let the torch go forward," Dad shrieks, "through the land of the brave and free/That niggers are liberated in the grave and in the tree."

Maybe the rednecks don't know the lyrics, but these kids do, as they mime every syllable, hurl every word right back at Dad, who of course ignores them from within his bubble. "Legends don't take requests or sign autographs," Murphy'd once famously scoffed to some second-rate rock rag. "Legends take hostages."

I'm on my toes, ready for anything, no doubt due to all that has gone down between this show and the last. Knowing Dad's secret makes me able to empathize. Maybe he believes his God wants him on the road howling—his equivalent of raising snakes to the Lord?—apparently till the bitter end. Of course, he hasn't said this. Despite all the chances for confession (mostly mine so far), Dad hasn't said any of the things I am hoping to hear. As always, talk is cheap, doing is all. I'd gone back to his hospital room after Murphy had left, and he silently suffered me as I related what Dr. Fritzius had said about what the "episode" might portend.

"Don't change nothin'," Dad muttered.

And that was that.

Fine—I've got my own pain right now after talking to Joanna, and if the Furies need to shed a little blood tonight, I guess I'm willing to bear witness to their idiocy, maybe even mingle some of my own (metaphorically speaking).

After "Mississippi," Dad begins endlessly tuning while the Furies stand, swaying with waving arms and pirouettes.

Someone finally shouts from a center table, "Why don't you assholes sit down?"

"This ain't the Grateful fucking Dead," another hollers.

"Deadheads give great head!" one Rhodes scholar slurs. "Hey, baby, come sit on my face."

Harsh laughter erupts. Dad is oblivious to crowd tension (he simply lacks a trouble detector, whereas the needle on mine is as responsive as a seismograph's). Patrick and Wendell cast nervous glances at each other and the crowd while they wait. Apparently *they* are in perfect tune.

"Silence, Philistines!" It comes from the light-skinned black girl, the one who wept at McGillicuddy's while Dad howled. Tall and long limbed, she wears large golden hoops as big as bracelets through her ears, clusters of studs in her nose above her sensual lips. Her smallish breasts are barely covered by a low-cut white top held in place by a single silver button. "He comes with a sword," she shouts, "like a mighty wind." The hecklers have no ready comeback, and finally Dad nods to the lead man, and the drummer counts off.

It's "Water and Blood."

My spine takes a hit. All the way back to Dad's conversion tour, it was the first hymn he wrote—I'd forgotten it entirely—and as it unfolds now, accompanied only by his fingerpicking, the heads of the other musicians bowed, I realize it is one of his best.

We all know the master endured the thorns,
the cross, the spear, the blazing scorn;
and blood poured silver on the mystery hill
where one world died and another was born.
Yes, the master, pregnant with truth,
tears flowing from his pains of birth,
delivered all of those who believed
by making water from blood,
turning sin to love.

Aware of movement, I look to my left and see only the black girl is dancing, her willowy bare arms weaving before her, fingers sculpting, then scooping, hazy blue air. Head thrown back, her face catches the light, and I stare at the most intimate public glimpse I've ever received, in church or roadhouse, of ecstasy and pain fused in a complex blend. Her body convulses, writhes, as she dips to the floor before my father. Dad sees—he must—but he's staring straight ahead into Israel-land, singing by rote, it seems, perhaps pondering which epistles from Paul to read tonight.

And she's *right there*, not only sharing his single spot but stealing it—I'm sure he's more than willing—her arms upraised, sitting on her haunches, bare soles of her feet so vulnerable that I can imagine them stepping her tenderly through thorns or fire. There's something in her movement, sensual as it is, that smacks of the holy, not only of those who raise snakes but those who walk the aisle of Suffering Christ Church of Holy Martyrs, rare as they are, and who kneel at the altar, even before I can step down from the pulpit to grip their sweaty palms. The *reached ones*, who've been taken somewhere far from the clutch of paltry lives. And certainly far from me. And watching the girl's head loll back once more, I struggle against the possibility that they possess what I have lost. To have God's ear and lose it . . .

The song ends, as it must. It's a full five seconds before applause fills the building to bursting, and they stand, rednecks and hippies, sober and drunk, washed and unwashed, lion and lamb. When their storm finally fades into mortar, brick, and termite-eaten beams, Dad has them back, just like that. To remind them this is a rock show, he counts off, and the drummer slams into "Tooth and Hail," a screaming, guitar-shrieking rocker to make Neil Young cover his ears. I have brought earplugs and am glad to use them.

Not a single drop of blood is shed.

* * *

After the show, two and a half hours without a break, I follow the band to the bus, where I find Wendell yelling at Murphy.

"Those kids aren't the fuckin' show. Their asses oughta be kicked out—you saw 'em tonight—there coulda been big trouble."

Murphy is in good form.

"Those kids buy drinks, dipshit. And tickets. That pays the bar; bar pays us; I pay you; you pay your alimony; everybody's happy, eh?"

"A bar ain't an arena, man." It's Javier Hayes, the drummer, who's spoken.

Murphy cuts his eyes to the huge black man. "Need some good coke, do you?"

Javier glares right back. "That's *your* department. I got a wife and three kids back in Flint to feed."

"Well, they'd be a Pamper or two short this week without paying customers. They're your employers, Mr. Hayes, to which you owe your allegiance."

"Shit, I don't owe no self-mutilating faggots no 'legiance. I work for Mr. Jones, period."

Now all eyes turn to Dad sitting at the little foldout table, nursing what looks like coffee but is probably herbal tea. I have to admit the three days in the hospital for observation did him good. Amazing that he hasn't already disappeared into his back room for evening devotions. Dad dirties his hands with such trivia as audience antics as seldom as possible. Now he remains silent, eyes unfocused.

"I don't mind 'em much myself." It's Patrick. When the others look toward him, I inwardly groan. He'll pay for this later. It seems to me the boy's chord changes are a half second slow, and he keeps his eyes clamped on Wendell's left hand a lot. All the lead man has to do is turn his back, and the cheating guitarist will be screwed. If Dad notices—and, while he often appears not to know what planet he's on, he hears everything, or he used to. He once reamed a rhythm man for deadening notes and forbade him to play bar chords beyond the fifth fret. Wendell and Javier wait, handing the boy all the rope he wants.

"Hell, they're fun! Never know what the fuck they'll do next. They make shows inna-resting. I mean, not that they're not already, Mr. Jones, the way you mix it up and keep it spontaneous. Shit, they're like those girls that used to scream at the Beatles. They're—"

"They cut themselves." I can't believe it's my voice.

Murphy is grinning. I've shown my cards, and he has an ace. "So what? They buy tickets, give the media something to write about—hell, Reverend, they *like* to bleed. Right, boss?"

All eyes follow Murphy's gaze. Dad appears to be studying the bottom of his mug for cracks. I want to vomit, purge myself of all I've so far witnessed.

"They're doing this—or they think they are—for some reason." I look right at my father, but his eyes stay averted. I know I need to stay calm, but the power slips through my hands like greased rope. "I don't know what it is, but it's very sick. And"—I hate the rising whine of my voice—"mark my words, someone's going to get hurt, if they're not stopped."

Though I look at each of them in turn, Murphy is the only one who returns my gaze, smirking. Dad still does not look up. I cannot believe he knows and will do nothing.

"All right, then."

And with no clear idea of where I am going, I open the door, hop down the steps, and find myself surrounded. Half blinded in the security lights' glow, I first glimpse as if through fog a tall boy, his head completely shaved, face crosshatched by zigzag lines that look like sutures made by a drunken doctor, his nose, lip, ears, and cheek studded with silver and gold. Eyes adjusting, I make out a shorter boy in a long coat, grinning like an imbecile. From between them steps the half-black girl who chastised the crowd tonight. She squints at me, her mouth hard. "Tell Israel we request an audience with him," she says. Her voice, low and throaty, quivers slightly.

I shake my head. "I'm sorry. He needs to rest."

"You're his son," she hisses. "You can get him to come out."

I shiver in the thick, humid night air. Neither deacons', Murphy's, nor Dad's disapproval so chill my blood as this girl and her companions knowing my relationship to their god. As unlikely as it is, I wonder if they heard what went on inside the bus moments ago.

"Please," I say lamely. "He's exhausted. He gives everything onstage. He needs to rest."

"Liar!" It's the tall boy with the piercings. "Tell him—"

"We have a gift for him," interjects the shorter boy, "when he's rested enough to receive it." Though high, his voice has a quiet authority. Even the black girl is silenced, hugging herself. "I'm

Emanuel," he says, lifting his arms, palms heavenward, tilting his head back into the light. "And we are The Holy Theatre of Transcendent Joy."

He offers his hand, and though I half expect it to be holding a blade, it's empty. Whatever the gift, it isn't going to be presented to me.

"I'm Thom," I say, squeezing his soft fingers.

"I'm sure we'll enjoy a long, intimate acquaintance, Thom. But I sense you would like to know what we're about, n'est-ce pas?"

Struck dumb, I can't answer, wanting desperately to get back on the bus.

"Ready, my friends?"

The other two begin to clap quietly—and sway. Smiling, the boy turns to me and delivers his speech in a mesmerizing monotone.

"These frightened, haunted longings, these gleaming, glassless eyes staring from bodiless bone casings; these husks of men ghosting these hollowed-out streets, blood-pooled alleys, and Limberlost towers—who are they? And why do they watch us, minions of the postmodern madness below, who know they're lost and damned—and freely confess it? But wait!—we know there's dignity in salvation; yes, and nobility too. We look higher than corporate castles and media monoliths to glean meaning from the cruel cosmos. We love the Lord, you see, but not a god of bottom-lineism, a god of menace and meanness, a punishing huckster whose son's sacrifices mean nothing more than a commodification of his body fluids. Far from it. We believe in trans-*send*-ence, a floating-to-the-top essence, a latte foam at the zenith where heaven hems earth; we believe in a god who rocks, who's hip, who loves humans more than they love themselves, who loves them like spouses, like favored children, for whom forgiveness is the essence of breath; who expects them to sin, nay, *craves* their sin so He can be the Big Jive Daddy of the Biggest

Bang, so He can grasp man to his breast and say, 'Son, I love you just the same.'"

"*Just the same,*" the two harmonize behind him.

"God depends on man for love, it's as simple as that. Why else make him up out of photons and protons, comet dust and star jism? God would be suicidal without us, for we are endlessly interesting, zanily creative. We amuse him; we synthesize, cannibalize, concoct, and steal; we plagiarize, convert, collaborate, spurt, and spew; we're fresh, replete, flush, and effete. We strip down, build up, complexify, conquer, plan coups, kill, annihilate. And God can't predict a nickel of it—oh, the Big Banger grasps the gist; after all, He crafted us out of dust and mush; baling wire and duct tape, but like a rock supergroup—think CS&N, Emerson, Lake and Palmer; for Chrissake, the Beatles with Billy Preston!—we're more than the sum of our parts; we are stardust; we are golden. Once set in motion, once wound up, we twirl like tops, spin like light, whiz like electrons, spritz like synapses as elastic and plastic sometimes as majestic as molecular dancers."

"*JUST THE SAAAAME,*" they crescendo, arms raised, fingers aquiver as if my father is onstage before them. The black girl's eyes bore into mine as if willing me dead. The grinning boy before me spins, eyes closed, coat billowing, before continuing.

"What would God be without us? We give Him meaning—I know it's hubris to say, but there it is. For what it's worth. Call it the contribution of Gen X, Y, or Z, whatever you want to call my ilk and me. It took a zillion years to get to this place of making—of ultimate art—but here we are. We've cobbled together God out of his own myths, conjured Him from the fog of his own misunderstanding, and now we require him to shine his beneficent countenance our way. And he is too holy not to comply, nothing if not a Great Good Guy. We have made him this way, call it the most successful collaboration of all time, the ultimate Martin and Lewis, Lennon-McCartney, Wilbur and Orville vaudeville act: man and woman and God, locked forever in solid embrace—we without meaning, he without love, strike me down if this be not true!"

When he falls backward, they catch him, then fling him forward, back onto his feet. My entire body tingles from toe tips to bald spot. When he thrusts his hand at me again, I flinch. There is no escaping it, so I lift my arm from my side. The boy clasps my hand firmly as he bows slightly.

"Good night and God bless, Thom."

"Good night." Eager to get away, I'm held a moment longer by Emanuel's expectant smile. "And thank you for . . ." Not until I say the final word does its truth dawn on me—this performance was meant for my father. ". . . for the gift." With a flourish, I extend my arm to include all three actors in this bizarre production. And while both boys bow, the black girl refuses to look at me, dissing as well as dismissing me. If it weren't for her, I might've actually taken their request to Dad and let him decide. *No way*, I think, glancing at her furious profile. She wants blood, and right now it feels like mine.

When I strike the door with my fist, it instantly opens. Patrick sits in the driver's seat. Grabbing the rail, I bound up the steps. "Close it," I hiss.

"Dangerous, you think?" the guitarist says before taking a swig on his longneck.

"I can't tell."

"I think they're kinda cute."

Sliding into a seat, I glance over my shoulder, see the endless card game is in progress, sans Dad. "Not a word to my father, all right?"

"Scout's fuckin' honor, Rev," he says and crosses himself with his beer. "They can go kill their stupid selves for all I care."

* * *

Sunday night's gig is at an even worse dive, The Green Door, near Chesapeake on the Ohio River. No arena within miles. After trying to sleep on the bus while the band laughed and drank at the rear, I don't want to see any of them for a while, so as soon as we pull up to the rear of the joint, I take off wandering through the town. It's an unseasonably warm December morning, near seventy with enough sunshine to make atheists pray, and I find a coffee shop with outside seating that actually sells Italian roast and the *New York Times*. I consider calling Henry or Maxine, but I decide to give it a while longer. This weather won't last, and it's too perfect to pollute with bad news.

I'm in the middle of an article on the growth of "sports arena" churches when I sense someone standing near me, hum-singing "Amazing Grace." I look up, expecting to see Patrick grinning at me.

"Mind if we join you, Reverend Thom?"

Lowering the paper, I squint hard to see a tall figure with the sun directly behind him. When I shade my eyes, the tall figure comes into focus. "You're from last night."

He nods. "I'm Judge."

Wearing a tight, blazing-white, sleeveless T-shirt and small gold hoops in each ear, he towers above me. As the sun goes behind a cloud, his blade-ravaged face looks as thready as leaf veins. It takes some doing not to stare, so I look past him, where I've seen a shadow of someone else. As if aware she's been spotted, the biracial girl steps forward. In daylight, wearing a purple jogging suit, with a red headband taming her curly, brownish-blonde hair, she looks much more conventional than her companion. Hands in the pockets of the satiny jacket, head partly lowered, she's schoolgirl shy. Gone is the rage that radiated off her like heat from an engine last night. My heart lifts: she's come seeking a truce.

I gesture expansively. "Please sit down."

As he pulls out the chair across from me and sits down, I notice the couple draws alarmed glances from my fellow caffeine sippers. At least I think they're a couple, though I'm not totally sure—he doesn't introduce her. She sits on my left, closer to her companion than to me. He rubs his shiny head, and for a moment I think he's studying the front-page headlines. Then I realize he's waiting for *me* to say something.

"Fantastic morning, isn't it?" I smile, but he just stares.

"We wanted *you* last night," he says, "but Emanuel said no."

"Me?" I feel my neck tingle. "What on earth for?"

Sitting forward, he laces bony fingers on the table and stares coldly at me for a good three seconds. I can almost imagine a swastika tattooed on his forehead, and it makes laughter well in my chest until I recall how he was the first of them to draw blood, even if it *was* his own. The memory is no consolation, but it does suppress the rising bubble in my throat.

"Cleansing," he finally says.

Though my heart stutters at the image of myself as their live sacrifice, I decide he isn't going to get a rise out of me.

"Why?" I take a sip, holding my cup with both hands to keep it steady. Though I glance at the girl, her face is as impassive as the deafest of my parishioners, her anger of last night apparently gone.

He cocks his head. "You bring bad energy to the altar."

"Altar?"

"Where the father is," the girl says softly. "That's the place of death and rebirth."

"The father?" I ask, inwardly cringing. The lingering image of live sacrifice has reduced me to blurting stupid questions.

"She means Israel," Judge says, his eyes gleaming now with undisguised contempt, making the scars on his face even harsher. Recovering a bit, I decide to deflect their hatred, if that's what it is. Turning my body slightly away from the boy, I address her more directly.

"Rebirth, you said. Is that what the Theatre is about, being born again?"

With a glance she deflects the question to him. If they aren't lovers, then perhaps . . . a hierarchy? (Did Emanuel authorize this visit?)

"Saint Paul says 'to die is to live,'" he says.

"Well, not exactly . . ."

"That's what he *meant*." It is the loudest she's spoken so far, and some of last night's venom is back. "The father embodies death," she continues, "in his music, in his life."

I take a deep breath. "My dad is a seeker, a—"

"Aren't you a preacher?" Her eyes have become slits. "Haven't you found the truth?"

I marvel that she doesn't put me more on the defensive, but here in the daylight, away from spotlights, bleeding feedback and razors, she just seems very young. But I still feel the full heat of the boy's gaze.

"Some," I reply. "Beware those who know all."

Judge suddenly sits back, chair legs screeching, and folds his arms. "You sound like a damned agnostic. *We* believe."

Feeling the first trickle of sweat down my side, I take another sip. When it sloshes and almost spills, I set the cup down for good. "Believing is good. But not everyone shares the same beliefs." My smile barely moves muscles. "That's the source of a lot of trouble in the world."

"Now you're talking like an atheist." His lip curls into a sneer. "The only belief worth anything is the one you'll die to defend."

"Why are you so intent on death?" I open my hands, hoping they won't see the tiny tremor. "Shouldn't one's innermost spirit be about life?" *Lighten up*, I almost say, before she leans forward and hisses through clenched teeth.

"Hasn't the father taught you anything? Death *is* life."

I can't help myself; it *is* Sunday morning, after all. And they probably won't kill me here before witnesses. "To die to sin— materialism, drunkenness, lust—that's what Paul meant. Not physically taking your life. That's refusing God's greatest gift." I want to use her name but realize I don't know it. When the boy scrapes his chair forward again, I turn toward him in relief, but he's glaring again.

"You just don't get it, do you, man?"

Though the fire in his eyes has grown steadily, it helps that I'm now seeing a nineteen-year-old on the lam from school, job, and society— in other words, Dad at his age. The veins at his temples throb. I try not to see the scars as he leans forward, gripping the table as if about to turn it over. "Your father's heart is mostly dead, yet it still speaks. It's guiding us. For now, we follow."

It's the first thing he's been right about. During the Big One, Dad experienced only minor pain all night; he'd even slept. By the time he stopped the bus in Raleigh, North Carolina, the next day, the heart attack had been going on for several hours. Though he was immediately sent to emergency surgery, much damage had already occurred. I'd never asked Dr. Fritzius how he could continue to live with that much damage. Apparently he could; he had. Taking my eyes off Judge, I glance at the girl for a moment and see fleetingly her mouth is open, her eyes full. Observing me observe her, she clamps her mouth closed and quickly blinks; she will show the Philistine nothing. Still I'd like to salvage something—leave a toe in the door.

"I forget which of Dad's early songs says, 'The only good leader's the one between your ears.'"

"'Off the Limits,'" Judge says, with the glazed eyes of the idolater. "He also said, 'You'll know your god by the scars on your heart.'"

I wave the words away like gnats. Scripture-quoting contests are for first-year seminarians. "He also says his songs mostly have to do with whether he had a good bowel movement that day, or—"

She stands up fast, jostling the table, spilling coffee, and drawing stares. Spit flies when she speaks: "You don't deserve to be his son. Our gift was wasted on you. His songs are prophecy, and tonight we gift *him*."

Judge and I watch her blend into the crowd and disappear. He stands slowly, unfolds himself to his full height.

"Why is she—"

"You have something she wants."

Now I'm *really* amazed. "What in heaven's name could that be?"

Placing his palms on the table, he leans so far forward I feel the breath from the single word.

"Access."

Despite the boy's breathing down my neck, I shiver.

"Reverend, she'd give her soul to speak with Mr. Israel Jones."

"I'm sorry." I open my hands. "He doesn't have much to say to anyone—even to me."

"She calls him father," he says, "but she's furious with him."

Straightening, he opens his mouth, but before speaking darts his eyes to the side. Is it the girl or the grinning Emanuel he fears? Finally he decides.

"Tonight he will be given a gift he can't refuse."

Before I can react, he fades into the crowd and is gone. Glancing left and right, I see I'm alone. Above, the sky's greyed considerably, and the temperature has begun dropping.

* * *

Murphy sighs when I tell him. "Skip, if you'd only seen the crazies I've seen, but all right. If it makes you happy, I'll hire some security." He stands up, claps me on the shoulder like I'm twelve. At least he doesn't tousle my hair. "We'll be ready."

Somehow I feel worse, not better.

* * *

Ready for nothing, it turns out. It's a miserable show—due to my dad, not the Theatre of Transcendent Joy. Murphy's response to Judge's threat is to recruit several bodyguards from the crowd: big, beefy, bodybuilder types with menacing tattoos.

I'm a basket case while Dad, clearly off his game, lurches through mind-and-ear-boggling tonal shifts, sandwiching "St. John's Carnival"—narrated by a junkie St. John who sees the Four Horsemen of the Apocalypse as a pimp, prostitute, pornographer, and pedophilic priest—between "Face the Wind" and "Girl from the Moors," two of his earliest romantic ballads that everyone from Sinatra to Costello has covered. He stumbles a couple of times and barely strums, totally confusing the band, who are accustomed to responding to their leader's least lip curl or head bob. Dad is someplace else. In retrospect, maybe he knows it's coming, knows he is warm-up for whatever the Furies have planned (did Murphy leak what I told him?).

Dad doesn't take a break, which is fine with the packed house—patrons who drink and talk and mostly ignore him, as if he's some local kid playing for tips. The last twenty minutes consist of one horrible, long jam of "The Road to Hell is Paved With Good Inventions," during which he howls some. It is spooky and nerve fraying if you are paying attention but easier to take than a cappella solos with the audience actually listening.

I abandon my usual spot behind the band to take a table in the rear (earplugs in place), and though they are present, the Furies are at a long table, actually two tables put together, off to the left. And they stay seated, seem subdued, facing forward, their entire beings soaking up every nuance of their hero's mad screeching, made even worse because the whole performance is so mediocre, unlike his mind-numbingly bad shows where he played five songs and preached the rest of the time, or played nothing but hits so unrecognizably rearranged that half the audience left before intermission.

Surely even God heaves a sigh of relief when it is finally over. The blade bearers behaved, and Boss can only do better next time. Murphy materializes during the last fifteen minutes, standing behind my table at the bar, a half-empty fifth of Beam beside him. When he winks at me, I can't return it. I'm too tired, the lowest I've yet felt. Why aren't I glad that Judge and the gang didn't fulfill their prophecy?

Since there is no back exit, much less a dressing room, Dad leans the Gibson against his amp, ambles offstage, and makes his way through the middle of the room after the obligatory encore, a half-hearted version of a half-assed song, "Sonnet for a Summer Séance." So nobody except me (and maybe Murphy) is paying much attention when shadows from the right and left converge on him. Something gold glints on the taller figure's face, when a nearby door opens, flashing light for a second. The bald head gleams. It's Judge and the biracial girl meeting Dad midway in the room.

I rise on rubber legs, knowing it's too late, already feeling as if I'm underwater, imagining the cap gun shots of a cheap pistol, as in the endlessly repeated video of Reagan's shooting by Hinckley. Backlit by golden light from the bandstand, the two meet Dad at exactly the same moment. Frozen by my mind's time lapse, the vignette unspools like ancient newsreel. Reaching him first, the girl raises her arm, slowly, slowly. While my own arm lifts, and I point helplessly, she thrusts out her hand. I imagine the pistol, tiny, a child's toy the same size as the one Ruby pointed at Oswald.

But it is only a piece of paper, which Dad accepts, staring hard into her face. I relax a little, forgetting, as Dad apparently has too, the boy on the left. As if swiping a credit card, Judge reaches up and strokes Dad's cheek like a gentle barber. I almost laugh—is he testing Dad's beard?—until I see the dark track when he lowers his hand. Too late, I find my voice.

"Stop him!" I point like an idiot, but the boy has already melted back into the crowd.

Murphy's stool hits the floor behind me, and we get to Dad at exactly the same time. The girl too has disappeared.

"God*dammit*, where's the fucking bouncers?" Murphy has his arms raised stiffly beside his ears, an aging alkie Karate Kid. Dad stands staring at his blood-gleaming fingers.

"Let me see what they did," I say and step closer. Dad jumps back, clamping his cheek protectively. A perfectly understandable response, yet it still hurts like hell.

Murphy barrels right up, knocks his hand away, and studies the wound.

"You're all right, Boss," he croons. "It's just a scratch. But I'm gonna rip those fuckers another asshole when I find 'em."

He hands Dad a filthy handkerchief and turns his furious gaze outward. One of his goons finally lurches toward us. "What the hell'd I hire you for, dipshit! Didn't I say to stay close to 'im?"

The guy's about two-fifty and six four, with enough tattoos on his bulging arms for about a half-dozen frat boys, but he steps back when Murphy approaches. "Git outside and search cars. Bust heads if you have to. Find those fucking kids and bring them to me *NOW*."

"Maybe we should call the cops," I say.

Turning suddenly, Murphy seizes my arm. His eyes are wild, and I steady myself for a blow. Then he lets go. "I can handle this."

After signaling to another guy wearing denim and chains, the bouncer heads out the side door. Turning, I see the club's owner and Murphy leading Dad out, arms around his waist. He still holds the handkerchief to his cheek, and though tempted to follow, I don't. Judge did what he'd meant to do—exactly that and no more. My father is now marked, claimed, baptized, and bought—one of them.

Chapter Eleven

When I get to my hotel room, I find two messages on my cell. Any communication following what I just witnessed can't be good. I say the serenity prayer and punch in the password.

"Good evening, Thomas." Another night, Mr. Owens's polite baritone might've been comforting. Tonight it's jangling. I flop onto the bed. "I hope you're having a good day. I wanted to update you on the adjudication process. But first, I must tell you that Brother Ron continues to astound."

I close my eyes and lie back on the bed, tuning out while the deacon compares Reverend Jenkins to the young Billy Graham. Up until my leave-taking, I too used words like adjudication, walked on eggshells, and kept my doubts to myself, having lost my only confidante since ending my counseling sessions with Jo. I feel like shaking Henry, but it passes, and I laugh instead, finally releasing the tension of watching my father bleed. *Lighten up.* There ensues an uncharacteristic pause. I sit up.

"It was decided by the board that, in light of Mrs. Strickland's failure to, um, clear things up satisfactorily, they have some questions to ask you, Reverend. I regret this, knowing you're no doubt distracted by other responsibilities, but it looks like your presence is required at the next deacons' meeting Wednesday morning at eleven. I know that's only three days from now. I'm dreadfully sorry not to give you more notice."

The second message is from Maxine.

"I thought you should know, Reverend J."—she takes a deep breath—"that the Stricklands are separated. Phyllis Winthrop's daughter Deena babysits on days when Jo has choir practice—well, Jo called Phyllis and said her services won't be needed. 'Their father has them,' she said, 'and he *will* have them *to his apartment* on Thursdays from now on.'"

She pauses—out of kindness, I know. If Jo hadn't already told me this news, I'd sure need Max's forbearance now. After clearing her throat, she continues.

"Since calling you home, deacons've moved in the gallows. The guillotine is on order." I sense her radar scanning, as her voice lowers. "Perry Mason thinks he's got grounds to convict. Be prepared."

I open my eyes and study the white, cracked, water-stained ceiling. *Be prepared.* Like the good Boy Scout I never was. But I find myself glad to hear it's come at last, that I'll need to drop everything, remove myself from the tour at its lowest (I hope) moment. I stand up so fast I see stars. I want those deacons here *now*. Fixating on the fat jowls of Kenneth Branch, I long to . . . but then another face superimposes itself onto Ken's.

Ronald Jenkins. I'm defenseless against the wave of envy burning upward from my gut, heating my neck and face.

I know my transgressions, and my sin is ever before me.

Walking to the window, I see nothing but the usual dreary urban landscape of parking lot, dumpster, and blighted, dying pines. It's raining again, and the temperature has been steadily dropping since twilight. How has Dad endured this wasteland for more than four decades? But his mind has been his only real landscape for so long—all his life, I imagine. The external world is irrelevant. He hardly seems to notice it. (Except maybe now when it's come at him with a blade.)

BAM BAM BAM.

I lurch and almost fall but for the dresser. It has to be Murphy, come to accuse me for my role in the security breakdown. After the deacon's call, I'm ready for him. Flinging the door open, I behold a sheepish, bare-chested boy I at first mistake for Judge. But there are no scars; this boy's cheeks are as smooth as a baby's.

"Sorry to disturb you, Reverend, but . . . are you busy?"

"Come on in." Patrick enters tentatively, as if the air might be tainted by lingering ecclesiastical flatulence. I resist the urge to lay my hand on his shoulder and steer him.

"Have a seat, Pat." I have no idea if anyone calls him that. At that moment, he's a kid, just like (I dearly hope) the deluded Judge.

He sits on the bed, and I pull out a desk chair. "Well, the shit hit the fan, Reverend—pardon my French—and I thought you'd like to know."

I try for a good deep breath, but it's too painful.

"Boss fired Murphy."

"He's done it before. Many times."

The boy shakes his head. "Not while I been on board. He got in his Caddy and roared out of here like a bat out of a bell."

"It might take a day or two, but Murphy can't live without this. It's his life."

The boy looks down, then up, right into my eyes. His desire to believe me is touching.

"I hope so. I'm not sure things will happen, y'know, without a manager." He pauses. "Maybe you'd like to take over while he's gone."

My laugh is like a shot, and I see he is hurt. "I'm sorry, but . . . tell my dad and his band where to go and what to do? My father has never listened to me about anything." Then I think of Dad in the hospital room telling me his secret and almost relent. "Anyway, I've got to go home for a while."

"But you'll come back?" His eyes glitter.

I haven't until that moment decided. "I'll be back. I promise. And so will Murphy, guaranteed." I stand. "Until then, you guys can hold things together." I walk him to the door. "So what set off the fireworks?"

He shrugs. "Big fight over what happened tonight."

"I suppose Murphy wants tighter security, more bodyguards?"

"He wants the rest of the tour canceled."

I sag against the doorjamb. *"What?"*

"He compared it to what happened after Lennon was shot, when the others decided it wasn't safe to go out for a while. 'Lay low until the scum settles' is what he said."

"I can imagine what my father said to that."

Standing in the hall now, the boy cuts his eyes to his left, caught in the middle of a family feud. "Reverend, he didn't say nothing. He just walked over to within a foot of Murphy and stared."

I see it, feel it.

"Finally Murphy busts out, 'So, I'm fired, or what?' And when Boss doesn't say nothing, he turns around and slinks out slow, looking over his shoulder like he expected Mr. Jones to beg him back."

I shake my head. That'll happen when hell becomes a theme park. "Where's the next gig?" I ask.

"Chapel Hill."

I brighten. "Abshire's?"

"I think so."

I clap him on the shoulder. "I may be back before then, but Abshire's is a good gig. Eddie Abshire owns the joint—along with his son Jake. It's run as tight as a boot camp. First glint of a blade, and those kids are history." I begin closing the door. "But I'll call Eddie in the morning and let him know his old pal's dragging a Trojan horse full of blood-hungry Greeks behind him."

Pat's eyes gleam in the dull hallway lamp. Tears? If so, they aren't enough to make me stay. Ken Branch and his bullies are beating up on Jo in my absence; I am going to make them answer for that.

"One more thing, Reverend Thom." He cuts his eyes to the left again, but the coast guard must have things under control. "If it don't go good without Murphy, Wendell's talking about quitting. If he goes, so will Javier, probably Tully too."

Here you are, Dad: a full-scale mutiny. Keep it up and there'll be nothing between you and the narrow blade. Now I seize the kid's shoulder and squeeze. "But he'll have *you*, Patrick."

The kid's glassy eyes shine. "Fuggin' A." He drops his head. "'Scuse my French, Reverend."

"Good night . . . rather, good morning, Patrick." And I gently close the door.

* * *

It is well after two when I ease into the hallway and slip down to Dad's room. After Patrick's visit, I tried praying for an hour—on my knees at the desk, lying on the bed, in the shower. Not even a busy signal. After tapping lightly, I hear Dad growl.

"It's open."

Inside, the overhead light and desk lamp are on. He lies on the farthest bed, fully clothed, facing the wall, knees drawn up like a child's. The flesh showing between cuff and sock is shockingly white. A living corpse. Getting cut in public must take it out of you. It occurs to me that he expects me to be Murphy, left the door unlocked for him.

"Dad, I've got to go home, but I'll be back. Some business I've got to take care of. I'll hook back up with you in Chapel Hill."

He doesn't respond. Is he regretting letting Murphy go? Is he pissed at me for abandoning his sinking ship? Did he tell me everything he is ever going to in his hospital room? I'd like to ask about his cut, but figure he's in no mood. Surely Mother Murphy got it all patched up before he left.

That's when I see, propped on the nightstand, a curling photograph. Instantly I know it's what the girl handed him a few hours ago. And maybe the reason Dad is facedown against the wall. Tiptoeing over, I pick up the fading Polaroid as if it might disintegrate. The beautiful black woman's eyes glare a challenge at the photographer, though her mouth is clamped closed. Her child, though, about five, could not look more different. Her wide, gap-toothed grin says *yes*. Her dark, laughing eyes say *life*. Her curly, blondish-brown hair says *soft*. Is this unearthly gorgeous girl just another in the long procession of his wannabe children? So how much does she want? (Lord, Lord, have I turned into Murphy?)

"Dad, is that girl—"

His voice is like a thunderclap. *"NO."*

I lower myself to a sitting position on the other bed and wait. But there is no more. I decide to let semisleeping dogs lie.

"I'm in some trouble," I say to his back. "It concerns the young lady I spoke of at the retreat."

Despite the lights blazing in the room, darkness enters me. Do I want him to comment, to advise? But in the ensuing silence he neither faces me nor moves. Maybe he doesn't want me to see his face with its new injury. (Embarrassed? Ashamed?) I shudder, as if it were me that inflicted it.

"Plus there's this substitute pastor there—a young, charismatic guy, who they'd probably love to replace me with. I can't let them do that without at least telling them the whole truth."

And what earthly good, Dad's black coat seems to say, *has telling the truth ever done anyone? Only what they* feel *is true matters.* I grin, enjoying the silent dialogue with Dad's back. I need to chat with it more often, even if its opinions do tend more toward Pilate than Jesus.

"And the truth is, though I love this woman, I have never touched her. It's been strictly Platonic."

You touched her with your heart.

The back has me again. (I notice now his shoulders rising and falling more rapidly—in response to my words? Or is he asleep?)

"I know I can't have her, but I don't want her husband to have her either. He treats her like a slave. I want her to be free to—"

To what?

"—seek God's will."

Bull. Shit.

All the brightness drains away, and I listen hard and stare at the black coat. I seem able to see between its shiny threads and glimpse his tattered shirt beneath, then sweaty wifebeater beneath that. What if I pray right now? Do I expect God to come running down that hallway, nightshirt billowing, grey mane down around His shoulders like some big-haired headbanger? God mostly listens, AA taught me. There are really only two prayers, according to the old-timers: *pleasepleaseplease* and *thankyouthankyouthankyou,* and the second is by far the more important. But I am not feeling very grateful; I'm afraid. Afraid to stay and afraid to go back.

"Anyhow, I'm going home to see what I can do for her."

I rise, bed squeaking. I've got to leave before I do something rash like grab him and turn him over. *Show me your face, father!* (Wouldn't everyone be better off if I smothered him with a pillow?)

My hand's on the doorknob when I stop. Just one word. One word and I stay. But there's nothing, so I go.

*   *   *

Within minutes, I'm packed. The night manager helps me rent the Taurus that'll get me back to New Pres. Within an hour, I go from rain to snow back to rain again, the road becoming a fuzzy blur. In the waning hours of the night, I pull into a rest stop and crash for ninety minutes, then go on, endlessly. At last, I pull up in front of the parsonage just as the sun rises, shut off the engine, and wait. The psalmist's words come.

> *I have come into deep waters*
> *I am weary with crying*
> *My eyes grow dim*
> *with waiting for my God.*

Light flakes have begun sticking to my windshield, and the Taurus's ticking engine is the only reply.

Chapter Twelve

I sleep almost all day Tuesday, rising to eat, pace, and watch mindless TV before retiring at midnight. Monday morning, I rise early to catch up on mail and messages at the parsonage, but mostly I watch cardinals flit from branch to branch with a purpose I envy. Snow stops at noon after accumulating only a couple of inches, and although it's cold enough in the house to keep my coat on, I don't even consider walking to the church, grateful no one will recognize the Taurus out front. Whenever I feel the urge to grab notebook, pen, and Bible and prepare a defense of myself for the deacons, I resist. Innocence requires no defense; innocence is its own defense. I want to walk into the lion's den empty, pure. I want to do it the way Dad would, the way Christ would. Somehow I make it, hovering above the space heater in my study, till Wednesday morning.

* * *

Holy Martyrs' church office is empty except for the two of us. Maxine actually comes around the desk to hug me. Then, back behind her desk, she cranes her neck to see into the hallway before whispering. "D-i-v-o-r-c-e. Perry Mason thinks he's got you on two counts: putting Joanna up to it and . . ." She didn't have to say it. Would I be surprised to find papers from Mim's lawyer among the mail I haven't sorted through yet? When I nod, she scrutinizes me sternly above her glasses.

"But you should know before they put you on the rack that baby-sitting has resumed." I must look clueless. After ray-gunning me with her eyes for several seconds, she adds: "Phyllis told me the Stricklands are back together."

"Oh, no." I regret the slip instantly, but Max doesn't lift a brow. I'm apparently not the only one who knows how bad Jo has it.

"Oh, *yes*. Now you'll be well armed when Kenny tries to pin a big D on you." She sits up straight, returning to her keyboard. "Don't let him."

I try to smile reassuringly, but she resumes typing.

* * *

We gather in Fellowship Hall at two long folding tables side by side. The silver Christmas tree left over from the sixties is up, and deacons' wives have hung greenery, festive lettering ("A King Is Born") and dramatic scenes depicting magi, manger, the star. Elder deacon Kenneth Branch sits at the tables' head, and the nine others range along both sides, with me at the other end facing Ken with Henry Owens on my left. We need only the Good Shepherd Himself to complete our Last Supper tableau.

"Well, gentlemen." Kenneth waits a beat for David Ames to quit chatting with Melvin Crouch. "Let's get right down to business," he says, becoming the small-town attorney.

He avoids my eyes as he's done since entering the room one minute before eleven. All the others showed up early, wrung my hand or hugged me, looking earnestly into my eyes when they asked about my father's health. (Word is out, thanks to Maxine and Henry. I no longer care what they think.) We all talked trivialities, and

I kept it light too, giving my standard answer about Dad's health: "He's doing as well as one can who's had two major heart incidents and a ministroke."

To which they all nodded sympathetically. They or their family members have had their own such incidents. The deacons of Holy Mart are no spring lambs, and the average age would be higher but for Jerry Tibbetts, an infant at thirty-two—he's the only one who had to leave work to attend. I loved the deacons for not probing deeply into my background. They'd accepted me for what I appeared to be: a youngish seminary grad willing to pastor in the wilds of rural Ohio. Not a single one had known, as far as I could tell, who my father was—or if they did, they hadn't said. I sure hadn't told them.

"Reverend Johnson." Ken looks at me at last, and though his mouth is firmly set in a half smile, his eyes say what his lips don't. "I'll be candid. Your relationship with Mrs. Strickland has caused a disturbance in the church—that you already know. What you may *not* know is the disturbance it's caused in her family. Mr. and Mrs. Strickland have separated."

I try for a face as empty as Israel Jones's at a press conference. Thanks to Maxine prepping me, I radiate neither shame nor joy. After waiting a second, he continues.

"Both still attend services at Suffering Christ but sit on opposite sides of the aisle." He sighs, removes his bifocals. "There's talk."

I don't look away when his piercing blue eyes say: *sower of discord.*

"The Strickland children are suffering, Reverend Johnson. Currently, they're living mostly with their mother, but should there be a divorce, the proceedings are sure to be . . ."

Bloody. Of course he's too squeamish to say it. Should I spill the beans right here, tell him they're back together and save myself?

". . . strained," the deacon concludes. "To the extent that we can, the church must help, to be seen as an institution that doesn't say,

'Hands off, it's none of our business,' or, like the police, 'We can't intervene until something happens.' We *have* intervened . . . spiritually. Now, hopefully with your cooperation, we must intervene materially."

I glance at Henry. He stares down at the table, looking miserable. He's gained weight, pants a little, and sweats easily. I half expect him to start weeping. I long to pat his shoulder but don't want to taint him. He'll remain here long after I am gone.

"Thank you, Reverend, for keeping a low profile recently. Your presence in the pulpit might've polarized the congregation further. Things are bad enough already. Fortunately, during your absence we've had a healer in our midst." He smiles left and right, acknowledging the nods of approbation. "Perhaps you'll stay for services tonight, and observe a young man richly blessed, bringing grace, even salvation, to a troubled congregation."

All of them hang their heads now. Bluntness, much less cruelty, is not the Holy Mart way. Ken is clearly in courtroom mode, letting his long-held dislike of me show. If he thinks I am going to flee with my tail between my legs, he's wrong. "I'd like that very much," I reply, which causes a few to glance guiltily my way.

"You won't be sorry, Mister Johnson," Ken replies. "He's a juggernaut for Jesus."

Now the talk's turned to Ron, I've become Mister instead of Reverend. It is all decided, then. No wonder they've been studying the table. Will they be shocked to hear the Stricklands are back together? Will it be enough for them?

"But we digress. In your own words, sir, would you tell us what Mrs. Strickland seemingly could not, though we tried to obtain her full testimony? Was there an ungodly relationship between the two of you?"

"God was there the whole time."

He doesn't blink. "Did your relationship enter the domain of the . . . extramarital?"

"We did not have sex."

"The extramarital includes a lot more than carnal relations. Did you exceed your responsibility as one bound by God to counsel one's sister only for the salvation of her soul? Ergo, did you suggest she leave her husband and destroy the sanctity of her marriage?"

I pause a beat, remembering my dialogue with Dad's coat. *When did the truth ever help anything?* Still . . .

"I told Jo—Mrs. Strickland—that it might be impossible to reconcile their conflicting desires and aspirations for their children."

Ken tents his fingers on the table. "That means divorce."

I return his stare. "Not necessarily. Besides, divorce is not always wrong."

He knows as well as I do that Holy Marters despise divorce the way most Catholics hate abortion. Henry is the only moderate present, and he's only two degrees left of Ken. "Would you want to explain to the"—*court?* He catches himself—"the board why you used pastoral counseling to split rather than save a Christian marriage?"

"Mrs. Strickland is an artist," I begin, "and Mr. Strickland is an auto mechanic. Her vision for her three children is that their upbringing be as close to the world of art—nature, God's world—as it can be. She wants them to be exposed to"—I can't say cultural; that'll conjure museums full of Mapplethorpes—"everything that opens a child's eyes—art, books, music, while Mr. Strickland considers all of that humanism, which takes kids' eyes off of God and puts them on the secular world."

Ken glances meaningfully around the table. I have paraphrased the opposition too well. Deacons mostly gaze at the walls or ceiling. Some doodle on notepads. Their worst suspicions have been confirmed. *Secular humanism.* Though good people, self-sacrificing and hardworking to a fault, none of them care a whit about art—New Prestonburg schools substituted miniclasses in how to pass state proficiency tests in the place of art and music; there is no longer a show choir at the high school, and their most ambitious school play in recent years was *Cinderella*. Jo knows she'll be sending her kids to Chillicothe for music lessons when the time comes.

"Parents often disagree, Mr. Johnson, and it's hardly grounds for divorce. Is there anything else we should know?"

I stare back. Now's the time to play the ace Maxine gave me. Even without lying, I could imply I'd helped the troubled young couple patch it up. Branch might even blink. But I've decided to play the hand I was dealt. Dad would.

"She told me a great deal more, but she told me in confidence. I will not betray that confidence."

"But, surely, to save—"

"No."

I look around. The deacons have heard enough: their preacher has chosen art, nature, and divorce over the Christian family; and the freedom to find your true family, in case it isn't the one you were born into. In effect, the first time I told a married woman it wasn't too late for her to choose how and with whom to raise her kids, I'd parted ways with Holy Mart. (And God? I'm not sure.)

"Is there anything else you can tell us, Mister Johnson?"

It is time for closing remarks. I take the deepest breath I can get in the airless room.

"Mr. Branch, I have problems similar to the Stricklands' in my own home." As if at a multicar pileup, they can't look away, though the sight surely sickens them. "My wife and I are not currently co-habiting." My sweet Lord, I am picking up Branch's stilted lawyer tone. I have time for only the briefest of prayers: *Help.* I gulp down air.

"Sometimes partners go in different directions, and sometimes that causes a parting of the ways for a while. But who on earth can say what God's will is for those partners? But I know as surely as I know God's saving me was real, that when a person sees suffering caused by injustice, especially suffering in children—and those kids will suffer under Dennis Strickland's hand—he must speak up. Especially when you're a so-called man of God."

When I pause, a little breathless, I feel that all-too-rare Sunday-morning surge when He seemed to burn away my ego entirely and sear my words with spirit. "God gave me a voice with which to speak as surely as He gave Moses, David, Paul, or"—all was lost, anyway, so I went ahead—"Jesus."

"Mr. Johnson!" Ken spreads his arms to gather in his Pharisees. "I can hardly equate a domestic, a *human,* situation—yours or the Stricklands'—to Christ's."

"I disagree, Mr. Branch." I keep my eyes on him. "Jesus was a man first, the Christ second."

I feel more than hear the sharp intake of breath that always accompanies heresy or truth. Has it really been Thomas the Doubter who's uttered what surely constitutes blasphemy inside these walls? Though my heart gongs within my chest, it does not quiver. Apparently it was I who said those words, and I do not hear Him telling me to recant, though, God knows, I am willing for one moment to forswear and save myself. Then I hear Dad speak from his sickbed right before I walked out after his first heart attack: "I will stand in the fire until God smites me with His sword." Staring at my prosecutor, I do not blink.

Relacing his fingers, Ken looks once more around the circle, satisfied, making brief eye contact with every member of the jury before he speaks.

"Reverend, would you mind waiting outside while we confer?"

Their verdict will be swift.

"I'll be upstairs in the sanctuary."

* * *

I turn on no lights. What leaks in from the iron-grey day outside is sufficient. The scent permeating this high-ceilinged room
is palpable: candle wax, old roses, and evergreen: I smell before see
the white pine that always stands to the left of the pulpit during
the entire month of December. Red-robed Jesus looks down from
the window on the right, the one I always turned to when I strayed
during a sermon. Like the professional shepherd He is, He led me
back, or I fancy He did.

Now I'm in the pulpit, facing empty pews. I imagine Jo sitting
with her kids, staring into my eyes as she had the first night she
ever came to get my counsel. *I feel I can trust you.* Would I have
done better by her, and would I be able to pray now, if I hadn't loved
her so deeply? Was it, in the end, just lust after all? Squeezing my
eyes shut, I grip the podium hard to keep standing. *Can the man
ever be fully denied to embrace the Christ?* Every cell in my body says
you took a vow. When I open my eyes, I behold not the old Suffering
Christ Church, where I've toiled so long for so little effect, but a new
church, conjured from somewhere deep inside.

Peering into dimness, I make out a figure sitting on the last row:
a man, his grey-black head bowed. Has the ghost come for a sermon? All right.

"I seek only peace—is that asking too much?" My voice echoes,
too loud. "A man needs to accept what he cannot change, but sometimes it's too hard, and he goes to God."

The bowed head in the back may as well be my Dad's, so sharply
do I feel rebuked. I keep my eyes forward.

"So here I am, naked before the jury. Yonder stand my judge and prosecutor. Here stands the sinner. Who will throw the first stone?"

"You've thrown stones all your life, Thom. But they've been pebbles. It's time to stand behind your words, your life."

I turn toward the voice (knowing it's only in the echoing sanctuary of my soul—I am overwrought but not crazy.) Steeped in recent memory, stunned by loss, my wife stares up at me, her eyes fierce.

"I am," I say. "I'm on the road with my father."

"I mean up *there*. I want to know if you'll ever show this congregation who you really are."

"I am their servant." My first misstep, and the floor shifts ever so slightly. *Watch it.* Below in Fellowship Hall, the conflagration rages. When I glance toward her, Jo doesn't look up, adjusting a child's collar, wiping a mouth, shushing and soothing. The voice continues inside my head.

"You are the son of a legend; you are a musician, poet, alcoholic, and"—I wait for it: *pastor? husband? lover?*—"a father."

My knees weaken, exactly as they used to during my earliest sermons, when, for a single moment, I took my eyes off Him. I grasp the sides of the podium harder. *I will stand in the fire . . .*

"My love, I am many things, but I am *not* a father."

"Thomas?"

When I turn, Henry stands in the doorway, looking stricken. I realize I've been speaking aloud, but I feel no embarrassment; I feel . . . euphoric.

"It's time, Reverend."

I smile at my friend, then look back. The pews are, of course, empty.

* * *

The prosecutor hardly waits till all are seated before speaking.

"We've agreed that, for the foreseeable future, Reverend Jenkins will lead Suffering Christ as its full-time pastor, if he's amenable to our terms, allowing you time off to tend to your father and seek God's will for your life."

"If I'm fired, Ken, just say so."

He smiles, tries but fails to keep smugness off his face. "Mister Johnson, this is a church, not a corporation. We don't fire people." He looks around at his colleagues, all of whom seem certain on this point. At least they aren't looking at walls and ceiling. "Thus, you'll be paid a stipend of one-fourth of your salary, for up to twelve months, in order to make your decision."

Mystified, I look at Henry, but he shrugs. I think I've been following the proceedings pretty well. "What decision?" I say.

Ken folds his arms. "That when and if you resume your duties, you make a vow before God—and us, in writing—to keep His children together in marriage, never to part them."

I think of my own parents, doomed from the outset. Together, they were in hell, though parting had killed my mom, as surely as if Dad had stabbed her. Still . . . is a vow a prison? If I'm to burn on this earth—and we all are, if we're alive—one must find the fire where he'll blaze the brightest. I know now that, as surely as Dad should not have vowed till death do us part to my mother, I will not vow to these men. My wife is right (how long has she known?): I am not now and have never been, not truly, their pastor.

And I won't use the last rag of truth—that the Stricklands are back together—because the real truth is, whether they remain together or not, I *would* part them if I could.

"Mr. Branch, the Stricklands' marriage, like my own, is between themselves and God. I have faith He will guide them out of their present trouble, but I also believe He will not force them to stay together." When I pause, I hear pinging on the window. The weather grew increasingly worse the farther I'd traveled north just three days ago: rain, then sleet, back to rain the last fifty miles. Now it is icy snowflakes. "You'll have my resignation by tomorrow."

"Thom, please." It's Henry. "We don't mean . . ."

Finding my legs stable, I stand as straight as I can and walk out. Easing the door closed, I merge with the hallway's darkness and breathe.

* * *

Afterward, in the pastor's study, I think Henry will cry. "I had no idea they'd be so vindictive."

"They weren't," I say, avoiding the photo of Mim that had lingered at the bottom of the drawer since I'd placed it there after she left. After a long walk through an ice-locked town, I'm feeling better. "Actually, Ken was pretty restrained for a prosecuting attorney."

My friend is vigorously rubbing his eyes. "He's an estate planner, not a prosecutor."

"Until today." I smile tightly, feeling the muscle above the right side of my upper lip twitch. I throw Mim's photo facedown in the box. "You want to go hear Reverend Jenkins preach?"

Henry carefully replaces his glasses. "If you do."

* * *

Prayer meeting is held in the chapel, since a much smaller group attends than Sunday services in the sanctuary. When we sneak in late and sit in the next-to-last row, Ella Mae Bailey is reciting a long list of friends and family needing prayer. At eighty-something, she knows most of the town. So this is what prayer meeting looks like when you aren't in charge. I observe young Ron, standing in the aisle between the first two rows, one hand on the front pew, and study him closely for signs of impatience. But as Ella drones on, he looks relaxed (as I never was, anticipating the unexpected with a hypervigilance that I called dedication). His eyes never leave her powdered, wrinkled face.

After we've sat a few moments, Henry nudges me, tips his head toward my left. When my eyes land on Joanna's flaming hair, I can't breathe. Beside her sit the children, resplendent as jewels. Dennis sits close beside her, his arm on the back of the pew, extending past the girls, his fingers fondling her shoulder. I release my breath slowly. Glancing right, I see Henry has been watching me.

"You knew, didn't you?" he whispers.

When I don't answer, he faces forward and crosses his arms, his mouth tight. I hope he's not too disappointed, but I don't care whether he understands or not. Maybe it's because I'm not in charge, but I feel free sitting here with a strange pastor at the helm of my ship. I clap my eyes forward onto Ron Jenkins's angelic face. A shadow of a smile not the least bit condescending lights his unremarkable features: gaunt, sallow cheeks with deep-set eyes that gleam when he leans his head back and lets them catch light, as he is doing now, his long pianist's fingers tented as he prays the opening prayer. All heads bow but mine. I let my eyes roam among the few dozen congregants, those who dutifully come whenever the church doors are open.

But I carefully keep my eyes away from the family on the third pew from the front and to my left. Images come, unbidden, of Joanna's many faces: entreating, smiling, frowning, sorrowing as she laid out her hopes and fears. I hear not a word of Ron's prayer but come to in time to hear his message.

"I'm grateful for all the joy and health we have here at Holy Martyrs, and I anticipate being more joyous as these prayers are answered." He pauses. "But as all who believe in Him know, they won't always be answered the way we desire. Some of those we just prayed for will leave us. Not all of our sons and daughters serving in the military will come home. All things pass. Life is neither permanent nor free of suffering."

Watch it, Ron. However, all eyes remain uplifted, all bodies silent, even the children, who either watch, eyes glazed, mouths opened slightly, or keep their eyes in their laps, scribbling on old bulletins.

"So, my friends, we must come to grips with our mortality, fully aware we are part of God's creation: all must pass away for the master to rule.

"Still, we offer these prayers. What we're really saying to God is, 'We witness our brother's and sister's pains and lift up our hearts to you, not so you'll do *our* bidding and heal them but give us the strength to bear our suffering, all of it.' Now the first step is seeing it, facing it. But we don't want to. We want things perfect."

The easier, softer way. I slowly relax.

"We want," he says, looking right at me, "to be unconscious."

I feel my mind divide, half of it critical, jealous even; and half excited, eager. It is what I came to, also, in my ministry: when does dependence on God become overdependence, denial even, of our own responsibility to be awake? But I thought the congregation would consider it psychobabble, even blasphemy; thus, I explicated safe parables in a corny, modern way. Ron is grinning all over himself.

"We are all, even the eldest among us, still children—God's

children, of course—but kids with skinned knees who want Daddy to fix our boo-boos, right?"

Sympathetic laughter. It hurts a little to see how thoroughly he has them charmed. I'm charmed too, not even worrying, for the time being, what I'll say to Jo if our paths cross before I get out of town. (*If* I get out of town; when Henry and I walked over, the wind was blowing snow horizontally, reducing visibility.)

"It shows itself in our prayer life. 'Do this, Lord. Do that.' Natural, maybe—but wrong. If God is God, He knows all; He's got the facts, ma'am. And what He does with them is up to Him. So what's that leave for us? Gratitude. Ninety-five percent of prayer should be grateful praise. Then what's left for us to *do* in this Christian life?"

They are leaning forward. Beside me, Henry sits, softly wheezing. It's like waiting for Dad's first onstage howl.

"Find one's path—oh, God will lead you—and stick with it, sunshine or storm. False paths will rise to claim us for a time—they may even be decorated with images of Christ, might even contain crosses for us to bear—but if they don't contain the seeds of our crucifixion, then we must leave that path and begin again."

As he tilts his head once more into the light, his forehead shines. There is only one crucifixion, Bub; one's mundane problems hardly compare. But they're chewing on it. You can hear the turning of a hymnal's page in the silence before he speaks again.

"God be with you, friends, in finding your paths to Calvary; and if there is no blood shed—I do not mean this literally, though in some cases it could come to that—you haven't fully surrendered. Let He who shed His blood for us be your mentor, your guide. He won't take you only so far and leave you. He'll take you all the way. Now, if you'll bow once more in prayer . . ."

This time I do.

Afterward, I try to get out fast, but when Henry blocks the aisle, talking to Harvey Wells, whom he apparently hasn't seen in years, I fight back my need to escape. If crucifixion is coming, let it begin tonight. So when Joanna and Dennis start down the aisle, I relax, or try to, neither averting my eyes nor altering my stance. It makes me sad seeing that hardly anyone speaks to her, but so inward looking is her demeanor, I'm not surprised. She comes straight toward me, her eyes narrowed, brow furrowed.

"Reverend Johnson," she says meekly, "you're home." My heart falls. Hair held back tightly by barrettes, she's wearing blue eye shadow beneath thick glasses (where are her contacts? Then I remember: Dennis doesn't like them). She is barely recognizable as the fiery, wild-haired creature who came to my study last winter. God forgive me, I cannot look at the man standing beside her. I've surrendered her cause; surely she hoped I wouldn't.

"Not for long," I hear myself say. "My father needs me. I'm going back."

A silence ensues that, before Ron's sermon, before my inquisition, before my vision in the sanctuary, would've been death itself. But I'm pretty certain my crucifixion lies on down the road, that my father will lead me to it, and it's not coming tonight. As for hers . . .

She looks up into her husband's face, and I resist the urge to look away. Instead I follow her gaze. Dennis bends down, listening to something the youngest, Kayla, is saying to him. Jo takes a step toward me, whispers so that only I can hear. "Dennis forgave me."

I am frozen; I have no voice.

When Dennis straightens, Jo steps back beside him and takes her daughters' hands. Now she smiles, and I see I've been wrong again. Jo isn't judging me; Jo has chosen. The seeds of her crucifixion surround her on all sides. Now I know what I must do.

Seizing Dennis's hand, I squeeze it between both of mine. His nails are blackened with oil and grease, his fingers rough as coarse-grit sandpaper.

"God bless you."

"And you, Reverend."

It's hard to forgive those we've harmed, but meeting the eyes of the man on whom I've blamed my sins is not as terrible as I've imagined. He returns my smile, I drop his hand, and it's over. Jo's face is as pale as Henry's was earlier. I've surrendered her cause, and though it's what she wanted, she feels the cruelty of her choice. Only a day (a lifetime) ago, I would've said something rash, mumbled some impossible promise. Since I can't save everybody (anybody?), I offer what I have.

"God bless you both . . . and the girls."

Releasing her daughters' hands, she takes her husband's arm and guides her family out the door. Neck burning, I lean on the pew while Henry drones on. Now, watching Ron Jenkins make his handshaking way up the aisle, I am wild to escape, but my friend still blocks my path.

"Excuse me, Henry, but I really need to go."

But by the time he's moved his wide self into the aisle, Ron is on us like a raptor.

"It is a joy to have you among us, Reverend Johnson." He takes my hand firmly and speaks quietly, his face full of concern. Perhaps my biggest surprise: I believe him.

"And how is your father?"

I shake off Joanna and Dennis, deacons and ghosts. "He's not out of the woods yet, but there's hope," I answer, hearing myself as a listener, amazed. It sounds like Dad is nursing a hangnail rather than howling onstage with a half-dead heart and free-floating blood clot heading for his brain. It'd be almost funny if it weren't tragic. I notice Ron still has my hand—one of my tricks to capture somebody who hopes to flee the holy fool.

"I'll keep on praying for him," he says, his first utterance that smacks of preacherly rote.

"But not that he be spared?" It's out before I can squelch it.

He doesn't catch on for a second. Then he remembers what he said earlier. "Amen," he whispers even lower, and finally releases my hand. His blue eyes burn like the fire at the center of opal. "I'm glad you came tonight, Reverend Johnson."

I gaze longingly toward the doorway.

"It's awful hard to let someone else take your crop to market, isn't it?" Ron continues. "I'm sorry your father called you away. But you'll be back in the pulpit before you know it. As a matter of fact, that's what I wanted to ask you. I overheard you tell the Stricklands that you're going back, but if you're in town till Sunday, would you honor us by preaching?" He reads my face like a repentant sinner's. "It'd be a tremendous blessing—for all of us. It might strengthen you . . . for what lies ahead."

The seeds of our crucifixion.

His offer is real. He doesn't know what the deacons are up to. They'll wait till tomorrow to offer him my job. I lay my hand on Ron's shoulder.

"Reverend Jenkins, I'm moved by your offer, and, though my soul is more than half a quart low at the moment, I'm tempted. But the pulpit is yours—and rightly so."

He starts to say something but closes his mouth when I squeeze his bony shoulder. I won't tell him the truth, that I suspect I'll never preach again. He'll protest, I'll argue, and that will break both our hearts. Then my hand tingles, just as it does when I contemplate picking up a guitar during Dad's shows—never say never?

"May I take a rain check?"

"Of course, Reverend."

"Despite what the board of deacons might say?"

His blue eyes glitter. "Deacons don't tell us what to do. God does."

I look toward the door through which Joanna and her family just disappeared.

"I hope so, Ron," I say. "I truly hope so."

Chapter Thirteen

It is a great relief to get back to the parsonage. Henry asked me if I was all right at least a half-dozen times between chapel and parking lot before I finally got rid of him. Then I walked the twenty or thirty steps home, pleased to find the wind abated and hardly a flake of snow falling. After closing the door behind me, I inhale: dusty books and wood polish. Before she left, Mim had kept the antique ice chest and barrister's bookcases inherited from her Italian grandmother gleaming. Along with the incredible relief of being alone at last, I feel a quick, sharp stab in my gut: no food smell at all—no scent whatsoever lingers of garlic, olive oil, and marinara.

She left last April, right before Easter. In retrospect, I'd seen it coming: long silences between us; her increasing, then total, absence from services; her retreat to her basement study, where she read Thích Nhất Hạnh and the Dalai Lama, and practiced yoga for hours. (I hadn't set foot in the room since her departure, knowing I'd find the books and her mats gone, only bare parquet floor—waxed to a glossy sheen, of course.) And the driving to Harless, to the community college, where she took classes in comparative religion, ceramics, world literature, tai chi—I finally told her they should put her on staff. Why, I asked, did she need to spend so much time there? Was it too much to expect her presence at an occasional service or meet-and-greet? Her silence said yes. And then she confessed: The Dharma House wasn't *on* campus but *near* campus. The wife of the pastor at Suffering Christ Church of Holy Martyrs was worshipping (or whatever they did) Buddha. Not *worshipping,* she said emphatically, shaking her head, *studying.* Whatever. I said she'd have to choose, knowing she already had.

Inhaling deeper, I detect a slight, wavering treble note in all that baritone dust—her herbal teas: Bengal Spice, elderberry, Lemon Zinger, peach. A coffee man, I strayed into her tea cabinet seldom, never on purpose, but when I did, their thick fragrance enveloped me like fresh flowers. Maybe I'll see if she took all her teas later. Right now their lingering scent might reduce me to a weeping, wailing wretch. Maybe tomorrow. (But then, tomorrow, God willing, I'll be gone.)

After all that has happened, I don't expect to be ambushed by remnants of a life I consider dead and gone. (One consolation: that Joanna and I began our "ungodly relationship" a month after Mim left. Still, a man withdraws his heart from one woman well before he offers it to another.) I decide to do what any other recovering alkie would do the day he gets a pink slip: go to bed.

My foot is on the first step, hand on the banister, when I hear, as clearly as if she stands behind me, my wife speaking again that word I'd imagined her saying in the sanctuary earlier. *Father.* And my overweary brain fires an image straight off the slick, glossy pages of a magazine: a bottle of Jim Beam sitting on a deep, rich, cherrywood table, a roaring fireplace in the background. The liquid fire shimmers like sunset on a lake. A woman in a black, low-cut dress drapes herself across a Victorian fainting couch to the right of the fireplace. And I know exactly where my ex (for that's how I think of her now, though the official documents remain to be filed, read, witnessed, and signed) kept her bourbon: below the sink with the mousetraps, Raid, and roach motels.

In the kitchen, I stride to the sink and pause. Maybe she took it with her, and I'll be saved. (*HALT*, AA calls the booze triggers: Hungry, Angry, Lonely, Tired. I have them all tonight—so what? Where is AA's easy god when you need him?)

Mornings following blackouts were hell: remembering nothing, I had only my wife's total freeze-out to leave it to my imagination what I'd done. *Why?* her tight mouth had said. But she never asked it aloud. She had a lot to lose too by questioning our unspoken deal, for the more I drank, the less I required her to be the pastor's wife. Was she secretly driving to Harless even then? To see whom?

Closing my eyes, both hands on the counter supporting me, I feel it hovering at the periphery where it's lurked for six years. I bend over, spread my legs slightly. Anyone looking in the window will think I am bracing myself to be flogged.

Come . . . now.

And I see Mim's grey face, the lines at her mouth, carved into her forehead, as she lies spent and lifeless on the hospital bed. For the thousandth time, I ask myself: is it my fault for not wanting the child more?

Oh, but Mim wanted her so much! At thirty-two, relieved of some of the duties if not the label "pastor's wife," she changed. She gradually quit teaching Sunday school, began building her library, taking yoga at the Y . . . and holding babies. *I do hospital visits too.* She wanted me to believe it was a concession. But as more and more of her time was spent visiting the newborns, I saw what was happening. And it was remarkable, for she'd sworn she never wanted children and that her own upbringing (not to mention mine) with Grandma the witch was not conducive to our ever being parents. "People who've never been children have no business having them," she'd said even before we married. I agreed. I felt flummoxed around children, as if they were another species.

Then she changed her mind: we *would* make good parents—because of, not despite, our wounds. And because of her great beauty and aliveness at those times, her naked body beside mine in the matrimonial bed, I began to relent, slowly traveling from one side of a circle to the other, navigating the endless pros and cons. Having a baby is never about pros and cons. Finally it was about how it made me feel to think about someone else. Mim, I'm sure, had her own complex reasons, but it just looked like she was addicted to infants' smell and feel (all that *holding*, cuddling, coddling, cooing, and burping—I'd just sit and grin stupidly for a few minutes, look at my watch, mumble about "my hospital rounds," and take off, whether any of my flock were in the hospital or not).

That didn't mean I didn't want a child; it meant I had serious questions. About myself. Reasonable questions, like the total lack of qualifications, newness of my sobriety, and whether I could get outside my own skin enough to submit to a need as consuming as a child's. All I felt in the presence of Mim's holding and hugging was embarrassment verging on shame. I never once asked to hold one of those newbies, and Mim never offered. Maybe she knew if she did, she'd never get pregnant.

It took a year of nearly nonstop screwing (she loved the irreverence: "This is functional fucking, Reverend Johnson. We're not enjoying this—we're making a baby!"). And I enjoyed it, the best sex of our marriage, wild and unashamed. And slowly, surely, I crossed the circle, became ready to be thrown into the terrifying unknown without guide. (I prayed God and Mim knew what they were doing.)

It took a year, but finally, at thirty-five, Mim was pregnant with David Catherine—the first name mine, for the king of Psalms, if it were a boy; the second hers, for her mother, if a girl—and she threw herself into it, as she'd thrown herself into making my vocation the focus of our lives in the beginning. She carried the entire household weight for years: taxes, cars, shopping, cooking, cleaning, as well as potlucks and prayer chains. All I had to do was give myself 150 percent to a job that'll take two hundred if you let it. I let it. I was out to avenge Dad's failure to be my father, mine to be his son.

Then I became a father. For three days.

My heart seizes, and I am bent double. Darkness rises from the floor. I become aware of the refrigerator's hum, passing traffic, a car stereo's booming bass thumping in the center of my chest. Every synapse seems to be firing. Dad stands outside Whitechapel Church, eyes in shadow. *You can't forget.*

I squeeze my eyes shut, and the screen goes blessedly black. *Who, Dad: whom can't we forget?* Your mother and father? Mine? My wife? My daughter? The key to forgetting is sitting right on the counter in front of me. All I have to do is open my eyes, reach out, unscrew the cap, and forgetfulness is mine. I will get what I deserve.

But I keep them closed. My mind lapses silent—for five minutes or maybe an hour. Finally I hear kids yelling down the street and open my eyes. The kitchen is saturated with golden light gilding the honey-oak cabinets. Dimly reflected in the window is a balding, middle-aged man, bent as if by a great blow.

"Catherine." My voice crackles like crumpled parchment. Releasing the edge of the sink, I stand up straight; blood returns to my fingers, spreads upward from my gut. Louder now:

"Catherine Joy Johnson."

I wait, but He doesn't strike me down. I sag up the stairs, fall on the bed, and sleep like one sepulchred.

* * *

I awake to the sound of pots and pans banging. The cold bedroom blooms with the scents of bacon and coffee. Downstairs, the fridge door opens and closes. Pulling aside drapes, I see my old Buick wagon parked behind the Taurus, and my heart swells. *Mim.* I hadn't minded her taking it, since it's only a few steps to the church, and I hadn't anywhere to go until the call came. Looking again, I calculate the snow's depth at about three inches, and the sun is shining. Maybe it'll all be gone by the time I have to leave. (If I leave.)

Rising quickly, I run fingers through my hair, think about brushing my teeth but don't. Easing downstairs to avoid creaking, I hope to surprise her, but she hears me coming, despite my stealth. My wife speaks without turning away from the stove.

"Heard about your father and your deacon problem. Folks are talking about it over at Harless."

"The Dharma House?"

She nods. I recall the time we visited the old remodeled Victorian mansion on ecumenical Sunday a couple years ago. Mim's eyes were as full of light during the chanting, prayer, and teaching as they were at our earliest romantic dinners. Her face shone like a bride's when the bald monk, a young American trained in Thailand, took both her hands and, staring into her eyes, held them for a long time. All this time she's been only ten miles away living in that "den of iniquity" (Kenneth Branch). With her priest. And I didn't know.

"So what are you doing here?" I ask too brightly.

"Making you breakfast."

She'll tell me in her own good time, so I bring her up to date on Dad. Her eyes widen when I describe the howling, but she laughs when I conclude with Murphy leaving.

"So the little pope fired himself," she says.

"Not exactly. You've seen Dad's stare of steel."

"On magazine and album covers. He looks so lost and sad. I look at that face and say, 'If anybody ever needed Prozac, it's him.'" She places the bacon on paper towels, crispy, not burnt, the way I like it. It amazes me to remember my wife has met my father only once.

She laughs her wheezy laugh, and my eyes fill (I hope I won't weep in her presence). I suddenly see myself standing, bent in half, five paces away at the sink. She lowers the plate before me and sits wearily. "Eat," she commands. The steam from the eggs and potatoes (with onions, peppers, and rosemary) makes me a little light-headed. I eat.

She stares in silence for several minutes. Finally: "I poured the bourbon down the drain."

My face flushes hotter still. *Damn.* I left it on the counter in plain view. She mistakes my shame for anger.

"Thom, if they throw you out, I don't want it to be over whiskey."

I lay down my fork, appetite gone. "They've already thrown me out. And it wasn't over whiskey, which, by the way, I didn't drink." I meet her steady gaze. "They're letting me go over a woman in the congregation. Joanna Strickland."

She jerks her head away, as if I slapped her. And the longer we sit, through the grandfather clock's loud ticking, the McPhersons' dog next door barking like gunfire, wrens' chatter on the feeder beyond the window, the more I feel I *have* struck her. And been struck back. The Dharma House. That priest who'd held her hands, her eyes.

"But they've got it wrong. We never had sex."

"Please don't—"

"Her husband wants her barefoot and pregnant for the rest of her life. And her children . . . benighted."

She continues to look out the window.

"I told her to leave him, and they fired me for it."

"Bastards!" She reaches across the table to cover my hand with hers.

I backpedal. "They actually offered me paid leave to go away and 'find myself.' But the only way I can get back into their good graces is to vow I'll never counsel anyone again to leave a Christian marriage, abusive husband or not. No D word, ever."

"No one could do that in good conscience," she says, closing her eyes.

I wait until she looks up. "Mim, what about us?"

Carefully, she retracts her hand. "I don't know."

I feel her going away, as we each have gone away so often, for longer and longer periods, she in the basement and me in my study, at the church, or hospital. (What about *him*? I can't say it.) I have to keep her here for a little while longer.

"Listen," I say, "I stood right there at the sink where you found the bottle and said her name. I said our daughter's name and waited to die."

She stares wide-eyed, her mouth slightly open.

"But I didn't." I hold on, wishing that I were sitting knee to knee with her, as I'd sat with Joanna the last time I counseled her. I long to tell her of my vision in the sanctuary yesterday—how she called me father—but I don't want to burden her. Instead, I say what I should've six years ago. "I chose to work instead of staying with you both. It was wrong, the biggest mistake of my life. It happened to us, and now we have to go on."

Her mouth opens to speak, but she doesn't say it: *You did go on—and let me die.*

"Mim, I can't pray."

"I know," she says. "I feel that."

"And now I don't have a job. It would be easy to say this is my punishment for abandoning my family."

One lovely eyebrow rises slightly.

"But I'm not going to, no more than I'm going to say it was God's will that—"

"Don't."

I backpedal again. "What I've learned from being on the road with Dad is I don't know God's will. I'm just staggering down the path, one step at a time." The chant comes as automatically as breath: "'One day at a time,'" I intone, "'for the rest of my life.'"

I said those words in the only lead I ever gave at a huge church AA meeting in Chillicothe. Terrified at the prospect of standing before a roomful of drunks and telling my hardest truth, I asked her to come. Lukewarm at my "conversion," my new friends, the incessant phone calls—one more thing we didn't share—she said she'd think about it. Just after I was introduced, she walked in and took the only remaining seat near the front. When it was over and the last person shook my hand, we walked to the parking lot where she cried in my arms until she shook, something she'd never done before and has never done since.

She rises, her chair screeching. "There's more food."

And she heaps my plate with more eggs, bacon, potatoes, stuffing me with God-and-wife substitute. There doesn't seem to be anything else to say, so I leave. I hang around the church all morning, not writing my resignation letter, missing Maxine, who's out with the flu. When I come home for lunch, the Buick is gone. All the dishes are washed, replaced in the cabinet, though the breakfast smells linger.

I sit heavily at the kitchen table, imagining Mim across from me, avoiding my eyes. I pushed too hard. Living amends—showing not just telling her I'd changed—is what I owe the mother of my child. It could take years. I am free to follow Dad to the ends of the earth, if that's what I decide to do. It takes every last bit of energy left to get me upstairs to pack, to get out of town before the weather gets even worse.

Chapter Fourteen

No color, only absence and shadows. He feels himself inside a maze of concrete passages and closed doors, at the heart of a grand labyrinth, and for several horrifying seconds, he has to gulp air. They are all out there, beyond the lights, waiting for him to embody the legend. He wants to spit on the floor, he hates that word so much (how would they like to be lauded as less than alive, more than dead?). Truth is, though, he's waiting for Him to show up, trusts that He will; hasn't He always? Meantime, no bright swirls, no wild coral swaths, iridescent indigos, or lavish yellow globules.

Well, all right.

He goes to tuning. When all else fails, tune the lute, stall, wait for the old bellyful of coals. Waiting is never wrong. Pause and silence help you carve music out of light. Words are only hangers to put clothes on, branches to grip and cling to, stones on which to scribble desperate, meaningless messages.

Doesn't everyone have a snake to sing? For that's what this old axe in his arms is for: to loose the snake coiled within his chest, the damned black thing. It makes him want to laugh, thinking about it, and he almost sees color, but maybe it's a camera flash at the edge of his vision. (Out there taking pictures. My God. Like filming a train wreck, but that makes his chest go giddy, and the serpent stirs.)

It's time, and he really only has one song to draw out in one long breath, one breath until death, which, if it doesn't come this night, will surely come another. Earning it, like every other thing. But closer, closer it stalks, and he can feel it, it's the wood and metal in his hands, it's their weight bearing down from beyond the knife-bearing light (which he will fling off with song—his voice is a sword, battling air). The sounds are steeping inside him, syllables rising. Words are way beyond, but they'll come closer and let him seize them, gathering within the sacred scar of his heart. There still may be enough.

He opens his mouth, and it is the song he wrote long ago for his son, his silver-and-silk-skinned, sleek, bonny boy whose baby flesh was Canaan, the Promised Land; the lost boy he'd left behind in golden light, the woman he let go. Now colors come, imposed over the silver shinings he sees among the gathered—money, watches, gold, and silver in their smiles—he can love them like this when all he has to do is open the passage and let the thing uncoil on the air. It came raging at times in sulfurous boil of fog; or bitter as mold and urine and sickly, evil yellow; but also, like snow, his lips shaping the vowels, tonguing consonants, with brutal, hot-breathed love. O, too much and his throat aches and closes. Too much, and the air glows pink, suffocating as a sarcophagus, and he'll be left hissing and spitting.

Not tonight. Tonight, the serpent lies soft against his ribs, leaving him room to breathe and bellow; it will be good and righteous, and he'll be shriven. He's curious to hear what they hear but has long since given that up, the vibe in his skull, the welling in his throat not at all what is caught when he bothers to listen to recordings, till, in disgust he quits lest he learns to shrink from what the world wants from him.

O gentle, quiet, and tender as the One can be too.

Divided, ten years in, whether it was devil or angel inside his chest, he no longer cares; now he simply serves.

Glad to have the opening song over, he feels the faint first stirring, knows there are many minutes and miles before Hero will be sated (snake's ironic name—it helps him live with it). Why o why, he ponders as he touches the tuning pegs, did God give us nerves?

To tune, to endlessly tremble like pinging forks to earth's pitch.

* * *

Abshire's is just as I remembered it, a huge, barnlike room seating around five hundred, with polished oak bars on each end, manned by a smiling staff of bartenders wearing white tux shirts with black armbands. The place is packed, and the tone is calm but upbeat. The crowd is closer to Dad's age than mine, with a lot of grey-haired (and bald) tie-dye and denim wearers. And though everyone (except me) avails themselves of the thirty-two selections of micro- and macrobrewery beers on tap, the place lacks the doomy feel of the bars Dad has played lately. Plus, this is a scheduled stop, not a rescheduled arena show. Abshire's is one of a handful of bars that "birthed the legend," as the marquee outside declares.

I've cut it close. I-77 South had been tricky, with patches of black ice. Thank God the ice turned to wet snow in Virginia, and I made better time. After returning the Taurus, then catching a cab, it's twenty minutes to showtime when I finally arrive.

"Thomas Johnson?" a portly guy with neatly clipped beard greets me as I stand staring around me. "*Reverend* Johnson?"

"Just Thom," I say, frazzled from road nerves. But when the smiling, clean-shaven man with the black ponytail takes my hand, I find myself warming to him.

"You don't remember me, but I'm Lee Carver, your father's bean counter. I was a big fan of Subterfuge, back in '88. Followed you around some in those days. I was just a junior accountant then."

Speechless, I return his grip. Someone who liked my music as well as my dad's?

"I'm the new Murphy." He glances behind him in mock fear. "Until he comes back, both barrels blazing." He laughs full bore. "And you know he will. He always does. But, listen, there's a table right over here for you."

Before I can take a step, he drops his bomb. "Your dad's solo tonight, by the way." He grins like the proud father of twins. "First time in over three decades." Then he takes off back to the delivery room.

Stunned, I look around—sure enough, no band equipment anywhere.

Patrick is waiting for me in the rear, a stone's throw from the smaller of two bars and the restrooms. I am touched. It is such a contrast to my first tour of duty and the mixed reception I'd gotten back north. (I had written but hadn't delivered my resignation letter; it now burns a hole in my pocket. Whether I am just messing with Kenneth Branch and the deacons, I'm not sure, but for now I am enjoying keeping my options open.)

"Well, you're looking at tonight's band," Patrick says. "Wendell's called a strike, and I'm the scab."

I pretend amazement.

"Boss knows. He's been in the back of the bus since we pulled in around noon. See, me and the others took off and sort of went on a tear, I guess." He grins proudly, and I realize he is very drunk. "Man, Chapel Hill has some great bars. Here's to the South." He raises his glass shakily. I lift an imaginary one.

"I finally got away from them guys—they was all drunker'n skunks, and Wendell was raising holy hell 'bout having to play these tiddlywinks places." His giggle turns into a sputtering cough. "That's what he said: tiddlywinks."

I glance at my watch. Ten minutes till showtime, and Dad is solo. Will he howl the whole time? "So, how did you get word to Dad about the strike?"

"Shent a message. That feller up there." He points a shaky finger at Carver, who is having a serious conversation with Eddie Abshire at the main bar. (I'd forgotten to call and alert Eddie to Dad's new groupies.) From his expression, the owner is just getting the news that Dad is performing sans band. It was 1965 when Dad had performed his last solo gig. I was about seven, and I remember him looking so small, the crowd so huge and scary, that I'd cried throughout the whole concert. Patrick is saying something.

"Them bastards, Wendell and Tully, and"—he belches—"Javier thinks Boss'll hire 'em back and pay 'em more. Shoot, I know better. I've studied Mr. Jones. When you're gone, you're gone." He draws his finger across his chin.

I don't tell him Murphy did all the firing. Murphy once told me that, if it were up to Dad, Billy Rod Fain would still be playing bass. An alkie with terrible stage fright, Billy Rod would remain relatively sober until about an hour before the gig, when he'd start chugging tequila; by the first song, he'd be unable to find the key to the simplest three-chord tune. Dad had liked BR's sense of humor—and his young Mexican wife—and had kept him on a good month before Murphy fired him, the manager even slapping the man in front of his kids.

I'm glad that I'm not panicking about Dad playing solo. Nobody else is. Eddie Abshire's taking it in stride, no doubt seduced by the silver-tongued accountant's golden bottom line: *The legend's first solo gig in thirty-five years . . . at Abshire's!*

"So why are you here, Pat?"

The boy acts as if I've impugned his honor. "Why am *I* here?" He points to his chest. "Why am I *here*?"

I like him so much better sober, but now that I no longer imbibe a quart or two of bourbon a day, I like everybody better sober. "Were you intending to play behind him tonight?" I say gently.

"Fuggin' A."

"I think Dad's going solo tonight, Patrick."

"Sholo?" He straightens, glances around him, looking for whoever'd made such a poor decision—he could've kept drinking with the boys if he'd known.

"He's done it before." I pat his arm. Even drunk as he is, the kid attracts more than repels me. "It's been awhile, but he'll be fine."

We lapse silent for a minute, and when he stands up suddenly, I start. He staggers toward the bar, then beyond, where he crashes into a guy wearing a ZZ Top beard, denim vest, and sunglasses, before lurching through the door marked Stallions. It's 9:01.

"La-dies and gen-tle-men, thank you for coming out tonight. I'm Eddie Abshire, and before the show starts and we welcome the Walt Whitman of Folk; the Rocker of Ages; the Poet of the Homeless, Helpless, Hung Up, and Hung Out to Dry, I've got some great news!"

The spattering of applause, the rising tension, dies down beneath Eddie's hands now patting the air before him.

"Abshire's has always been a special gig for him, he says, and this one is to be no exception, folks. Performing totally solo and acoustic for the first time in thirty-five years . . . *ISRAEL JONES!*"

The place goes bonkers. I see that, if there were ever a venue for a washed-up, has-been musician in dubious mental/spiritual/ physical health who's just lost his band, manager, and ability to write songs, this is it. These believers don't need glitz or glamour. They've come for the bona fide legend, and by God they are darn well gonna get him.

In the seconds before Dad emerges, I look around and even stand up to see better. But I can find no half-naked, nose-ringed, tattooed ones. I do, however, see a number of well-dressed young men, suit jackets concealing their muscles and perhaps more, their arms folded, leaning against the wall near the door and bandstand. None of them are drinking, and they smile politely, their eyes roving. Looks like Lee employs a classier demographic of bouncer than Murphy had, at least better dressed. Clearly the kids aren't with us—have they simply conceded the old hippies' bohemian enclave as a lost cause and taken the night off? Or has Dad's new management come up with a method of screening cults?

I accept God's grace and let it go. History is in the making, and I want to witness it. When Dad slinks out, his Gibson under his arm like Odysseus's great black bow, everyone in the place stands.

Is-ree-il. Is-ree-il. The chant turns to clapping, then stomping, and I think Jericho's walls might topple before a note is sung. But they hold as Dad stands glowering before us, tuning endlessly, then begins fumbling with his harmonica on its rack beneath his chin (the harp is back!). I watch in wonder this man that has brought pleasure—and transcendence, faith, salvation of sorts—to so many, and incredible pain and grief to a few. (The dim image of Mom staring out a limo window, rain streaking the glass, materializes momentarily before dissolving.) And he looks good, the tiny bandage on his cheek the only reminder of what happened before I left his side. (Why had I left? The reason now seems superfluous.)

Before Dad hits a lick, I realize something inside me has shifted. I'm seeing the man inside the black coat for a change, sans legend, sans parent-child baggage, sans crazed groupies and alkie spouse-manager. As he stands alone before a crowd of people that know every tune and can name all the albums' song titles in order; can describe each tour and rattle off set lists; can play you hours of bootlegged performances so bad—as well as wondrous—that you'll swear it's the neighbor kid's entire garage band playing through one tiny amp rather than the author of the anthems "Blue Sky Red," "Desert Swept By Rain," and "Sons in the Earth, Parts I & II." He looks so gawky and fragile and horribly awkward, like some deluded drunk backstage who's picked up a guitar and wandered into the spotlight just as an expectant audience rises to its feet screaming.

Caught in the spotlight. He asked for it, no mistake—mercilessly and viciously clawed his way to the top of the folk, then rock, heap. Murphy once joked in my presence that he'd left more corpses in his wake than all the military graves at Arlington. (I noticed Dad didn't laugh.)

As Dad stands there, the crowd begins to settle. At last he begins to strum a C chord—forever, it seems. (I shiver—will he howl or sing?) My sweet Lord . . . it is "Sons in the Earth," and he's singing . . .

Men rise, men fall, sons live, then burn
But they all come to live in the earth.
Men's missions take them far
Fathers see their boys for who they are,
One prays, one's gay, one's Abel, one's Cain,
One steals the father's body,
One inherits the body's soul.
Both are blessed, both die.
And they all come to live in the earth.

Tears rise, but when I see Patrick is back, slumped in his seat, grinning like a coked-up prophet, I fight them down. Following a furious harmonica blitz, Dad continues in great voice:

Old men cannot die
Till they see and feel the lie
That, though no longer young,
They'll not come to live in the earth.

So the old man dreams
Watching days drift away
Till he finally forgets
And fails to regret
That his son came to live in the earth.
He cannot speak when they come

to say that his boy is gone
And though he cries and tries
He cannot live to die to death
Never come to live in the earth.

His voice, coarse-grit sandpaper, resonates above the bright strings, releasing what lives inside his scarred chest, going back to his barest-bone, kid-skinny beginning. I imagine gleaming golden hair, wrinkle-free face, and a brand-new Gibson with near-zero miles on its frets. And no black coat.

When my father's fingers stop in midstrum, there's a space of maybe five seconds during which we hear eternity. Then we bring the house down. When Patrick leans over and drawls, "He's the real deal, ain't he?" tears are rolling down his rosy drunk's cheeks, and I know that, whether Dad howls tonight or not, it won't matter. God is out of the trunk. Can Beelzebub be far behind?

I watch the lines on Eddie Abshire's furrowed countenance smooth as the liquor and lyrics flow beneath my father's baleful stare. Dad even addresses the audience a few times, asking if we're all right (*Yes!*), if we don't mind hearing "old clunkers and clinkers" (*No!*), and don't think it's getting too warm (*Hell no!*).

"He don't need us," Patrick said at one point, shaking his head. I am pleased to see the boy hasn't touched another drop since his visit to the john. The first set has been mixed—with my father, it always is so—and he careens between tunes he should not sing, needing a band to "talk to," as he's famous for, forcing instruments to answer him, question him, scream back at him, making the music more than the sum of its parts. Some vocals devolve into a croak; some are songs with inane, air-brained lyrics or, worse, make me feel nothing: musical wallpaper. But feathered into the mix are jewels: memorable hits as sturdy as the day they were written; lyrically poetic, long-forgotten album songs and rockers reinterpreted: slowed down, maybe with new beat, new chords framing and freezing the words so you hear them anew.

I'm sitting inside a pink cloud, for once unconcerned about the future or past, when someone crouches beside me. I feel warm breath on my cheek, and hear before understanding the words. Lee Carver's face, so bright before, is drawn downward; even his eyes seem to sag. Something in the bathroom—will I come and take a look?

Thankfully, it isn't far to walk. I'm pushing on the door to Stallions when Lee gently guides me to Heifers. One of the two dark-suited young men standing beside the door nods grimly.

* * *

The room is a mess. The half-black girl from Emanuel's entourage lies where she must've slumped after doing her thing, with the blade lying beside her left arm. It's hard to believe that much blood could come from one small body (and, judging from the bloody sink, she'd stood before it as long as she could, letting her life leak down the drain). At some point, she slid down the wall, probably unconscious, and continued to bleed on the floor.

"Dead?" I murmur, tearing my eyes away.

Lee nods. "We had to break in. I thought you might know her."

"Why?" I'm instantly defensive.

His face is an anguished mask of misery. "I don't know."

"Get my father," I say.

His mouth drops. "I don't think it's—"

"Get him. I'll stay here."

Lee turns and is gone.

* * *

Before they come back, my mind is a dark, frozen crypt. The compassion I'd like to feel for the terrible waste lying in filth on the floor is complicated, first, by my father's denial in the motel room that she might have a legitimate claim to patrimony; and, second, by the girl's anger and seeming willingness to do him harm. *She may call him the father, but she's furious with him.*

I avoid looking at the floor at all costs. The bare bathroom bulb above my head is already interrogating me; my mind composes headlines; mourners pass before an open coffin. Part of me knows this will take some time to sort out, but when the door swings open, I stand with St. Peter at the gate, sword in hand.

Dad locks his eyes onto mine right away. *Help me bear it, son.* But I want him neck deep in it; I want those pale, spindly fingers that only know how to seize covered in the blood of this child who wandered within reach of his voice. I want to rip off that bandage, reveal the scab or scar beneath as his badge of transgression, want the blame laid at his feet like wilted roses and rotting flesh, and I want him to kneel and pick them up.

When my father's eyes leave mine at last and touch the body, I do not follow his gaze. I want to watch his reaction. I guess I've never really seen my father's face; at least, not *this* face. I've made the same mistake the journalists and biographers have: that the mask is him. Now I watch it burn away. His forehead grows shiny in the overhead neon glow, not sweat but just a shine. The flesh beneath his eyes drips like tallow toward the cheeks, which, encrusted with two to three days' growth of wispy, grey-blond beard, hang like slabs of meat. His mouth, that last bastion of angry rebellion, hangs open, an obscene slash in his lined, deflated face.

But it's my father's eyes that have the last word. Despite the vilest tongue in the history of rock, it is his eyes that fight most of his battles, vanquishing foes before he speaks a word. The eyes: cracked-glass, splintered window to the soul. (The cliché makes me closer to puking than the blood. It's too soft, too pretty, like religion until you bring the stink of Christ's rotting body right into the sanctuary.) And now, his eyes having soaked up enough, he turns his face toward me. They aren't a child's eyes—not innocence, exactly, nor emptiness—but they are open wide with a question. Now I want to shield him. But it's too late. Too late to save him from himself and too late for vengeance. I don't want to hear his question; I have my own.

"One more time," I say so low only he can hear, "is she or not?"

When he looks at the floor, I want for a moment to throw him up against the wall and throttle him, until I consider that possibly he's in shock.

Lee hovers near me. "Who is she?"

"One of the Furies," I say through clenched teeth. "This group of kids that've been following the tour for a while."

"I didn't see any kids," Lee says.

"They aren't here tonight. Or"—I nod toward the body—"not all of them."

"So there's no personal connection?"

I look at Dad. He glances around as if he's lost his sense of direction and can't find the door. He's gone somewhere else. It doesn't matter: he'll never tell me the truth, if he even knows it.

"I don't think so," I finally say.

"That's good."

I fill Lee in on the kids' razor-blade ways, concluding with Judge's cutting Dad at the Green Door.

He looks relieved. "A cult." He strokes his chin. "Couldn't be murder, then?"

"No chance. It's obviously suicide. There's nothing to worry about in terms of a lawsuit, paternity or otherwise. Their actions were always their own. Dad just did what he's been doing for four decades, playing and singing like the troubadour he is."

An odd thing has happened, a thing I would expect to terrify me but doesn't. I've become Murphy.

Lee avoids looking at Dad. "Except the new thing, that . . . sound he makes."

"It's part of his act, Lee."

"It could be seen as inciting them, Thom, egging them on."

Exciting them to violence. I look at Dad. He doesn't appear to hear, has even stopped looking for an exit, resigned to stand here in hell with the rest of us.

"Not legally." Hearing myself, I'm shocked. I can't completely deny that the girl on the floor could very well be my half sister. For all I know I have half sisters (and brothers) all over the world. And I'm trying to get Dad off on a technicality. But praying over the body, much less shedding tears, seems moot. He's alive, she's dead, and I'm witnessing Dad's orphan eyes. With Murphy gone, isn't my responsibility to *him*? I know it's probably a massive rationalization, but I'll have time to think about it on the bus.

"We'll handle it," I say firmly, "if there's anything to handle. And I'm not a reverend anymore." Lee's eyebrows arch. "Now let's get the cops."

Chapter Fifteen

It's a mess, but we handle it, me and poor Lee, who was, of course, bound to be baptized in Dad's waters, shorn of innocence and optimism—but not, I'd hoped, this soon. And I am reborn too: sheep to shepherd. Who else is there, with Murphy gone? Calmly we get the crowd to leave. Eddie tells them there's been an accident, an ambulance is coming, and that, in the interest of safety and security, we need to clear the aisles. I don't know whether it's the respect Abshire himself commands, or whether the Holy Spirit has descended once the devil fled, but the faithful leave quietly.

I am tempted to force everyone onto the bus right then and get on down the road when I see the buzzards flocking to the roadkill. The well-dressed gal and guy approaching me have TV news written all over them. Somebody made a phone call.

"No interviews," Lee snaps.

"Give us a minute," I say to them, taking Lee's arm and leading him a few paces away. "Do we want them to get this *only* from the cops?"

He scowls. "Preacher to spinmeister, huh?" Before I can retort, he grins. "So what do we say?"

"The straight scoop, pretty much—don't deny who she is, was: a fan and a follower."

"Nothing about them cutting your dad?"

I hesitate, feel the pressure when I look behind me. The paparazzi are proliferating as Eddie tries to herd them out the door. They aren't budging, and soon Abshire's might have ugliness on its hands—I don't want that; Eddie doesn't deserve it.

"What if somebody saw?" I whisper.

Lee's mouth was tight. "Play dumb."

I don't like it, but I catch a glimpse of Dad trying to get around Patrick, who is so far keeping him corralled. Already we hear sirens. Minutes are becoming seconds. Inexplicably, I still feel calm. "Get Dad on the bus with the kid guarding the door. You handle the cops, and I'll handle *them*."

Lee nods.

"I won't have to play dumb. I *am* dumb." I turn and face the rabble.

Give us Barabbas.

* * *

The media and cops are easy. Of course a bomb might go off in the next twenty-four hours, but at least we'll be hundreds of miles away by then. Dad is another story. Neither Patrick nor I can get him inside his room at the back of the bus, and his speech has become incoherent. We consider getting a doctor in case he really is in shock, but, an hour toward Pittsburgh, he regains his color and can concentrate well enough, apparently, to read his big, black, curly paged Bible and drink some tea. I call Lee, following the bus in his Beamer, and tell him it'll be best if we carry on, that if Dad falls down now, he'll never get back up. Since we have the day off tomorrow, I'm hopeful he can play the next gig; then we'll see. As for the media, if a storm strikes, we'll see what needs to be done and go from there. What else can we do? Nothing like Dad's troubles to take my mind off my own.

As we ride through the night in silence, I find myself missing the rest of the band, even though I appreciate the lack of cursing, smell of booze, and slap of cards. (Patrick falls asleep instantly—a small blessing.)

So we slide on up I-40 past High Point, the ice becoming rain, and I marvel how quickly I've thrown off one collar and put on another. I find myself still unable to focus on the dead girl—except for her body, all that blood. (Yes, for a while I see Mom in her bathtub, but it's as if repetition has dulled the shock. Also I'm not that wide-open boy anymore.) I'm seeing the girl as a problem, not as a person. I'll eventually collide with reality, who and what she really is, what Emanuel and his Circus are up to, Dad's responsibility in igniting all this, but for now, in these first sleepless hours, I find myself remarkably accepting, knowing what is down there at the end is death, Dad's for sure, and perhaps my own as well.

The cops got her name from the driver's license in her bra, Amanda LaKeisha Anthony. It bothers me that she not only was in the club alone, but there were no Furies outside either. Was she excommunicated? Worse fears nibble occasionally at my frazzled nerves—what exactly does taking her life have to do with my father?—but for now I dismiss them, lulled by the rocking sway of the bus (windy, rain again turning to horizontally blowing snow, the farther north we drive). Punch-drunk from an adrenaline hangover, I frown at my reflection in the glass and think of how warm Mim's hand felt on mine before she'd removed it. *Seeds of crucifixion.* The last sign I see says Fort Chiswell, Virginia.

* * *

I don't know how long my dozing trance lasts, but when I awaken again, I'm instantly alert. Yellow shafts are penetrating low-slung clouds. As far as I can tell, it is neither raining nor snow-ing, and we're no longer on the interstate. In fact, out the window it looks like the back road to hell. Snapping to attention, I wrench my neck so hard, white flashes behind my eyes. Whoever'd said rock and roll is a young man's game was spot on. It's taking a physical toll on my forty-year-old body. I glance around me. Pat-rick snores, mouth open—I'm touched by the sight of his blond-stubbled cheeks and bobbing Adam's apple. The only innocent left among us.

"Where are we, Kevin?" I ask the driver.

"Wild, wonderful West Virginia," he says brightly, tilting his head slightly, letting me see his right eye (I see him smile in the rearview).

"But . . . this isn't the interstate."

"Boss ordered a little detour . . . place called Lindsey."

I look around, but my father has no doubt retreated to his room at the back and is reading King James and beseeching his Lord. At least he'd better be.

"Aren't we supposed to be in Pittsburgh today?"

"No problem. We'll be at the arena before nightfall."

"What, an arena that didn't cancel!"

He shakes his head. "Not after last night." He hands me a news-paper. "Picked this up at the BP back a ways." He chuckles. "You were out cold."

It nearly leaps out of my trembling hands. At least the story is at the *bottom* of page one:

"Legend Lives, Fan Dies."

My heart begins to punch my chest like a crazed boxer. I devour the article quickly, glad that it isn't as lurid as the headline. It's re-markably true to the facts I gave. I sigh deeply, and Kevin shows me his profile again.

"Nothing like body count to stir the pot," he says, shaking his head.

I groan. "Do you realize how long it's been since Israel Jones was front-page news?"

"The divorce?"

What a period that was, with lawyers amassing like armies, smelling the scent of millions. And then, at the height of the battle, Dad settled out of court, giving Mom everything. Everything but what she'd really wanted.

Sitting back, I try to adjust my position so my hips aren't aching. As yellow light gathers outside, I make out images—aging grey trailers with pickups, Big Wheels, plastic Santas and reindeer parked out front. If I could meditate or pray, I'd feel better. And how is it, really, that I feel? As if I've been waiting and waiting for something—but it's been spoiled by the very waiting. Like Christmas, when, around ten or eleven, it becomes more than a kid can take. All the glitter and bows are there, same old shepherds and donkeys, but now you know too much, and you can't get the magic back. Worse, you see it's all a lie: there's no Santa, and December 25 is not Jesus's birthday. What was once magic is now death. Which isn't so bad in the abstract, but when you're forced to look at it up close (like last night), it becomes inescapably real.

And then I'm castigating myself for equating the loss of Christmas innocence with the death of that beautiful, angry girl. Pretty soon I'm pondering my own death, considering the blessed release from checkbooks, rectal exams, and taxes. As for what follows? If there's a heaven and you believed, you've won the lottery; if hell and you didn't, then you gambled and lost.

But if there's nothing but silence and worms?

Right now, silence and worms sounds good. Silence and worms and a pretty granite gravestone beneath an autumn, orange-leafed sugar maple beside my mom and daughter under blue-burnished Ohio sky. I'm actually feeling a bit better when Kevin pulls the Whale carefully off the two-lane. I am nearly as numb as my eleventh Christmas, when Mom decided to skip the whole "capitalist orgy" and treat Christmas just like an ordinary day. (It was far from ordinary: silence and worms. Plus our ordinary was always everyone else's exceptional.)

For a few moments, there is only the bus's diesel growl, which even drowns out Patrick's snoring. At last, I hear Dad's door open and his boots on the floor. I don't bother to turn around. His claw grips my shoulder.

"Come with me."

I don't ask where. The less I know, the better. When I stand, every muscle screams for release.

* * *

The gravel road up to Whitechapel Church looks a lot less forbidding in thin dawn light. We might be two hunters setting off, our breath tenting us, guns shouldered. We're halfway up before it hits me that we're not going to church. Even snake handlers can't worship 24–7, have jobs, kids, bills to pay, hogs to slop. If I'd been more than half-awake, I'd've borrowed a coat, because after being down South, I'm majorly chilled, though it's only on the edge of freezing. If Dad weren't still in shock, he probably would be too. He's wearing only the black mourning jacket. It occurs to me he slept in the same clothes he performed in last night, if he slept at all, which I doubt. Glancing at him, I do a double take. His face looks parchment yellow, as if mummified wrappings have just been removed. I shake my head. He looks only slightly more than half-alive, his breath coming shallowly as we climb higher, past the church.

* * *

Whitechapel Cemetery is no doubt beautiful in three seasons. I can imagine the rhododendron, oaks, locusts, and ash. But now, at the year's crossroads, I cannot imagine a starker landscape. There's something about graves on a hillside that is more poignant than when they lie on flat ground, as if the coffins below, riding shifting seas, might tip their occupants out. But the frozen ground beneath my loafers feels solid, and I'm huffing great shards of breath, even sweating a little, when we finally arrive at our destination: a small, low tombstone.

Wind lashes us. What in the name of God are we doing here? I gaze down.

Thomas Peter Johnson, 1919–1999.

I know Dad's father died five or six years ago. During the Golden Years before I turned five, I was in the frail man's presence a few times. He had seemed nearly invisible, looked out the window a lot, hummed, and muttered into his hand while others talked. Dad never looked at his father when the old man spoke.

"So I'm named for him." My voice is nearly lost on the wind. Dad's eyes never leave the stone. "The doubter and the denier, all in one."

I know not to say more. Dad is taking the stone right into his bones. Questions? Sure, I have a few. Who was my grandfather? Why didn't we ever see him again after those few visits when I was little? And where was Grandma? *Who* was Grandma? Ask my father such personal stuff? Heresy, even now after sharing a bloody bathroom and the bus ride from hell.

I wait, freezing again. The wind rattles the papery leaves like an audience begging for an encore. I could kick myself for failing to wear a real coat, but I guess I thought we were returning to the scene of the snakes; I'd not considered that Dad would celebrate Memorial Day in December. Truth told, I hadn't been thinking at all, and trying hard not to feel. At last he turns toward me.

"I can't die," he says. Then, not waiting for me to answer, he grips my forearm hard. This time his voice cracks. "Why won't you let me?"

The wind is howling now, and I almost go ahead and ask him why he turned his back on us and killed my mother. But as always something stops me. Is it guilt at my own culpability after becoming Murphy last night, the presence of the dead, or some remaining vestige of pastoral restraint? When I do speak, it comes out quivery as tremolo.

"It's not up to me. It's up to God."

Though I keep my eyes down, his are on me, glaring, burning. Waiting to be struck, or at least cursed, I stare at that stone, as if it might tell me who I am, from whom I have come, where bound. But stone will speak of these things before my father does, and after a few more moments, he takes his eyes off me. When the sky at last opens up and starts spitting snow, he turns and starts down the hill, bent and stiff, taking such baby steps that I think I need to help him. The weather must be locking up his joints. The car wreck that took him off the road around the time I was born was only one of many accidents. There was that stage in Amsterdam he'd fallen off of, dead drunk. And more than one horse had unsaddled him during the making of his one movie, a western. God knows how many women threw him out of bed (not enough). That last thought makes me smile despite myself. The old man before me is, to my eyes, the least sexy legend in America. I marvel at the transformation.

He stumbles halfway down, and I automatically touch his arm to steady him. He knocks my grasping fingers away and scowls, his razor eyes raking my face. I imagine Moses, mad as hell, descending from Sinai to find his traitorous tribe drunk on idols. (And where *is* his tribe?—scattered to the four winds.)

"I ain't dead yet."

I am glad my face is too frozen, for once, to betray me.

Chapter Sixteen

The U.S. Steel Tower rises before my tired eyes. Then we are crossing a bridge. What are the three rivers? Ohio, Allegheny, and . . . Mononga-something. Then I imagine *her* name in flaming block letters—Amanda LaKeisha Anthony—and her body, her copper glow gone grey . . . back on the bus, I was finally able to weep for her last night—perhaps all I needed was to stand before my grandfather's grave—which allowed me some measure of grief. Then: troubled dreams in which the dead girl struck a silver sword against a great gold gong.

I wipe the vision away, along with the dry crust at my eye corners. Welcome to the home of Carnegie and Mellon, Noll and Bradshaw, Pirates and Penguins. Another day in the land of rock and roll, lust, greed, and murder; another day with Dad (and, I hope, with Him). Fortunately, it looks like the storm only raked the Appalachians, leaving a thin, icy mix coating trees and streets.

"If it bleeds, it leads." Patrick chirps like a bird, with apparently no hint of a hangover. High on caffeine and sugar buns, he's just read the newspaper article.

"Tragic is magic!" Kevin crows.

"Please," I interrupt, "we're talking about someone's daughter, someone's best friend." *A child of God*, I don't say, feeling hypocritical.

They seem cowed. For five seconds.

"Death is always good for a rock career," Patrick muses. "Look at Elvis, Morrison, Cobain. And when it doesn't even have to be yours, it's great!" He glances nervously back toward Dad's cell. "Some chick croaks, and we fill an arena." Then he groans, covers his face. I think for a second he might've heard what he'd just said. But no.

"Holy shit, man," he says, "we don't have a band!"

I want to slap him. But my rage quickly escalates into shame. I've spent the past several hours since discovering the girl worrying about the effect on my father, the tour, myself. *Hypocrite. What if it were my own daughter lying there dead by her own hand?*

My own daughter. Now I've gone from anger to shame to . . . what? It becomes a glow in my chest (like when Mom covered me in herbs for a cold, as she said her mother had done). When it occurred in the pulpit while I preached, I called the feeling love; now I wonder if the hot dog I ate last night at the truck stop isn't giving me heartburn. I can't be feeling love *now*, can I? But I am: for *this* daughter, for my daughter, for all daughters. *What took so long?*

The center of my chest isn't the only thing burning. Israel Jones's house, if not ablaze, is smoldering, and all the waters of Jordan might be required to douse the flames. We need a Moses in the worst way. Actually, we need Jesus, but a rock and roll tour, unfortunately, isn't his usual gig.

We do get Judas, though. After pulling into the parking lot, Kevin parks between two SUVs halfway between the arena and the highway. Though we don't see any obvious media lurking, I decide I should scope things. Patrick, staring over my shoulder, snaps to attention. Glancing behind me, I see Dad, fully dressed, striding down the aisle. He bobs his head toward the door, and we follow him out.

* * *

Before we get to the arena's back door, I see Wendell Delp slouching against the wall, smoking. When the guitarist sees us, he stands up straight, tosses down his butt and crushes it, stroking the tattoo on his upper arm, a flaming Stratocaster with the initials JH inside, looking as wired as a pimp at a low-rent beauty pageant. Beside me, Dad looks rested, spiffy even, wearing his string tie with an abalone and eagle-feather bolo he bought in Tijuana eons ago (gracing the cover of *Dead and Alive*, his album of busted love and bloody divorce songs that was the final nail in Mom's coffin). I think he's dressed more for a wedding than the solemnity demanded by Amanda's passing, but I accept it as Dad. Who knows what strange synaptic surges might be produced by the suicide of an innocent in the mind of such a man? For one moment I wonder if he now considers it his duty to incite his followers even further. (Or whether he even knows what duty means.)

Wendell strides right up to Dad. "We're back, Boss, if you'll have us."

The man has balls, I'll give him that. I want Dad to kick them. Hard.

"Who the hell wants you?" It's Patrick, standing at Dad's shoulder.

"*You* should, motherfucker."

The voice isn't Wendell's. Murphy sidles through the open stage door as if on cue. He saunters over, reeking of nicotine, sweat, and garlic in the frosty morning air. He's probably visited Dante's seven circles during his all-too-brief absence. I fold my arms and wait.

"The show's sold out. As a matter of fact, Mr. Price is talking about adding another one day after tomorrow." Then the drunken lout remembers his status. "*If* y'all are interested."

"Who the hell do you think you are," Lee sputters, "to speak to Mr. Price on our behalf?" His face is redder than it was last night. I suppress a smile. Lee's a scrapper. But he's in way over his head.

Ignoring the accountant, Murphy steps closer. He knows exactly how close he can stand to the legend, about twenty-four inches, a foot closer than anyone else. Cross that line, and Dad's eyes fry your skin. "You shouldn't've had to see that mess in the bathroom last night," he says to my father. He glances at me for two seconds before returning his gaze to Dad. Part of me wishes I'd strangled Murphy when I had the chance at the hospital; another part of me is ashamed. The tiniest glimmer wants to believe God used me to hold my father's feet to the fire.

A quick peek at Dad verifies what my sinking heart knows: he's listening. For a second I'm flummoxed. How did Murphy know I'd been the one to show Dad his handiwork? Too late I remember Dad has a cell phone hidden inside his coat. Now the manager speaks in a low voice, not quite crooning. "Did you sleep at all last night, Boss?"

I find my eyes ping-ponging between them, mentally screaming at my father to resist this temptation, though I am powerless to speak; it would just make things worse.

"I need to give you this." And now Murphy takes one careful step closer, bold even for him. When he opens his gnarled claw of a hand, stars burst from his palm.

A diamond wedding ring.

"I kept it safe for you, the way I said I would." He stretches his hand toward Dad. "Now here, take it before I'm gone."

Dad closes his fist. "Tell Mr. Price," he says in a voice so scarred and choked by thousands of hours of songs he's sung, millions of miles waiting to sing songs, and hours spent mourning his losses, "we'll take another day."

And he turns and walks back toward the bus. All we can do is watch him go, growing smaller and frailer, his shuffling limp turning to a painful lurch before he finally makes it. When we turn back to Murphy, the spot on which he'd stood is empty except for an oily stain on the pavement.

* * *

With Dad buried inside his Bible on the bus, and Murphy sucking butt all over the arena, I have nothing to do but read—which I do for a couple of hours—then nap. Awakening, nearly panicked from a dream full of blood and black alleyways, I see it's late afternoon, early sun replaced by iron-grey clouds. After glancing back at Dad's closed door, I know I need to move *now*. Before I can will my feet to move, I'm off the bus. Standing here in my suit with wind slicing my cheeks, I feel more hurt than mad—how quickly Dad reclaimed his prodigal, when I thought we were getting along just fine without him. Well, okay, not fine with the girl's death and all, but that has nothing to do with management.

I find myself pacing the perimeter of the parking lot—I do and do not belong here. Anger at Dad has triggered anger at my deacons back home (I'm as homeless as he is right now), and I am trying my best not to think about any of that. Next thing you know, I'll be nursing a resentment the size of Heinz Field. My saving grace is the image of Ron Jenkins, his wide-open, welcoming face. Some Christians are real.

I am also avoiding looking at a whole host of female ghosts wanting to book time inside my skull: Amanda Anthony, Joanna Strickland, Mim . . . Mom.

I stop at the parking lot's far edge, where, oddly, several vehicles are parked. Employees ordered not to take up customer spaces?

Abandoned cars of lovers who rendezvoused here last night, shacked up in some no-tell, and forgot where they parked? Who knows? (No hidden hordes of Furies, I hope.) A vast sea of black asphalt now lies between me and the arena, which rises like an ugly spaceship crash-landed in the middle of Sprawldom. Eight lanes of traffic whip by, yet I somehow don't see anything but a swirl of color, the wind howling around me. It feels entirely inhuman, but I like it. Out here on the edge of the earth seems like as good as any place to make a call I've been putting off. Between an Insight and a Vibe, I hunker out of the wind and with frozen fingers pluck the tiny card from its place in my wallet, punch in digits. He picks up right away.

"Tony, this is Thom Johnson." When he doesn't reply, I add, "Israel's son."

"I saw the newspaper. How is he?"

I tell it all, including how I held my father's face to the fire, while Tony Romeo, Dad's ex-backup singer from the Holy Tour, the only musician he ever personally fired, listens in silence.

"God's will be done," he says when I'm finally finished.

I take a deep breath. "What I need to ask you is, do . . . do you think—I mean, knowing my father, is it possible that girl was—" My knees buckle, and I'm vibrating like an overloaded woofer.

"Her harlot mother was with everybody on the tour." His breath leaves him in a rush. "The child is more likely mine than his."

I don't tell him that the girl's fair complexion would seem to preclude that possibility. But Tony's simple willingness to take responsibility—so antithetical to a rock tour—restores me and I notice I'm shaking less.

"But Dad, he—"

"Skip, he was trying *very* hard. While we were involved in the usual madness, he was holed up inside the bus. I know you'll have trouble believing this, but he prayed *out loud*. And wept and sang spirituals. The first time Murphy ever told me this, I laughed, but his face said no joke, so we snuck inside and listened at your father's door and heard for ourselves."

I'm shaking badly again. If it were to be believed, a miracle: Dad growing his faith in the arrested adolescence of a rock tour, Babylon on a bus.

"Skip, you still there?"

"It's a lot to process."

"I love Israel. What can I do for him, for you?"

"Nothing more than what you've done. Which is a lot more than you know."

"Well." A pause. I imagine his huge golden shoulders slumping. "I know I don't have to tell *you* the power of prayer."

It would've hurt more, had I not been so numb.

"Hug him for me, will you, Skip?"

"I will, Tony."

"God bless you. Now go to your father."

Disconnected, I still see the big black man in my mind's eye, shimmering in his gold suit, singing his heart out on that Sunday morning before all this happened, when things were merely a crisis and not a catastrophe. Closing my eyes, I begin: "God, I've got to ask you—"

"Don't ask Him to do for you what you can do for yourself."

I turn, expecting to see Murphy or Patrick—anyone but Emanuel, wearing a long grey overcoat and a floppy-eared aviator's cap. Except for his scar-webbed face, he looks almost normal—absurd in his rummage sale rejects, but normal. He is and isn't real, a wraith floating through an urban wasteland. In my mind, I see Amanda's lifeless body, and the load falls. *He will come with a sword.* I approach so close I can smell the kid's breath, sweet as peaches. It takes everything I have not to grab him by his lapels and throw him against the Vibe.

"What did you have to do with Amanda Anthony's death?"

His stare remains vacant. "Prayer is irrelevant now. The Lord wants you to act."

"What made that girl want to die?"

"It's where we're all headed. She got there sooner rather than later."

His apparent lack of compassion would've infuriated me earlier, but Tony's talk did me good. "I want to meet your friends."

"Friends?" His lip curls.

"The ones who come with you to my father's shows."

His irises became pinpoints of blue flame. "They're not shows. They're real." Stepping back, he assesses me. I hope he can't smell my rage, for, if he knows how close to the fire he stands, he will surely flee. "You really want to know us, Reverend?"

I nod, lips quivering, my face a slab of meat. He steps back, lifts his arms heavenward, and recites.

"We are Israel's tribe, innocents all, none more perfect than our sister Amanda. We choose, are not chosen; we act, are not acted upon; we provide, are not provided for; we are not religious, we ARE religion. And from whence did we spring?" He pirouettes slowly, arms outspread. "We come from Detroit and Akron, Sarasota and Saint Paul, from affluence and poverty; from blue collar, white collar, and no collar at all—Amanda's mom is a high-class whore with a golden arm." He spins again, the hem of his coat flapping, throwing his head back and singing, "HER-O-IN!"

"And you, Emanuel?"

Sobering, he lowers his arms. "McDowell County, West Virginia, poor white trash. Born in a trailer in the middle of forty nights of rain. Damn thing floated downstream till it fetched up on a busted slag heap oozing out of the Herndon Mining Company."

"And I'm Jumpin' Jack Flash."

"*Listen*. Mama handed me up out of those baptizing waters of Cloudy Creek to Muriel 'Big Maw' Skaggs, a black granny who was already raising four of her own daughters' babes. Then the current sucked the trailer back into the slime, and I never saw my mother and little sister Penny again. Big Maw proclaimed me a miracle, named me Emanuel, and raised me right there on Cloudy—till a social worker showed up one day when I was seven and took me to the Pelfreys." He whirls faster, his silver-rimmed glasses flashing, then stops, arms outspread. "Another miracle: from Big Ma's collard greens and outhouse to Aurora Hills, possessing the state's lowest crime rate, highest per capita income, and best school system in Kanawha County, possibly the entire Mountain State."

It's like listening to an Israel Jones album—stunned numb, you shut down. Or you get up and turn it off before your head explodes or you fly off the planet. I admire the kid's art. He studied, after all, at the feet of the master. My disbelief is irrelevant. I bide my time until I can get my hands around the whole tribe. (Then what? Doesn't matter; for now, I connive.)

"Interesting history," I say. "It'd make a good song."

He comes closer. "You know what their schools taught me, Reverend? Hate and more hate, *insidious* hate. And I don't mean the normal kids' cruel treatment of trailer trash. I won't bore you with how many times they crammed me inside the dryers at the Laundromat. No, I mean the faculty and administrators, who, with every word, taught us to hate them, *them*, THEM. Gypsies, Jews, niggers, welfare scum, faggots, anybody not smart or white enough to be on the top of the heap. There were of course cliques, even in a rich school, the bottom being scions of men who were only managers rather than owners of mines or medical supply monoliths. Elias Pelfrey owned a prosthetic devices outfit, plus I was adopted, so I was a second-classer from day one: Rubber Dick, they called me. The boys called all the girls over to see my plastic penis. The name stuck all the way through high school—I fled as soon as I could. Your father called me with his message: be free and screw the system—screw all systems—and make your mark, for art IS life, there's no 'making it,' and the sweetest death is the one you give yourself. It's the ultimate control, Reverend Thom, you see now? We bleed to show him we understand."

Though it sickens me, I play his game. "And if you bleed to *death*?"

He spins on one foot, then faces me in a crouch. "Then we are free of the life most wear like weights. Come and meet the children of God."

* * *

An Aerostar turns out to be his ride, and though I expect sleeping bags, dirty clothes, and pizza boxes, it's empty except for electronics I dimly detect from the passenger seat. Surveillance equipment? The sight of it leaves me colder than the arena's empty acres of asphalt. Emanuel seems zany with joy, possibly drugs, effusing over the city, the day, the coming of Christmas next week.

"It's a phony holiday the tribe loves to hate. We hang out in malls, dressed in black, wearing buttons that say 'Christmas is Jihad,' 'Jesus hates Visa'—it's great! We don't say a word but make small purchases, which we give to Salvation Army, so no one can touch us as we spread the word."

I want to ask if he knows that Dad's Christianity is more conservative than Jimmy Carter's, that my father not only reads but apparently believes in much of the Bible—especially the Old Testament—but I don't have to say anything to keep him talking. I kick the box at my feet, realize it's full of wine bottles, reach down, and pick one up.

I whistle. "This is a far cry from Mad Dog."

Emanuel smirks but never takes his eyes off the road. "You're wondering how a band of indigents rate Bordeaux."

"Well," I say, returning the bottle to the box, "even Deadheads have their T-shirts and drugs."

"We ingest no stimulants besides wine, which is, of course, Christ's blood. And then only at meals. Since we don't accept global capitalism, an archaic, corrupt system whose seeds of destruction are brutally self-evident, we manipulate it as a means to an end. *The* end."

"Which is?"

"The end of all systems, the restoration of the One Lord Over All."

"So while you're awaiting the restoration, it's all right to eat, drink, and—"

"Use the system to screw the system."

"But how—?"

"Panhandle."

I shake my head. Their webbed faces would make most flee, screaming. He sees my incredulity and smiles.

"Israel's tribe is much larger than what you see here." He waves to include the van's contents. "We're in contact with others all over the world."

Despite the heater's prodigious output, I shiver. That itchy, panicked feeling I always get when I imagine hordes hovering above their keyboards, staring, stoned, into their monitors, seizes me by the throat. If he is to be believed, this ragtag band is the vanguard for a vast army of zealots looking to shed a lot of blood.

"No identity theft, I assume?"

"Nothing illegal or immoral."

Except sanctioned self-slaughter, I don't say as we bump across the rutted driveway of an abandoned shopping center with knee-high weeds growing through the blacktop. Appalled as I am at their hostile takeover of all my Dad stands for, I focus on the memory of Amanda's body on the bathroom floor, nurse my fury, and keep my mouth shut. I'm on a fact-finding mission. Whatever else happens, I must keep my horror—and my opinion—to myself. If I am patient, maybe I can delay the spread of this virus until Dad comes to his senses and . . .

We cut the corner beside empty stores, pass rusting dumpsters, until, turning into the back lot, we're confronted by flames—and next to it crouching figures. He screeches to a halt.

"Welcome, Reverend." He cuts the engine and looks at me, unsmiling. "Inferno or Paradisio, you decide."

* * *

They are gathered around the fire, eating silently. No one looks up, but in the glow I think I recognize a few faces: a totally bald girl with thick black eyebrows like furry arches above flashing eyes; a tall, thin, black-curly-headed boy with amazingly long arms and fingers gripping chopsticks as he devours goop from a little white box.

"Papa Chins!" Emanuel cries, joining the group, squatting to take Beanpole's sticks and tweeze out a huge glob of chop suey and slurp it down. "Lo," he intones, gesturing toward me standing beside him. "The Holy Reverend Thomas Johnson blesses us with a visit."

"Hey, Rev," Beanpole says, smacking his leader's hands and taking back his chopsticks. "Good to see you getting out some. That bus must get stuffy."

I nod and smile. The others ignore me, giving me time to get my bearings. The gathering feels otherworldly, as if I'm inside one of Dad's lightning-chain-of-free-association songs where the graphics, both bizarre and mundane, coalesce into a surreal landscape that is as horrific and comic as it is emotionally real. *Welcome to Israel-land; we are his children . . .*

Another van, a Plymouth Voyager, is parked a few paces away. A white boy with dreads is seated inside, the large door open, with the dome light on, clicking away on a laptop. I am looking for Judge. But there are no other bald heads besides the girl with the big brows.

"Where's Judge?" I ask.

Emanuel cocks his head.

"Bald guy, lots of piercings, jewelry? Defacer of legends?"

He looks around. "Anyone know somebody like that?"

Dead silence, no eye contact. I smile and glance around. I can wait. At one end of the circle, a red-haired girl has her long skirt hiked up to her crotch and, as nonchalantly as if she were shaving, is incising the inside of her thigh with her glinting blade. While I sneak glances, she carves with her right hand, soaks up the shimmering line of blood with her mitten, then slices again. Still munching, the boy follows my gaze.

"Kia does good work. You should see the mandala she did yesterday on Andromeda's belly."

"Or the Mary and Jesus I did on LaKeisha's back," the girl says, glancing up.

"Amanda LaKeisha Anthony," I say, "the girl who took her life?"

Kia scowls. "She might've told us. I'd've drawn it on somebody else."

Emanuel narrows his eyes, warning the girl, but her eyes are on her work. She shakes her head. "Crazy. She was eat up with anger."

For several seconds, there is silence, save the flames flapping like banners. I resist asking Kia questions with Emanuel's Tasers ready to fire. But Kia's disapproval tells me the dead girl was not universally beloved.

"Chinese carryout, huh?" I finally say, addressing them all. "Pretty yuppie stuff for a bunch of anarchists."

"Nobody says yuppie anymore." It's Beanpole, chewing open-mouthed. "We accept consumerism as a necessary phase to pass through on our way to complete metamorphosis."

And metamorphosis trumps basic concern for a troubled human being? But I bite my tongue and turn back toward Emanuel.

"Why didn't you come to the gig at Abshire's?"

"The owner's grandfather was a grand master of the KKK back in the fifties. They held meetings in that very building."

"Ironic that Amanda would choose such a place for her . . . metamorphosis."

"Actually, it was perfect. As she transformed, she cleansed the evil done to her people in that filthy temple with her blood."

"Life," I say, "not death, exists for the purpose of one's spiritual transformation."

It feels to me like I've thrown down the gauntlet, but he just grins.

"Your dad sings about this in 'The Only Holy Roller.' He says, 'When the day comes that Christ asks you to shed your own blood/ Will you throw your keys to the kingdom into the flood?'"

Such crap I've heard all my life. It disgusts me worse than their indifference to Amanda's death.

"What if my dad's lyrics don't mean anything?"

He tweezes up another mouthful of goo, inserts, and swallows. "What if the Bible was written by malicious politicians throughout history with their own agendas? What if the translation's often wrong, not only because of incompetence and human error, but intention, *evil* intention? Does that make its truths resonate less in the hearts of humankind throughout the centuries?"

"So truth is always in the eye of the beholder."

"Heart, Reverend. I said heart."

"A person's heart can be just as wrong as his head," I shoot back. "Haven't you ever been in love?" I feel a slash up my spine, thinking of Mim.

"Touché!" He tosses his empty box into an open trash bag.

"Just one more question," I say, feeling the moment slipping away. "Why all the cutting?"

He wipes his mouth on his sleeve. "Everything's just words without blood."

"So does that mean suicide is just one more option in the American smorgasbord of consumer choices?"

"Your words, Reverend, not mine."

"Dying to prove you're sincere is just plain silly."

"Sincere?" His lip curls again. "Is that all you think we're doing, trying to be *sincere*? That's what you and your churches do, act sincere. And I *do* mean act."

"Christ said, 'Let him without sin—'"

"And I say we *are* without sin, or as close as one gets in this world."

The ground shifts a half degree. When Emanuel smiles, I'm with Jesus in the temple, money changers everywhere, standing at a crossroads I often described from the pulpit but never hoped to see myself. Just as one's life passes before one's eyes, one last sermon scrolls across my mental screen.

. . . *when onlookers watch the pot boiling and do not lift one finger; when every truth is twisted to justify a lie; when arrogance is elevated to the level of religion; when suicide is encouraged, making it murder; then*

how is a man to act, caught between Old and New Testaments? Yea,
though his heart knows Jesus is right to say turn your cheek, the Lord of
Vengeance places the sword in the hand . . .

Emanuel reads the war in my face and steps closer. "Ours is Israel's message. Help us spread it."

I shove him aside and stumble toward the Voyager. Shapes blur, the sound of a vast sea roars in my ears, and I'm struggling against water rising to my knees . . . Now I'm at the van.

"Reverend . . . stop."

The boy in the van looks up but not in time. Tearing the laptop from his grip, I turn back toward the word twister's voice and lift it high above my head. Before I can dash it to the ground, they're on me.

* * *

On the drive back, Beanpole holds his blade to my carotid artery while Emanuel drives. For a while, my heart simmers, then withers. By the time we arrive at the arena, it has turned to ash. Their silence tells me there is nothing I can say to stop what is coming— something worse than I'd imagined, more than the machinations of a single, suicidal, ragtag mob—and not even Dad can prevent it. But when they drop me off beneath a portentous sunset, and I feel where the blade had pressed, my rage flames, blazing mightier than before—at kids who cut themselves and make up their own bloody religion; at self-righteous deacons, mutinous musicians, drunken managers, and legendary rock stars who strum their six-strings while the city burns. The Whale looms out of the darkness, and I stagger toward it, disoriented and angry, Lear on the cliffs of Dover. Hammering the heel of my hand against the unforgiving cold steel door, I holler like a kid throwing a fit.

"*DAAAAAAAADDDD.*"

I bang on the side of the bus till my hand aches. I'm not taking no for an answer. He's in there. Everybody else is dining and drinking in splendor somewhere in Steel City at Israel Jones's expense, but King David is on his throne.

Finally he comes, hunching forward, hand shielding eyes, trying to discern the identity of the madman outside. When the door flaps open, I storm aboard. He plops into the seat behind the driver's and smiles wearily, as if he knows exactly where I've been. Which just stokes my fires further. I don't even sit down before I blurt everything about my meeting while he stares into the middle distance, occasionally turning to glance out the window, fingering the red scar on his cheek (the bandage is gone). For once, I am relentless.

"They take you and Saint Paul literally when you say they must die to live." I give it a moment to soak in. "What are you going to do about them?"

He shows me his rough palms. "Nothing."

"You could try to stop them."

"Nobody stopped me."

"You weren't inciting thousands toward mass suicide."

"Might've, though, if I'd thought it was a good thing."

Another day I would've wanted to slug him. But we'd stood in that bloody bathroom together too recently. Plus, I seem to have spent my fury, at least for the time being. At the bottom of my anger, I find, is not Armageddon but Amanda Anthony. Easing myself into the seat across from him, I bend toward him.

"Dad, that dead girl . . ."

Turning away, he looks out the window into total darkness. I follow his gaze out onto the highway, the long road that led here. The parking lot lamps shine dully out of the black void. Another image, unbidden: Mom beating her fists on an arena's back door. And then . . . all that blood: two bathroom suicides—what were the odds? I see now that he's not going to answer, and for the time being at least I'll have to accept Tony's. But there are other things on my mind, a thousand other things.

"Dad, why did Murphy give you a diamond ring?"

"He was taking care of it for me."

"Ever heard of safety deposit boxes?" I may as well have said checking account or oil change—trivia from which legends are exempt.

He reaches into his inside pocket, pulls out the ring, and offers it like loose change. I lean forward. Without as much light to capture, the diamond is muted. I scrutinize the band, an intricate gold vine gripping the large stone. Tiny leafwork practically obliterated from long wear. An antique. Mom's?

Keeping his hand extended, he turns the stone so it catches the beam from the pole outside and flashes it in five different directions, like sun shafts penetrating a forest. I am four again, back in that pine grove where he wrote till noon while I played in the dirt, till the sun rose higher, until my clothes were sweat soaked. He would decide when we'd go back and Mom would make cheese and tomato sandwiches, chicken noodle soup, lemonade, and peanut butter crackers.

"Sky," I whisper. "My mother."

He retracts the hand holding the ring. "She was beautiful when she was carrying you." He looks up, his eyes glittering. "We called you Mel."

I stare stupidly.

"Melon in her belly."

Bending forward, I close his fingers around the stone, smothering the light. "Did you think that by leaving, you were saving us from all those people who wanted to get to you?"

His head dips toward his breast, and he shakes his head. When he looks up, he makes some sound deep in his throat. Maybe it's supposed to be a laugh.

"You don't remember your granddaddy, do you, Thomas?"

"Never knew him."

He sits up straighter, looks over my shoulder through the dark windshield. "My mother never satisfied my father. She was backward as all get-out. According to him, she didn't talk right, dress right, cook right. She mostly stayed home. Before I went to school she taught me old hymns and ballads on her granddaddy's 'dulci-mere,' as she called it. Then, when I went to school I'd come home and she'd have on the radio, singing along with Elvis or Patsy in the kitchen. Pretty soon, I was singing with her, and I'd tell her some-day I'd be better than those guys. I told her someday everybody in America would know her son's name."

And you thought that would be a good thing, I think but don't say. How can anyone see inside the hell they choose when they're sev-enteen?

"By the time I was in junior high, she liked it when I started bringing friends home, especially when we started playing guitars. She saved a couple dollars a week out of grocery money until she had enough for my first electric, a Silvertone from Earl's Pawn Shop. She'd sing too, and perform. Always before he'd get home from the flower shop."

"Your father was a florist?"

"Part-time. He tried to make a living selling life insurance, but in hard times, that was the first thing poor folks let go. Flowers were more dependable: funerals and weddings go on even in bad times. Got to where I hated the smell of roses, wished he'd been a butcher, even a miner."

I see it all, the kitchen's floral wallpaper, the Hotpoint stove, and chrome-polished toaster with embroidered butterfly cover. Had I actually been there? I had to've to see it so vividly now.

"Anyhow, Raymond Caudill had been bringing his brother's old, beat-up Harmony over after school, and we'd work out songs. Ma really loved 'The End of the World' by Skeeter Davis. Ray knew it and asked Ma if she could sing it. Well, she did—with her eyes closed, head thrown back, and arms held out beside her like she was beseeching Jesus. She showed me there was a lot more to singing than just your voice—she wrapped her whole body and soul around that song. It was impossible to look away. When I glanced over at Ray, he was grinning, and I could tell he was as knocked out as I was. We played it over and over, all three of us in some sort of trance, and we lost track of time.

"When the door flung open at five fifteen, I knew the old man had been standing out on the porch listening, 'cause the look on his face would've blistered paint. Ray unplugged, grabbed his case, and ran out the door with his axe under his arm.

"'Where the hell did he get this?' the old man said, picking my guitar up off the couch where I'd laid it. She didn't answer, but he knew."

I imagine her head hanging exactly the way my mother's had, as she sat at the table while Dad ate behind his book or newspaper.

"Then he threw it on the floor. When Mom jumped, he turned quick as a cat and slapped her so hard she fell. Before I could move, he yanked me up by the arm and shoved me into the hall. 'You're taking this goddamn thing back tomorrow,' he hollered. Then he screamed for another hour about how she shamed him, while I waited in my room for him to hit her again, telling myself that, if he did, I'd be on him like lightning."

He looks hard at me. "I's a damn coward. After that, I was never allowed to have anybody over when he wasn't home. It was like he'd caught Ma whoring."

He hugs himself, as if freezing. I can't move a muscle, don't want to disturb one molecule of air. We might both burst into flame.

"Things got a lot quieter in the house. He sold the radio—we'd never had TV, which he despised. Nobody ever said a word while we ate. Then he'd read the paper and work on sales figures till he went to bed. Two or three nights a week I'd go over to Ray's, where I kept my equipment—we had a decent band by that time. Old man never asked what I did outside the house. But Ma never sang again. Music was banished from her life."

He looks at my hand on his shoulder. I don't remember putting it there, and now I take it back.

"Ninth grade, September I think it was, near my fifteenth birthday. We were waiting at the breakfast table for him, when he came in madder'n a scalded dog.

"'Why didn't you polish my goddamn shoes like I told you?' he roars at her. 'You know I have a big meeting today.'

"When he lifted his hand, I rose out of my chair—not all the way—about six inches. Our eyes locked, and we looked at each other long enough to say words that can't be taken back. Then he lowered that hand and walked to his place at the head of the table and sat down, dipped out his oatmeal, and ate. Nobody said a thing, but once or twice he and I caught each other's eyes as we passed the applesauce. He seemed to be saying *you sure?* while I told him with my eyes *touch her, and I'll kill you.* As far as I know, he never again laid a hand on her. But after that, she never left the house, never went back to church, even had the groceries delivered. When I's a junior, she got brain cancer and was gone fast. He let her people take her back to West Virginia. 'Too far to go out there in the sticks,' he said. 'Besides, I got work and you got school.'"

He let his body uncoil from its tight crouch. I let myself breathe a little.

"We killed her, Thomas—and didn't even go to her funeral."

When he opens his hand, the diamond, out of the light, lies dead in his hand. He opens his mouth to speak but can't seem to get his lips around any words—what he needs is to howl, but we are nowhere near a stage. He's begun to shake.

"If you'd stayed with us, you wouldn't have hit anybody," I say. "You're not him."

His head is low. It would've been easy to touch his head, let the warmth from my fingers enter him. But I couldn't've taken it if he'd shrugged me off. At last we hear loud voices, car doors slamming. The band is back, and from the sound of things, they're drunker than lords.

"Here, son." He holds his fisted hand toward me. I might've knocked it away but for his eyes. "He gave it to me after her funeral."

Of course. *His* mother's, not mine.

"The sonuvabitch said, 'Y'all were more married than she and I ever were.'"

I stand to find my legs are granite. "I'll keep it for you."

He holds out his hand, a trembling claw, slowly opens it, and drops the ring into my waiting palm. It's heavier than I'd expected, and warm, very warm.

Chapter Seventeen

In my dream, I am in a debate between God and the devil, who is dressed in the outfit George Harrison wore on the Beatles' *Sgt. Pepper* album, right down to the tricornered hat. The "spiritual Beatle" is actually Satan! He has God shaking his shaggy head over the advantages of leading a life of dissolution, the last one being you're never a hypocrite. I am waiting to hear God's comeback, but someone starts banging a gong. That's when I realize I slept on the bus (bad decision—the band had been fired up about how they were gonna melt the beams in the arena tomorrow night—*tonight*, I think, my stomach lurching like I'm in an elevator whose cables have snapped), and someone is pounding on the side of the bus.

"What the hairy fuck?"

It's Patrick, shirtless and in reindeer boxers, wiping condensation off the window to see out. Now the banging is accompanied by shouts. He glances at me. "You better do something, dude. That bitch might have a gun."

After all that's already gone down, a gun doesn't actually worry me too much, but he's right. Murphy didn't stay for the party last night; Lee headed back to the Big Apple shortly after Dad restored the ex-manager's authority. Since I've not been officially demoted, I am still kind of an assistant. When I stand up, I find myself fully clothed. Looking around, I see the other half-dressed musicians groaning and clutching their heads. Silently I thank God for the billionth time for sobriety. If I were more awake, less under the influence of Satan's flashy arguments, surely I wouldn't go out. Though I step into searing, silver sunlight and breathtaking cold, I've actually reentered hell.

"I want that bold-ass motherfucker out here right now."

She is the most beautiful black woman I've ever seen, tall, statuesque, and thin in a fur coat. High cheekbones complement her wide mouth, lips pulled back over perfect white teeth. Her eyes are smoking Colt .45s.

"Which one?" I ask lamely.

"Whose bus is this, fool? Israel Jones—that lyin', cheapskate bastard who never takes care of his own, that piss-poor excuse for a father."

Raising my palms outward to ward her off, I glance behind me— no reinforcements; Patrick closed the door as soon as I stepped down—but I find my head cleared somewhat by the frigid air. Her curses are congealing before us as she berates me.

"Ma'am, please calm down. He's not on the bus."

I'm shocked at my lie—and disappointed, as is, no doubt, God. But she lets her arms fall to her sides, and her tall figure sags. Best of all, her gorgeous lips close, and her mouth corners turn down. (It is a sensual mouth, a mouth with character, I think, a mouth that expresses a lot without words—as it is now doing.)

"Where is the jackass?" She glances around her, toward the traffic just getting started. "At the Hilton?"

"I'm not at liberty to say—security reasons."

She claps her glare back on me. "Who the hell are you—James Bond?"

"I'm his . . . assistant manager." Even in my thin suit, I realize I'm not cold. Her eyes currently provide all the heat I need.

When she steps closer, I smell her. Jasmine, cigarettes, pepper-mint, vanilla, and a hint of . . . (I swear) sulfur. Though George-as-Satan says *give her his head*, God frowns. I go with God; she'll get to Dad over my dead body.

"Well, then, maybe *you* can help me, Mr. Assistant."

I fold my arms. "Possibly." That fast, I'm Murphy.

"Your *cli*-ent," she enunciates carefully, "is the father of my daughter."

This is something I can handle. I've seen the little pope handle it a hundred times. All you do is ask if they've had a blood test; it always cows them. I become pastoral polite. "And who is your daughter, ma'am?"

Another step closer. The woman is definitely in my face, and even though she has a beautiful one, and has enjoyed excellent den-tal care all her life, I really need her to step back and let me breathe.

"My daughter *was*," she says in a breathy whisper, "Amanda LaKeisha Anthony."

Tears spill down her beautiful cheeks. "Amanda Anthony *Jones*." She pulls herself to her full height. "I am Diamond Anthony."

Of course I knew it already—had seen that photo in Dad's room—knew it but didn't allow the knowledge entry. I barely have the strength to reach behind me and hammer on the door. "Open it," I yell before saying to her, "He's here."

She just nods, had known it all along.

* * *

"Amanda was brought up knowing who her father was." Her back is rigid, her posture as perfect as her teeth. "I don't believe in lying to children. She knew what I am too. Do you know, Israel, what I became when you turned me out?"

Dad shakes his head, stubbled and bleary eyed (he's probably been up talking to Moses, David, and Paul all night, unable to sleep). She leans forward slightly, no doubt desiring to get in his face as she had mine. I am glad to be relegated to a supporting role. Though I wonder if he'll kill me later for letting her in, I don't care. As soon as she presented her credentials, my collar reasserted itself. If what she said was true, she had a right.

"I'm a hooker, Israel, a very high-priced hooker. In Miami." She laughs at his wide-eyed bleariness, then glances toward the open door, taking in the squalor of the bus—beer cans, liquor bottles, pizza wrappers, the stench left by snoring drunks, which her perfume thankfully dilutes (no sulfur, since she stepped inside). "You couldn't even afford me now." She chuckles, then her eyes and face change, a shadow crossing her features, mouth hardening. "But, then again, your stock, I understand, is now rising. Booked into an arena, not one but *two* nights! It must feel good after a dry spell." She locks merciless eyes on him. "It must be very hard on a legend to have a dry spell."

He just stares back, occasionally glancing at his hands. He looks remarkably calm, though I find myself breathing shallowly. Her voice, still low, is gaining tensile strength.

"Nothing like a fifteen-year-old girl's death to attract attention to a legend in decline, possibly even a *has-been* legend, a legend whose actions lately haven't been all that legendary."

The rising tide of her emotion is overflowing the room to fill the entire bus. One wrong word from my father might be all it will take to get her back to where she was when I stepped down to talk to her.

"I don't know her," he finally rasps, the first words he's uttered in hours, since those hard words last night.

I feel her start, though she doesn't appear to move a muscle. "Oh, of course you don't. You didn't want to know, and since you didn't want to know, I didn't want you to know either. What is a little girl to a legend? What is an ignorant, pregnant background singer to the great Israel Jones? Girls are a dime a dozen, children are pennies."

When she thrusts her head forward at him, I see a striking viper. Ice coats my spine. Is *she* the woman who called me at the parsonage?

"They're everywhere, aren't they, my love—you've peopled the earth with children. What does one or two or twelve more matter? I'm not stupid. When you sent me away—or that cockroach of a manager sent me away—I knew better than to communicate with you. I'd never get through *him*. But *she*—" Her voice catches, like a lace dress on briars, and rips just a little. "Keesha wanted to communicate with you. Oh, she wasn't a fool like me. She knew that a legend has an endless appetite, that his emptiness must be filled. More drugs, more thrills, more *cunt*."

Dad is on the ropes, and he is bleeding. In the harsh light of the neon bulb above us, he looks as old as Moses the night he tossed the reins to Joshua and croaked. I sense that he's not defending himself because if not guilty of this crime, he's guilty of others, parentage of her child no doubt only one grievance to which he knows this woman, and many others like her, is entitled. Though I agree in principle, should I still stop it? She sits back, scowling, while another tear tracks down her cheek.

"So she ran away to follow you. Had I known, I would've tried to stop her. Any good mother would've, you're saying, as qualified as you are to judge others' parenting skills." She turns to me, her smile a serrated knife. "Amanda was raised by her granny in Atlanta. I visited her regularly. Not an ideal situation, I know," she admits, looking at me hard. "But after your *cli*-ent introduced me to show business, I pursued it—I guess you could say the bug had bitten. From performer to whore." Her painful laugh fills the cabin.

"Not a stretch at all. And, believe me, Israel," she says, turning toward him, "whoring is certainly show business."

"He's not my client," I say, "he's my father."

She doesn't blink. "I know. And I feel very, very sorry for you." Her voice becomes even lower, controlled, almost a growl. "Since Israel Jones is incapable of love." She lets it hang for several seconds. Dad never takes his eyes off his hands. "I can only imagine what your life has been, what your mother's life was like, poor thing. But pity has its limits, doesn't it? Looking at starving orphans, day after day, so fucking needy—our charity is exhausted. That's probably how your father saw me twenty years ago. It's the way he sees you now, hanging around waiting for a pat on the head."

My face heats beneath her gaze. She can't be the woman who called me. She doesn't want my father helped; she wants him dead—his son too. I can't blame her.

"You're wondering what I'm doing here, especially on the eve of the legend's greatest comeback. I've just come to tell you that your daughter, our daughter, followed you to North Carolina, apparently, to make contact with you—that's what she told her granny, as a matter of fact, only hours before she entered that bathroom. She said over the phone, *very* firm, *very* upbeat, 'I've been afraid, but this time, I'm really going to let him know who I am.' Apparently she couldn't do it. You've followed the media?" She glances the question to me. "Keesha had problems—what orphaned child doesn't? Her teachers—especially her treatment center counselors—yes, Israel, your daughter was addicted to drugs—always accused her of 'acting out.' That's all I heard from her granny, my mother, 'openly aggressive to girls, sexually inappropriate with boys.' Fighting and fucking from twelve on. Maybe you gave her the drug gene, Israel, but I'll take credit for the aggression. My daughter was me all over. And you."

How much, lady? Murphy would ask if he were here. *How much do you want to get the hell off the bus?* Thank God he isn't.

She stands up and smooths her skirt. A glance at Dad tells me the bleeding has, for the moment, stopped.

When she looks down at him, she is suddenly almost shy. I see that she still loves him, though she'd never admit it. When she speaks, it's almost tender. "I just wanted to make sure you knew who that girl in the roadhouse bathroom was, not that it matters to you."

Dad's face is a wearier version of the man in the bar bathroom with one foot in hell.

"But do me one favor and don't come to the funeral. You are not welcome."

And she walks out, her high heels clunky on the bus's laminate floor. The door is open, and she steps right off. When I look at him, Dad is shaking his head.

"No one needs—" I begin.

"She stayed high the whole tour—the only pay she wanted was smack. She doesn't even know it wasn't me. Coulda been anybody, anybody with junk on 'em."

"What intoxicants were you ingesting then? Are you saying you were celibate?"

He looks up sharply. "None, and yes. But I'm to blame, just the same. I've ruined ever' child or woman that's come close."

"Thanks a lot."

He blinks. "I don't mean you."

"I'm your child, aren't I?"

"Yes. No."—wagging his head as if he were articulating it for the first time—"More like my conscience."

My throat fills with flames. "I wasn't *your* father, you were *mine*."

"All I ever been is a guy who sings what he hears in his head. What'd you expect from me?"

Now I'm shaking, holding onto the wall, looking at him through a hard rain. But I can't say a thing, not yet. We sit there a long time without speaking. When I straighten up suddenly, he jerks his head left, as if expecting a blow. It's out of me before I can stop it.

"God damn you, Dad."

His teeth are terrible when he smiles. "He has."

It strikes me as sentimental and childish. "If He has, it's because you want it."

"Deserve. I deserve His wrath."

"There's grace."

"Not for me."

"You don't want it."

"Prob'ly not."

I cross my arms to keep from trembling. "A man's heart can choose," I say.

"For a while, maybe. Repeat the past enough, you're condemned."

"Grace doesn't come with a limited warranty."

"When I let Ma die, I was a kid. When I let your mother die, I was grown. I chose. Forever."

"Nothing is—"

"Isn't this what you been wanting me to say?"

"No. Yes, but . . ." A cloud of wasps clogs my throat. "There's still time to . . ."

He rises, squeezes my shoulder hard. "You thought it would make you happy, didn't you?" He shakes his head. "Truth never does, son."

"But it can save you if—"

"Then go save them that can believe it."

I can barely look at him now. His eyes and face have gone to beseeching, like last night when we'd stood in the bathroom.

(Had it only been twenty-four hours ago?) *Let me die in peace, condemned.*

I stand weakly, resist the urge to grab him by the lapels, shake him, and scream, *you don't have to die an apostate.* When I place my hand on his shoulder, he lets me keep it there for five, six seconds. Then I follow Diamond Anthony's path out the door.

* * *

I nearly bump into Murphy storming up the steps of the bus. I must look like Dostoyevsky after the firing squad didn't shoot him after all. The manager must be used to it. He shows me his gold tooth.

"There's a woman here to see you," he says.

"She just left."

His brow furrows. "Little brunette white woman 'bout your age?"

I ooze onto the seat. He's already back on the pavement. "Don't move," he hollers. "I'll get her."

* * *

Within moments he's back, leading my wife on his arm, chatting her up like a favorite niece. I'm not even surprised, just numb. "I see the news even reached Harless." I try to smile.

She doesn't reply, and though my wife is usually the politest person on the planet, I see she's impatient. She sits on the seat behind the steering wheel where Dad sat last night. Her body sags, her chin dipping toward her chest. After the initial shock, I'm growing calmer. After Diamond and Amanda Anthony, I think I can take anything now.

"Joanna left with the children."

Blackness seizes me, and I leave the earth for maybe three

seconds. I come back to neon whiteness, drained of all color. She is still talking, hasn't noticed I've been gone.

". . . apparently left while Dennis was at work, didn't tell a soul where they were going."

I'd surrendered Jo after Ron's sermon that night. Not till now did I realize that she'd wanted me to give her a sign, tell her she was wrong, save her. Then, like words unscrolling on a screen: *It's not up to me; it's up to God.*

"Thom . . . are you all right?"

I glance around. The walls look solid again. I smell Mim's herbal shampoo, the Lemon Zinger tea on her breath. I unfist my hands, take a breath deep into my belly.

"I'm okay." And I am. "They'll get a fresh start. Holy Mart can be vindictive. She needs a place where she won't be judged for what we did."

Now her eyes really widen. And though I long to remind her that Jo and I only talked, I know that what we had for that brief span was more intimate than sex. Mim will believe what she needs to believe.

"And you," I say, "what about . . . your priest?"

She turns her head, showing me a lovely pink cheek that I desperately want to touch. "He sent me away."

"What?" Incongruous as it seems, I want to punch the guy. Doesn't he know what he's throwing away?

"He said"—she looks over my shoulder for the words somewhere outside—"that, for some, it's best to seek God in their own tradition."

"Oh, right, as if—"

Her warm hand back on mine. "He's right."

I see in her eyes it's over with the priest. And as the moment lingers, I let myself enjoy her hand on mine. A long, comfortable silence ensues. Finally, I look at her.

"How'd you ever find me?"

She smiles wryly. "Just punched in israeljones.com—voila! The whole schedule, right up to the minute."

Cyberspace. I get a quick flash of Emanuel, pirouetting under a glowering sky.

"But Jo's not the only reason I came."

I wait. She retracts her hand.

"I let myself into the parsonage and stood at the sink, right where you said you stood, where I found the bourbon bottle? I said her name just like you did." She takes a deep breath. "I said our daughter's name."

It doesn't matter that her face is melting in my silver gaze. We scrunch closer on the edge of our seats until our knees touch, and we clasp hands, mine cold, hers thankfully warm. We sit and don't say a word for the longest time.

* * *

As it turns out, my wife has one more thing to say. I eagerly lay my hand on her arm as she unlocks the car. "I'm going back with you," I say, deciding right then.

Without looking at me, she gently unclasps my fingers before getting in, closing the door, and rolling down the window.

"Not yet, Thom. You've got to walk all the way to Calvary. See, I wish I had, when I had the chance—but I got scared and ran. So I'm walking toward it now, and it's harder. You'll know when it's time. Not now."

Then she grabs my arm and brings my face to where she can reach it. The kiss is neither long nor short—but it's a breath on dormant embers. "Why not drive back tomorrow?" I say. "We can get a room."

Her eyes widen at the *we*. She pauses for a moment. Finally: "They say there's a storm coming."

I roll not only my eyes but my entire head. "There's always a storm coming."

"I'll see you when it's over, Thom." After rolling the window back up, she flutters her fingers and drives away.

I stand there stricken for a few long moments, waiting for what comes next, when a voice speaks, high and calm: *False paths will rise to claim us for a time*—Scripture? Perhaps a long-forgotten Psalm?—*but if they don't contain the seeds of our crucifixion, then we must leave that path and begin again.*

I recognize the voice of Ron Jenkins—only a man, a preacher like me, struggling for the right words to give lonely men hope. Bowing my head, I'm wrapped in silence, while around me the sound of traffic rises like wind on the raging sea.

Chapter Eighteen

Later, I linger over coffee at Priscilla's Pancakes down the road from the arena, watching the snow fall straight down. Maybe Mim was right about the storm, but since she didn't stay, I don't care if hell freezes over. I ran into Murphy after walking Mim to her car, and he said he'd meet me here when he was through "making arrangements."

During my third cup of coffee, something hits me. Everything else might be screwed up (I haven't checked the paper yet for more stories about Dad), but I don't think I am separated any longer. We didn't actually agree on anything, of course, but wasn't reconciliation the real reason she'd driven so far? To see my face when she told me Joanna is gone and Catherine is back? I feel like Jonah recently hurled back into the world. If surrender is what God wants from me, he's got it. My wife has let our dead baby girl into the house. I am a sober man, joyous and free.

But she hadn't let me go home with her. *Walk all the way to Calvary.* With my father? Or was more implied?

Squeezing my eyes closed, I see Dad's face before I stalked out an hour ago. I know I need to forgive him, but his stubbornness infuriates me. Before I can think any more (a good thing), I hear vinyl squeak and open my eyes to see Murphy sitting across from me.

"Well, she won't make a stink."

I stare. Had Mim considered making a stink? To whom?

"I caught her in time, thank God. The wench was considering a press conference to name Boss a deadbeat dad."

Oh. That stink.

Murphy is preening, he's so pleased with himself. He lights a cigarette and waves it. "Soon's her taxi pulled into the lot, I knew she was trouble. Good thing ol' Murph never sleeps, 'cause trouble sure as hell don't."

We both feel a presence and look up. When the waitress begins lowering plates to the table, I dimly recall ordering food. Glistening eggs and leather-skinned link sausages make me nauseous, but I grin at the youngish blond. Her wide-open smile reminds me of Mim at her age, flirting with me in the college cafeteria where we'd met.

"Something for you, sir?" she asks Murphy.

"Coffee," he says, never turning his eyes off me. "Black."

After she whisks away, I fork a bite of egg just to be doing something. Despite my euphoria a moment ago, Mim's absence and Dad's pigheadedness have left me depressed.

"Plus, we settled on the cheap."

I lower the fork. "*Murphy*, I met Diamond Anthony. And she didn't ask for a dime. She said she just wanted Dad to know, that's all. And to stay away from the funeral."

"'Course she didn't ask for nothin'. She'd already seen me. I gave her a percentage of the till tonight." He blows smoke toward me, and I know I can't eat a bite. "A *low* percentage."

I sigh. And I believed her when she'd said she just wanted my father to know.

"And *your* percentage?"

He's indignant. "I don't get a dime unless we're three-quarters full tomorrow night."

When I lower my eyes to play with the salt shaker, he leans forward. "The girl wasn't his, Skip."

I'm so glad I've talked to Tony and don't have to disbelieve him. "So why'd you come back?"

He sits back. The hand holding the cigarette shakes like he's trying to write words in the air. "To help him one last time."

"A little dramatic, Murph."

But he's grinning up at the blond placing his steaming cup before him.

"Thanks, sugar."

I shove the plate away, promising myself to eat something later. "Can I borrow the Caddy for a while today?"

"You pretty good in this kinda weather?"

I follow his gaze outside, where the snow's begun piling up. "Lots of practice lately."

He nods, hunches above his cup, like a weight lifter steeling himself. Then, surrounding the mug with both hands, he lifts it. A spoonful sloshes onto the saucer and table.

"My boy Conor in 'Frisco wants me to come out and help run his store. A goddamn health food store! I'm gonna be peddlin' tofu and granola!"

"So you really are leaving after this gig?"

"If Boss's boost back into the public eye comes off as good as I think it will, he can call his shots from here on out. My guess is, after what's happened, he'll retire in a blaze of glory."

"Not likely."

"I asked him if he wants to come with me. He's thinking about it."

"Two elder statesmen of rock and roll growing old together?"

I half expect him to try to punch me again, but he's shaking so hard I know I can easily dodge it.

"I don't expect you to understand, Skip—I mean, I don't understand it myself, but somehow your father and me just ended up in this sinking dinghy together and . . . here we are—married!"

His fingers, when he spreads them, are horribly yellow. His face looks yellow too, even his eyes. Every cell in his body has to be nicotine saturated. I wonder if Conor Kelleher knows his old man might be bringing home a withered bride. But it will never happen. Doesn't Murphy know Dad is married to the road, that when he calls it never ending, he means it—till death do us part? I'm about to say as much when it finally dawns on me that I am witnessing something so incredible that, for the moment, it defies words. Murphy's face, usually puffy and sagging, seems leaner, almost skeletal, every line visible. I lean toward him and sniff. Nothing but nicotine.

"Murphy, did you quit drinking?"

He cuts his eyes toward the door. Is he going to tuck his tail and run?

His laugh comes out a cross between a growl and a gasp. "If I go west, Conor said I got to come sober. So I did detox at a private hospital in Lexington. And now AA. I'm doing ninety meetings in ninety days."

Decades ago, Murphy tried AA—and returned with stories he made endless drunken fun of, to the delight of Dad and the band. Now I'm struck dumb. Murphy at Betty Ford? Hazelden? Clapton's place at Antigua?

He leans forward. "I know what you're thinking: 'He won't make it,' right?"

There's no use trying to bullshit a bullshitter. He tries that laugh again, but it comes out angry. "It worked for you, didn't it, Reverend?"

It all flashes before me: endless meetings, shrinks, counselors, lectures—talk, talk, talk—all of it surreal. Until one day it began to take hold. Made a decision to turn our will and our lives over to *the care* of God. I remember thinking that day, and all the others till I was able to stand on my own two feet: I abandoned God, but God never abandoned me. Now Murphy is studying me as if I'm a specimen under glass: Recovering Drunk, Early Twenty-First Century.

I shrug. "Only requirement's a desire to stop drinking."

His eyes shift to the table, then toward a crying infant, anywhere to avoid looking at mine. "Hospital wanted me for eight weeks, so I split without telling nobody. I felt Boss callin'. But I think I got it down." He tries to look at his watch, but his newly sober eyes are having a hard time focusing on a moving target. He gives up.

"Got the time, Skip?"

"Ten-oh-five."

"Shit." He rises, spilling more coffee. "Meetin's at a church down the street." Hauling out a wallet so ancient that it actually zips, he manages to tweeze out a bill. "My treat."

He tosses down a twenty and the Caddy keys, and takes off. I see myself seven years ago staggering out the door on the same stiff, new legs and shake my head at the wonders this day hath already wrought, wondering what's next.

* * *

It isn't that hard to find the abandoned shopping center, but there is nothing in the lot behind it to say that the tribe squatted here. The snow has already covered the burnt place where they built the fire. I stand in the cold for a few minutes, looking around at the ruins, wondering where they've gone to gather their forces for battle.

"They left this morning."

I nearly jump out of my skin. When I turn, there stands Beanpole, hands in the pockets of his hoodie, looking pretty normal without his friends sitting around slashing themselves.

"Why?"

He shrugs. "Gotta keep on the move. 'Cops can't hit a moving target,' Emanuel says." He laughs. "Heck, they can't hit a stationary target in this town."

"You the clean-up man?"

"Defector. Look, I'm sorry about—" Cocking his head, he holds an invisible blade to his neck.

"I knew you were just being a good Indian." When I grin, he does too. "Is it that easy to unjoin the tribe?"

"I'm not the first. My little brother Judge went first."

I do a double take. Sure enough: shear his wild hair, give him hoops and piercings, and he's the twin of the boy who cut my father at the Green Door.

"And Amanda before him?" I wait; silence has worked well for me lately. He looks around as if for help. I half expect a dumpster lid to lift and Emanuel's head to appear. But there is no help.

"Actually, y'know, she was never one of us." He laughs unconvincingly. "She never cut herself."

"I noticed."

"She was beautiful. It wasn't hard to see why Judge latched right on to her."

"They were lovers?"

He nods. "You gotta understand, Reverend, my brother's bipolar. Plus, he was on heroin by the time he was thirteen. Rehab, shrinks, jail. He nearly killed a kid at school. For complimenting his tattoo."

"And he cut a legend with a razor."

"He did it for Amanda. In her worst rages, she said she wanted to kill your father. Well, Judge mighta heard that louder than the other—that she just wanted him to admit he *was* her father, 'acknowledge her heritage.' But Judge heard kill, and, well, he couldn't resist at least showing your dad—and her—that he could do the deed, if she'd let him."

I'm shivering as if we stand in the center of Siberia. Flakes as big as quarters shroud our shoulders. I can't help a quick glance around the lot, but only the dumpsters seem to be listening. "So where is he now?"

"Probably on his way home—Mom lives outside DC. Our folks're divorced, and he's her baby. She gives him money, whatever he needs."

"And you?"

He shrugs. "Got finals on Monday—I go to UNC Greensboro— and even though I haven't been to class in a few weeks, I think I can pass calc. And maybe bio."

I have a million more questions, but before I can get my mouth to stop quivering, he speaks.

"Look, Rev, you seem pretty cool. I thought I'd tell you to watch your dad's back. They're planning something tonight, but I don't know what. I ain't exactly in the inner circle anymore."

I know he could be conning me; maybe Emanuel stationed him here to plant disinformation or worse (Furies hidden in the dumpster awaiting a signal to attack). Maybe I'm just being paranoid.

"By the way, I guess you figured out that Keesh was your sister?"

Quiche? "What'd you call her?"

"Keesh, short for LaKeisha, Amanda's middle name. Everybody in the Theatre has nicknames—all except Emanuel. How can you improve on that, right? Plus, since it was his black mama that gave it to him and all . . ."

I'm not listening. Keesh—Keesha—was the name Dad muttered in his sleep on the way to the retreat. *Damn.* He knew who she was even before he saw the photo—knew and did nothing. Now I get an even bigger flash. "Do you know if she ever considered calling me?"

He shakes his head and grins. "She hated your guts. You were her rival."

But I'm not listening. I'm back in my pastor's study that Wednesday evening hearing that smoky voice urging me to go look after my father. My half sister's voice. The boy is blathering.

". . . so I decided to call myself Star-Strider, since my major's astronomy. Always been interested in stars and stuff."

"How're you getting home?"

"I don't know." He looks around, hugs himself. "Hitch or something."

"I'll give you a ride to the bus station."

"Won't do me any good. No money."

"God provides."

"Sweet."

* * *

After dropping Star-Strider at the Greyhound station, I cruise the city for hours, down East Carson, past gaudy bars and shops, up to Mount Washington for a bird's-eye of the Allegheny, Ohio, and—oh, yes, I remember now: the Monongahela—the black water shrouded in horizontal, cold, blowing snow. I even tempt the devil in the Hill District, daring degenerates to mess with me when I stop at a light.

Finally I emerge from my trance and begin looking for shelter from the storm. Since it got dark, temps have fallen to the twenties, according to the radio, ten to twelve inches predicted. I need to grieve Amanda "Keesha" Anthony, a seriously troubled child-woman responsible for all that's happened to me in the last three weeks (if indeed it was she who called me, and I think it was)—all that is leading me and my father somewhere, though I still can't fathom where. Though what I *really* want, remembering that kiss, is to go home to Mim.

But despite all that has happened, all that lies ahead, I find myself numb to everything but Dad. And although I've run away, just as I did after the Big One, I know I need to go back and try again. But before I can, I need to do something with this anger. *It is a spiritual axiom that every time we are disturbed, no matter what the cause, there is something wrong with us.* Maybe I need an AA meeting, but then I remember the reason I quit. Finding a god of their own understanding is crucial to those who feel scorn toward religion, but to Reverend Thomas Johnson, a seminary-trained drunk, a superhero is not supernatural. My higher power, I decided, must be independent of mere imagination; He's real, or He isn't. Right now I wonder if I am guilty of splitting hairs. Surely, any god is better than none. While the need to pray is a physical craving in my belly, I've lacked bread for so long I may not recognize it when I taste it. All the way, Mim said. So I start looking for the path.

* * *

After forty-five minutes, I pull over suddenly, horns blaring behind me, into a church parking lot. I'm in the middle of a residential section with boxy brick ranches with snow-fringed, gaudy, gold-and-silver wreaths and plastic Santas on the doors. The church is clapboard and brick with three words on the kiosk out front. *O Holy Night.*

The back door isn't locked, and the hallway between tiny classrooms is deserted. As soon as I step into the suffocating warmth of the steam-heated dark sanctuary, it feels familiar. It smells like God: wood polish, hymnals, stale perfume, and sweat. Yet I'm trembling all over.

As I head for the front pew, lights come on, nearly blinding me.

"May I help you, brother?"

I turn to face a large, bearded, bald man in wine-colored vestments. His thick glasses shine, and his smile competes with the blazing lights. "I'd like to pray, if that's all right." My fear makes me sound angry.

He nods. "I'll turn the lights back off. I'm working in the office down the hall if you need anything." As he turns to go, my heart leaps toward him, and I blurt:

"I'm Reverend Thomas Johnson, Holy Martyrs Church, New Prestonburg, Ohio." It isn't a total lie; I haven't resigned yet.

He steps forward, robes swishing, and takes my hand in his very warm one. "Garth Harmon, Reverend. I'm assistant pastor here at Sacred Space."

"Sacred Space?"

He chuckles good-naturedly. "We're supposedly nondenominational, but I like to say we're multidenominational. American Baptist, Zen Buddhist, and everything in between. Just about anybody's god can be found here."

I smile at the irony: I'm back to AA. "I love your sign's . . . simplicity."

He bows slightly, hands tented chest high. "Brother Stephen's idea—he's the real high holy honcho at SS. I'm just God's grunt. Steve is . . . concise." His puckish smile radiates the complexity of his relationship with the boss man. I think of my own congregation and feel a quick stab of regret: my first Christmas in a decade without them. "Sorry he's not here. He would be, but—"

"Garth, do you believe you should forgive anyone for anything?"

I like it that he hesitates. "Saint Paul says if we don't forgive others, God won't forgive us."

"I'm trying to forgive my father for killing my mother." God bless him; he doesn't even lift an eyebrow. "And someone else . . . a girl. He killed her too. Not literally. But he's responsible for her death nonetheless."

Garth nods gravely, and his eyes don't change. That's all it takes.

"When I was five, he left us, and my mother never got over it. She lived only for his return. He was—*is*—a world-famous musician. We followed him from city to city, motel to motel, waiting outside coliseums, arenas, bars, and hotels for a glimpse of him."

Garth nods, his hands laced above his slight paunch, his body absorbing the sound of my voice.

"Finally, after about six months of chasing him, we were waiting outside an arena in Baltimore. By this time we were living in Mom's old Toyota Tercel hatchback. It wasn't till after the divorce we'd get the money, the mansion, the servants, and bodyguards. A man comes over to us. And Mom rolls down the window.

"'We're trying to see'"—I hesitate to say my father's name, but the channel is open—"'Israel Jones,' she said. And when she saw his eyes glance at me, she said, totally blowing it, 'my son's father.'"

I think God's grunt raises one eyebrow at the legend's name, but I might be mistaken. I swallow hard and go on.

"The guy says, 'Yeah, you and everybody else who spreads her legs for the boss.' It killed her—after all, this was the first time we'd actually been spoken to by one of Dad's bodyguards. Usually we were shooed away by arena and hotel security. It took everything she had to say, 'I'm his wife.' My mother, the wife of the famous man, had, by this time, become the most timid mouse in America. The guy laughed. 'Israel ain't got no wife,' he snarled. 'And as for mother of his children, take a number.'"

"'I don't want anything from him,' Mom pleaded. 'I only want to see him for one minute. Please. I'll do anything.'

"He'd been pulling away, but now he saunters back, lays his hand on the top of the car, and leans close. 'Anything?' She wouldn't look at me sitting beside her. And though I was five and a half and oozing fear, he didn't look at me.

"'Follow me,' he says and heads for the back door.

"'Stay right here. I'll be back in a few minutes,' she said, then got out of the car. I waited and waited, even got out and pounded on that door, but no one ever came. When she came out half an hour later, she didn't look so good, but she said she'd seen my father and he'd said he was coming home soon. She celebrated by buying me a chocolate milkshake at McDonald's. I was nineteen, just before she committed suicide, when she finally told me she'd never got any further than some crummy, stinking broom closet right inside that door. The guy was a chauffeur for the opening act. She'd heard me banging but couldn't do anything. She even heard my father up the hall laughing in his dressing room. He was probably high, probably with one of his little . . ."

I think of Diamond Anthony, then of her daughter lying in her blood, and I nearly lose it. Garth's eyes are magnified behind his lenses.

"*Damn him,*" Garth says, hands balled into fists.

I guess I look surprised to hear the second-in-command cursing. He immediately looks contrite. "I'm sorry, Reverend. It just makes me so mad. My father left us—my mother, brother, and three sisters—before I was born."

"So you know—"

"Let's pray for forgiveness."

I hit the brakes. "I don't know if I can forgive him yet."

"Not him, Reverend. Yourself."

And before I know it he reaches behind us, turns off the overhead lights, and leads me forward into darkness.

Chapter Nineteen

I'm glad to see security guards patting everyone down at the arena's front door—and not at all surprised that the show is going on despite the weather. Province of the young and immortal, rock and roll stops for nothing, short of a closed airport—or maybe death. The Furies will have their blades wrapped and tucked inside their bodies' dark places. I shiver into my jacket as I head around back. The Whale is pulled up right at the stage doors with the motor running. Not for the first time, I miss Gunnar, arms folded, watching. The first person I run into is Patrick, leaning against the wall, smoking.

"Have you seen the crowd?" he crows, practically glowing.

"Have you seen Dad—or Murphy?"

"Nobody gets to see Boss before a show. He comes out when he's good and ready."

"Well, Boss is gonna see me." Turning, I slam my hand against the door, not caring if I smash the glass. It opens, and I see Kevin's startled face before I hurtle right past him. By the time the driver catches up with me, I've already banged on the sacred portal. His hand is on my arm when the door opens. In the greenish glow of the bus lights, Dad looks pale enough to be wearing whiteface.

"Boss, I tried—"

"It's all right, Kevin. Come on in, son."

I walk inside and perch on his bed. After closing the door he turns to face me, leaning against the wall.

"I found out something today," I say.

He waits, thumbs in his pockets.

"I think I know what I'm doing here . . . on the tour."

He gazes down at the toes of his boots.

"Keesha," I say.

Glancing up, he looks helpless again, like he did in the bathroom that night facing her blood. Rage shotguns through me, then is gone. I'm nearly breathless when I say, "She called me back in November. She's the reason I came. We owe her."

He nods, his expression unchanged.

"*You* could've called me, Dad."

He gazes over my shoulder. "I could now."

It isn't nearly enough, but it *is* something. For once, I allow all that's unspoken to remain that way. Finally:

"I think those kids might be planning something tonight." He doesn't even honor it with a shrug. I glance at my watch: ten minutes to showtime. They're probably out there already. I stand up. Before I can talk myself out of it, I clasp him to me roughly, devouring his musty scent, like old books, his three-day-old beard gritting against my cheek. He feels so breakable, so boneless. His hands remain at his sides, but it doesn't bother me. Finally I let him go and step backward.

I start to turn away, but he grasps my forearms tight, holds me where I stand. This close to my father the legend, I think my eyes might burst. When I think I've witnessed all his faces, he has one more, this one strangely young—only a few centimeters away from laughter, not mocking but real, the kind of look that says, "Nothing don't mean nothing. Let's go get a drink." Something in my chest releases, and I feel the wet, warm tracks down my cheeks. He speaks in a raspy whisper. "God bless you, son."

"I'll pray for you, Dad," I manage to get out, and something like hope blooms on his face for a moment before he lets me go and turns away.

*　*　*

Oglebay Arena is not your first-class coliseum, making it exactly right for the third-class has-been Dad was until Abshire's. The place holds about five thousand, so a sellout doesn't mean all that much, but it *is* an arena, and Dad *is* playing two nights. The floor has no chairs, and the first five hundred to buy tickets are allowed to mill about in front of the stage—a terrible idea, but even I know if kids can't mosh, mingle, and thrash, they won't come. They're even smoking, though of course it isn't allowed. A dump.

I find Murphy and threaten him within an inch of his life if anything happens. Praying with Garth and being blessed by my father has me feeling almost plugged back in.

"Skipper, stop! I'll be right here. I ain't going nowhere."

I make the man sweat—no easy task. "Get me on the floor." I turn and stalk off, waiting for him to follow. To my surprise, he does.

*　*　*

In the press of bodies, I don't see any obvious Furies, but most people are wearing coats, and the house lights have already gone off, so I can't be sure. The mob is ten-twelve deep in front of the stage. Maybe they're already up close, palming blades, ready to start carving. Suddenly the place erupts. When I look toward the stage, Dad lurches into the light, looking frail in that damned black coat, strapping on his guitar in the spotlight, back to the audience. What a long, strange road, I think—for us all. I fold my arms. Furies are either here or they aren't. When Dad ducks his head between his axe and its strap, I imagine for a moment a noose.

* * *

He can feel them out there, though he's turned off sound for now. Or has it focused to a needle point. He finds the right harp, shoves it in its rack, walks to the mic center stage, and strums, waits. At the edge of the spot, he sees burning, but no yellow or orange, just searing white, like newsprint burning. Indigo's a long way off. Time to find the first song.

Strums some more. But what is the song? He never worries about that. It always comes, embodied in voice, wearing words, for the thing to be pleased, appeased. And he feels it coiled tight in his belly, inside his head, oddly comforting in its sleek sameness, predictable as the pain before the vein explodes. Like heartburn.

Heart. Burn. It starts . . . a little. He stops strumming, grasps a tuning peg, feels the restlessness in the room, the drunkenness, the high, shrill whine—all the baggage they've brought, all their sick legend lust. He's only a troubadour, don't they know that? Tune some more.

Something at the periphery, glint of silver. Camera zooms to edge of stage. The glint is . . . a gleaming blade. Around his heart Hero quivers, flicks a tongue. Gonna be interesting. And now he knows the first song will be "Earth." Of course. Sons are . . .

Caught in the light, he can't see a thing—not unusual—but tonight he needs to see to sing. What the hell? Can't start putting conditions on him now. Hero stirs, uncoils, is in his throat.

O God, you will not despise . . . My sin is ever before me. Against you, alone . . . blameless when you pass judgment.

And then they are beside him, the pain-in-the-ass band, worst he can remember putting up with, though he loves them anyway. And sound roars as they plug in. He smiles, saved (damn throat and arm still hurt). And now the song without words, without voice, without love, without loss. He only has to bear it—will not wait and will not ask—and for now that seems possible, at least for a little longer, just a bit longer now . . .

* * *

Mesmerized, I watch my father tune, choose his harmonica, insert it in the rack, as he's done a million times, every cell in my body tingling. I'm not sure if it's just fear that the Furies will try something or something worse I feel. When he turns around, though, I think I know. Something about his eyes through the smoky haze. My heart's suddenly wild. The mask is gone . . . my father is scared.

Now he's stopped strumming, and I realize he can't remember the song he started. He can't remember *any* song. Not only can he not write them anymore; now he can't remember them. My temples throb. But just when he's stretched their patience to breaking, out come Wendell, Javier, and Patrick to joyous shrieks. Here in the pit, I smell hunger. After what happened to the girl two nights ago, they want blood. If the legend wants to deliver himself to them, that's fine. The band plays full tilt—praise the Lord my earplugs are in place—and it's the same old instrumental, "Dead Man's Blues." For the time being the man in the spotlight is safe playing without the mask, with terror, for his life.

* * *

He laughs soundlessly, remembering those wooden crates at the front of the church where they keep the pit vipers until the preacher decrees it is time to touch, to lift, to kiss. Same here. Hero's out of the box, and all shall see his power. The pressure at his center releases as the band cranks up "Dead Man." He lurches side to side in a several-foot radius before the mic. As weight leaves him, he wonders how much longer he can stand. No way of knowing. He isn't looking ahead—the moment is the only eternity there is. Keep pumping till you shoot it all.

Suddenly he is enjoying himself, able to strum again, his fingers striking air as often as strings. Hero's unholy length extends from behind his tongue to his belly, where the serpent's tail must be. Never been so fully exposed, so out of the cage. Stay on top and ride the wave . . .

Flash of red. He stumbles at the edge of the pit. Sound slows, warps, speeds up. And pain spews, a toothache throughout his body, permeating every vein. Uncoiled from his heart, the poison spreads. Released from its grip, the center gives. Bright red spumes fountain before him, on the music's rising rim . . .

What I did not steal must I now restore?

And there the other thing sits, tearing flesh in its bloody beak, glaring at him with ruby eyes. If it stays, he will stand and play; if it flies, he will follow.

Even unto death.

* * *

Wearing hoodies, the Furies, I see, have positioned themselves at Dad's feet. Any moment now one of them will leap onstage and put the blade to his throat. And there's nothing anyone can do.

A sudden roar goes up from the crowd, and I know something has happened. Gotta get up there. Shouldering through the mob, I run into a wall.

"Watch it, fuckhead."

The guy is well over six feet and weighs at least three hundred. Not only can I not get around him—I can't even see around him. I feint right, dodge left, and skirt Goliath. Finally I can see the stage. The place where my father had stood for over forty years is empty. I nearly knock the giant to the ground getting around him again.

* * *

Although wind is whipping the snow sideways, the door to the bus is open. *What?—he would never leave it unclosed.* Then I see the smashed side window. *Someone followed him, broke in behind him.* As soon as I put my foot on the first step, I feel unreal, as if I am acting in a play, or watching one. By the second step, I consider going back for help, but now that I'm committed, I haul myself into the aisle. No lights are on, and I see the door to his cell is partly open. I hear a voice, quiet, calm, nearly crooning. And rustling . . . clothes being loosened, removed. *Thank God. Security, paramedics.* I stumble forward, thrust the door open, and face the back of Dad's black coat.

For a second I'm thrown into confusion. If this is Dad standing before me, whose feet are protruding off the end of the bed? But every detail, worse than the last, unfolds as revelation. Muscles in the broad back before me bunch, release. Heavy breathing, as from hard labor, fills the room. I taste as much as smell a sharp, bright scent. My brain slowly conveys that the back I am staring at isn't Dad's—*someone is wearing his coat.* Glancing at the feet at the end of the bed again, I see that, yes, those are his pitiful boots. Why is the medic wearing Dad's coat?

My mouth is open to speak, when he turns. I lurch backward a step. It's the boy named Judge. He is smiling, his eyes luminous and large, pupils hugely dilated. Despite what my eyes see, my brain is all too eager to share his joy. Like an idiot, I tentatively smile back. He speaks.

"Reverend Thom? Father's here. See him sleep?"

Then he steps aside. My father's face is frozen in awe: Moses on Sinai; Saul at Damascus; Mom in her tub, water turned to blood. Dead as stone. The cut is so deep, I marvel that head and body haven't parted. (Even in my insanity, I wonder: why is there no blood?)

"I fly, Holy Father, toward your heavenly throne," Judge incants, blade held high, head back, eyes closed. "Your servant now sleepeth, findeth repose in your loving arms. Spotless as the lamb, baptized in your water."

The black floor rises, but before it can swallow me, I am on him like thunder, like gravity, like the slashing sea on Pharaoh's army.

Chapter Twenty

It is like surfacing from a long, lazy stroll on the ocean's bottom, slipping softly through the silent, seaweed world of glowing bodies and fluttering fins. The air there was thick, warm, and weightless—full of speechless joy. I was with others of my kind; we needed neither oxygen tanks nor mask as we floated through an endless current while sudden colors flared around us. I awaken with the sight of it all still in my mind, overjoyed to find Mim beside me.

"Did you see . . . ?" I lift my arm—it weighs a ton—and my hand reaching out to my wife is a bear's paw, has no fingers, will not flex. I retract it quickly, afraid I'll claw the white flesh of her face.

"What, Thom? What did you see?"

Language fails me utterly, and I laugh. *See,* I say inside my head, the images still imprinted on my optic nerve: *Aren't they beautiful?*

She sits forward and brushes hair out of my face. I feel stiffness above, as if a hat sits on my head, but I know better than to lift a hand. I've glimpsed the other one. Both are bandaged, letting me know what is on my head. My mind knows something that my eyes don't want to let in just yet.

"I've been to the bottom of the sea," I finally get out.

Her eyes show me better than any mirror what I don't want to see. I cling stubbornly to my ocean, already fading.

"Creatures . . . light . . . waving colors."

She nods, her mouth flexing into a momentary smile, fear slowly morphing into something I can't read. A great weariness sits on me like weights, as if my entire body is encased in sand.

I say to her, "A dream."

"You've been out for hours."

Light leaking through the blinds behind her tells me it is late morning. Sunday. Last night . . . the black coat, the open eyes, the great, gaping wound.

"Dad?"

Her eyes stay right with me. "He's gone, Thom."

I nod. "Why'd they drug me?" I try that laugh again. It sounds angry. "I knew he was dead. I saw him, for Christ's sake. I saw"—better watch it; Mim's eyes hold a lot more than Dad's death—"everything." The sandbags on my chest make breathing so hard.

Mim's eyes cut to the door. Finally she decides. "When you found your father, do you remember that someone else was there?"

I swallow hard and nod. Orange flame inside my skull. "That boy."

Her lips are tight as she nods, rocking her whole body. It must be bad, if she's waiting for *me* to tell *her*.

"He's upstairs, Thom. In intensive care. You attacked him. That's why he's in ICU, he had so many broken bones, facial damage—he's already had one plastic surgery, will have at least two more before . . ."

So. I am lucky to escape with paws for hands and a bloody cap on my head (and whatever else—my sandbagged body is slowly awakening to aches and pains like the ones I'd had after a fender bender years ago). Poor, sweet Mim—doesn't she know I can bear anything now?

"He murdered my father."

She glances again toward the doorway. When she looks back up, her eyes are gentle. "Under questioning, the boy said your father was dead already. There's to be an autopsy. Some think it might've been a stroke."

Though every nerve, cell, and synapse screams in protest, I see in my mind's eye there was no blood. Neither on the knife nor on my father. Not one drop anywhere in that accursed place. In the greatest irony yet, *I* am the murderer, not the deranged one with the knife. (Not murderer, no. He will not let me have that romantic delusion. I struck, but I did not slay.)

"Still . . ." My tongue is chalk. "He cut my father. Twice he cut him."

She nods. "I know, honey. I know." Her hand on my cheek is cool as rain.

All is silent, except someone laughing in the hall. My eyes are clamped closed. It was so warm where I'd been on the bottom of the sea, so full of energy and light. I open my eyes, and at that moment, with gold and silver streaming around her, my wife's body burns like the edges of a solar eclipse. I suddenly remember something, can't believe I've forgotten.

"Where's Murphy?"

I try to sit up, but Mim firmly pushes me back. "Oh, Thom." For the first time she looks truly stressed. "He got here an hour after you were admitted, but with you sedated and the weather so bad, he was afraid his flight might be canceled." I must look clueless. She quickly adds, "California. He said you knew."

So: he wasn't just jawing, after all. He'd already booked the flight before the Whale even pulled into Pitt. It makes me think of something else.

"How'd you get back here so fast, Mim?"

"I didn't get far before the snow got bad. I'd just checked in at the Holiday when Murphy called."

"You and Murphy, huh?"

She nods, but it doesn't surprise me much. And I thought it'd probably been Maxine who'd tracked my movements for her.

"But . . . the bus, the band . . ."

Her hand, gently stroking my cheek, feels good. She grins crookedly. "Manager to the end, Murphy said he split last night's take with the band four ways. 'Severance pay,' he said. And he left you something."

I lift a hand to interrupt. Maybe his plane hasn't taken off, maybe we can page him, make him explain things so I can understand if not accept how they went so horribly wrong. But Mim is dangling keys with a green rabbit's foot in front of my nose. And she's finally crying.

* * *

In the next twenty-four hours, I ask to see Judge over and over. Mim shakes her head, her mouth as tight as the sutures I've seen along my scalp when the lanky nurse Everett, after he'd changed the dressing, brought me a mirror. ("Looks like you went a coupla rounds with Tyson," he said, grimacing. "But I should see the other guy, right?" I hung my head, hoping he didn't know the other guy was a boy half my age.)

"There are guards," my wife says, spoon poised inches from my mouth. "He's charged with desecration of a corpse. Besides, you already beat him up. Once is enough."

Not having hands has many advantages. I am treated, every meal, to the sight of her chest when she leans forward to feed me.

Her creamy flesh is lightly freckled—how could I have forgotten *that?* Miracle.

"I'm thinking about moving out west," Mim says, holding the water glass for me. I immediately choke and begin to cough. She reaches, beats my back. "Lina Wolfe, a friend from Dharma House, moved to Port Townsend, Washington, to cofound a sort of ashram, more inclusive, both eastern and western traditions. If I could afford to live there, I'd go."

Even after I regain my breath, I cannot ask her: *why not stay here . . . with me?* But I have no home beyond this hospital room to offer. She reads my mind.

"Oh, by the way, there's somebody to see you. I told him I wanted to feed you a little first."

She's out the door before I can respond. I don't question it, don't feel I have a right to question anything. I've surrendered to patient status, letting myself be done for. Steeling myself for the cops, I'm startled when a very large man in a tight suit walks two paces into the room and stops, snap-brim hat in his hand.

"I hope I haven't come at a bad time, Reverend."

I'm amazed. "You've come a long way, Henry."

"I have the time, and the church paid for the flight."

"Please . . . sit down."

He sits in Mim's plastic chair, clearly uncomfortable. I don't smile or say anything to help him. So we both wait in silence. Finally he speaks.

"I'm so sorry about your father. I had no idea how a man like that lived." He lowers his head, glances back up. "There's a lot being said in the media."

I wonder whether the devils showed any restraint whatever, whether the true cause of his death was overshadowed by the sad boy who'd thought he was the Lord's liberator and heir apparent to the king's throne. "Dad's health was up and down for a long time."

Henry nods. "Passed away at his peak, some are saying."

What can I say? For me, he peaked in that pine woods thirty-five years ago. The silence lies heavy on us. Without our pastor-deacon roles to help us out, we're adrift, and Henry is a shy man. As Dad was. Which makes me smile. If the adoring public only knew how introverted many of their idols are, and how fame drives them into rooms no bigger than the size of a sarcophagus.

"Thomas, I've come on behalf of the church."

"In this weather. That's very kind of you. And of them."

"They've changed their minds, the deacons."

I wince. They've probably decided to rescind my meager allowance until I "find myself," or whatever Ken Branch said at the Inquisition. I will my face shut, won't show this man, their emissary, a thing.

"They want you to lead us again," he says gently. "They sent me . . . to ask."

I laugh—at first a short, staccato snort, but then, once the way is cleared, others follow in a long string. After a moment of red-faced shock, Henry joins me—and I'm surprised, then ecstatic at the relief it gives us, like a magnificent fart following great gastrointestinal pain; like orgasm; like waking up and finding that, though you have caused grave harm, you have not murdered. Before it's over, Mim even peers inside (it touches me that she is waiting so close by), but she seems to decide the therapeutic benefits of laughter are worth loosening a few stitches and goes away. Finally we settle down, casting sideways glances at each other. I let the tears remain on my cheeks.

"So they've stooped to pity."

He shakes his head. "Mrs. Strickland wrote a letter before she left the area. In no uncertain terms, she clarified that the relationship between the two of you, though personal, was entirely professional."

"No sex, you mean."

His eyes don't waver. "Yes."

I actually manage to lift my right hand. "Why would they believe her, if not out of pity? It won't last, Henry. It would be poison if I—"

"Mr. Strickland signed it too. As a matter of fact, he's the one that hand delivered it to Maxine. I was there too, in the office."

My body sinks into the sheets, into the mattress, my spirit leaking through the box springs, through the floor, down, down . . .

"He doesn't look well."

Dennis Strickland, bereft of wife and children, doing the right thing. Noble. Scary. Miraculous. I feel bubbles of giddy mirth welling up in me again like hiccups. If I am not careful, I'll soon dissolve into guffaws that Henry might misconstrue as joy over Dennis's tragedy. All hope gone, and he's come to set me free.

"And Deacon Branch?"

"He walked out without saying a word after we voted."

It makes me reflect on my congregation, the people I've faced so many Sundays and Wednesdays; and I know, without the slightest sentimentality—the knowledge is accompanied by hardly any emotion at all—that, while it's been hard, I have loved serving them. Then I get a flash of Ken Branch sitting at the head of that jury's table, fingers laced, calmly convicting me. It seems to have taken place eons ago. It makes me imagine the boy upstairs in ICU. In my mind's eye, he has no face. If Ken Branch is evil, so am I; so is my entire congregation, judges and juries, would-be murderers all.

A clean break is tempting. Dad would do it, Murphy would, no looking back. Without a yoke, maybe I can change my wife's mind about Port Townsend. But something holds me back.

"I don't know, Henry. I just don't know."

"Can I tell them you'll at least think about it?"

"Yes." I pat his liver-spotted hand. He stares at the bandage, silent. Now that he's said what he came to say, his discomfort returns. When he stands, his hat drops from his lap, and when he stands back up after bending, his face is red-splotchy, his eyes full. If he hadn't fled with a quick wave of three fingers, I might've recommitted my life to the ministry in a heartbeat. I hardly have time to ponder the implications of that before the phone rings. Twisting myself, knocking things off the table, I manage to pick up by shoveling with both hands.

"Skip?"

It's like a mild shot to the heart, and I lie back. "Where are you, Murphy?"

"Balmy sixty-two degrees out here. Angel Island shinin' like new money in the bay. Cloudy with a small chance of pree-cip. Beats the hell outta where you're at." His laugh sounds more like a moan.

"How's Conor?"

"Acts like he's glad to see me."

"Good for you, Murph."

What we aren't saying leaks out of the phone like poison gas. My eyes burn and my nose is itching furiously, but I can't scratch. My hands, useless appendages, want to clench, grip, and squeeze. "I couldn't believe it: Dad dies and you run away."

"I couldn't face you, Skip. I tried. It happened on my watch."

If he starts crying, what will happen to us? "*He* let it happen," I say. "Wanted it to happen. And we let him have what he wanted . . . as usual."

The silence is thick, and my lids are heavy, heavy.

"We's all parties to a mercy killin', then, you're sayin'?"

A part of me wants to argue, but it's outvoted by the rest of me that wants to sleep. Murphy's voice has its old edge back. He's with his son; he'll be all right.

"Thanks for the Caddy. I need a car now. Sounds like Mim's not staying."

I hear him exhale smoke. "I sold the goddamn Whale to a junkyard—piece o' shit, anyway. Didn't want it showing up on eBay: 'Israel Jones's last ride.'"

"Sounds like you thought of everything." I'm almost asleep when he speaks again.

"Them birthday cards? Israel picked 'em out. Took him a god-damn hour ever' time."

"If there's a funeral or something—" I yawn so big I'm surprised my mouth corners don't split. "I'll let you know." Just as my head is falling away from the phone, I hear his last words.

"Thom, something you should know: your daddy had a vasec-tomy in '91 before the Holy Tour. He didn't want nobody to know till he was dead. He said nobody'd want to listen to a rocker with his nuts cut off."

"Thank you, Murph . . . for everything. Please . . . keep in touch." And I am gone, gone.

* * *

I struggle above the waterline, gulping air. I slept fitfully—that pill they'd brought me—only to be pursued by faceless beings in black, flowing robes, down corridors, through doors, up ladders, across rooftops of a thousand-eyed, dark city. After supper Mim had returned to tell me that, according to the *Pittsburgh Post-Gazette*, au-thorities seemed inclined to believe Judge's desperate lie that Dad was already dead when the boy got there. In the dull glow of the light leaking in from the hallway, objects seem carved from granite. Mim is long gone, though I feel someone in the room with me. Behind my eyelids I behold a crimson river. I reach for, find a light, snap it on, and see stars.

"Hello, Reverend Thom."

How I keep my composure I'll never know. The boy congeals from the room's shadows to stand at the foot of the bed. We stare at each other for a good five seconds before I finally get enough spit in my mouth to speak.

"Emanuel." I lie back, ashamed to be panting. "I thought—"

"You thought I was Judge, your dad's accused murderer."

"Accused!"

"Your father was dead before Judge reached his side."

"And how do you or anyone else know that for sure?"

"Israel surrendered his body a long time ago. He'd been seeking permission to depart for some time."

"You have no right—"

"We all played our roles, my friend, yourself included."

"You could've stopped—"

"Nothing on earth could've stopped it, Reverend."

My mouth feels caked with blood, my tongue with scabs.

"The sons of the father were meant to collide," he continues calmly. "It was prophesied: 'One will tear, one yield.'"

"Who prophesied?"

He bends toward me, squinting. When he touches my head, I flinch and knock his hand away. "Looks like Judge did some damage too."

"Not as much as you," I croak.

He steps back and crosses his arms. "Now, Reverend Thom, don't talk out of your head."

"The damage you did to two lives; three, counting my father."

Tenting his fingers prayerfully, he closes his eyes. "He was mine too."

The initial panic of waking to feel his presence is dissipating. Also, I am listening to a voice—Mim's? God's? *Be still.* Even if I do awake some night to find Judge leering over me with his razor, I will never strike him again. Once nearly cost my sanity; twice will cost my soul. It's like a needle to my spine when the boy begins to sing in a quavering tenor:

One prays, one's gay;
One's Abel, one's Cain;
One steals the body,
One swallows the soul;
Both blessed, both die,
All come to live in the earth.

His voice is so like the folksinger's from three decades ago, it is as if Dad is in the room with us. I am stunned.

"The song is all you, Thomas, *you.* Once your anger heals, you'll look in the mirror and see him staring right back. As for our friend Judge, I've been with him. And, believe me, he looks a lot worse than you do. He wants me to tell you something."

"I don't need to hear from my father's murderer."

"Judge is many things, but he's no murderer. You should know that."

I hold my tongue. What else can I do? My wife, God, AA—the very air conspires against my righteous rage.

"He just wanted to taste what you ate on a daily basis," he continues. "Poignant, isn't it? That's why he put it on."

"Poignant, yes, that he saw fit to cut a good man's throat."

"Oh, he should never have done it, put on the coat. And don't worry—he'll do time for abuse of a corpse. It was a stupid attempt to steal the son's birthright. Before he went under the knife for his facial surgery, I told Judge as much. In the name of our dearly beloved father, I entreat you to forgive him."

He sits beside me on the bed, so close I imagine I can smell his sweet-peaches breath. "I know it's probably too early, Reverend, but think about it."

"What about Amanda Anthony?" I say in a raspy old man's whisper.

"A sad, lost soul."

"You knew—"

"We knew she was with us but not of us, even using us. We admired her passion and her strength. But when she married Judge . . ."

"*Married?*"

"In a simple civil ceremony at the Kanawha County Courthouse the day before Israel played his aborted concert in Charleston, West Virginia. In fact, I was the only witness to their union."

I find myself unable to lift my head from the pillow. "You knew he was bipolar?"

"The mentally ill need love too." His stare turns hard. "As well as the unacknowledged offspring of rock stars."

I don't bother to correct him. "You knew everything and didn't help her."

He spreads his hands, palms up. "Reverend, we're all just driving in the dark with our high beams on. Me, you, Keesha, Judge— we were, *are*, God's unwitting instruments."

He drops his right hand inches from my left; I don't bother to move it. "So what's next?" I ask.

He sighs. "You of all people will not be surprised that it was only Israel holding our little congregation together. They've scattered to the four winds."

"The cyberhordes?"

His smile is wide. "Hyperbole to impress you."

"Tell Judge I don't want to kill him anymore, that . . ."

He waits, lifting one eyebrow.

"That's all."

Before I can lift a finger to stop him, he bends and kisses my forehead. "Be well, brother."

I close my eyes to be rid of the sight of him. When I open them, he's gone.

Chapter Twenty-One

Mim and I arrive in New Prestonburg on the twenty-first of December. (I drove the Caddy behind her the whole way, relieved we didn't have to talk.) We enter a frigid house, and it takes hours for the furnace to restore some semblance of heat, but the place never truly warms up. Mim sleeps downstairs, me up. I don't awaken till nearly noon. Opening my eyes on the unfamiliar sight of the parsonage's bedroom, I find my olfactory sense overwhelmed with the smells of rosemary, basil, oregano, and garlic, and, lingering above all, sweet, yeasty bread. She's making Neapolitan ragù, my favorite, for dinner.

Staring at the nightstand, I glimpse the dumped contents of my pockets: wallet, keys, rabbit's foot, coins, and my grandmother's wedding ring. Since Dad gave it to me, I've carried it as if it were no more important than pocket change. Now, staring at the cut stone embering in its puddle of grey light, I know its fire might melt ice.

* * *

I waste the day in my study, reading mail and old newspapers, and fretting. But whenever I remember, I pat my jacket pocket to feel the ring's warm weight. By the time she calls me to set the table, it's well past dark. I put on Miles Davis, *Kind of Blue*. She lights candles. We eat as if starved, enough to hibernate till spring. We talk little during the meal, and though I try to flirt, her expression remains solemn. By the time we finally put down forks and knives, we haven't spoken for a while.

"I want you to have something," I say, startling her out of reverie. I bring it forth, open my palm. Light prisms. Her eyes widen, but she makes no move. My lips begin to quiver. The cold, temporarily banished by the steaming food, returns with a vengeance.

"Dad gave it to me. It was his mother's."

"It's beautiful." She reaches forward slowly, traces the twining vine with her fingertip. "I've never seen anything like it."

"I want you to have it."

Retracting her hand, she sits back and hugs herself. I hadn't planned beyond the offer. Now I see that I should have. "It doesn't mean forever, just that we're together now."

"Thom. I'm the one who called you. At the beginning of December."

I study my open hand: flesh, metal, stone. Outside, an engine roars to life. The driver gasses it, shifts out of park. The sound is so thick and muffled, I know there is snow, maybe lots of it, outside. When I tilt my palm, rays shoot around the room. Her words echo from far away, through cotton, almost as if I've drunk a bottle of wine.

"Murphy called me one day—God knows how he found my number. He sounded so tired and sad. When I said he should call you, he said you hated him, and although I tried hard, I couldn't talk him out of it. He *begged* me. I couldn't say no."

The food, the light, Mim's eyes—all make it easy to part with my former conviction. I see now that I never totally believed Keisha was the caller. But my wife?

"Mim, *exciting* . . . violence?"

When she smiles, it makes her look very young. "I was trying to fool you and act mysterious at the same time. I had no clue it would work!"

Reflection from the streetlight outside illuminates the table, the tendons in her wrist. Finally, she reaches forward, gently closes my hand, snuffing out the light.

"Not yet, all right?"

My hand, unconnected from my arm and my brain, moves into my lap. Standing, she stacks plates, silver, glasses, and is gone. I imagine the snow outside falling straight down. I blow out the candles and walk stiffly upstairs, bent like an old man. Lying on top of the bed, fully clothed, I wait and listen for a long time, still clutching Grandma's ring. Finally, I place it under the pillow and sleep.

* * *

The next day, I wander over to the church office, take one look at my desk—apparently Ron hasn't touched it—and ask Maxine if any Holy Marters are in the hospital.

"Adrian Baldridge," she says. "He got pretty sick around the time you went on your little trip."

I smile at her euphemism for my exile. "What's wrong with Adrian?"

"Upper resp." She quit typing long enough to raise an eyebrow, ever so slightly. "Everyone's hush-hush. They say he's dying."

I sit down fast, suddenly weak and light-headed. Maybe it's Dad's death, or the fact that I just sauntered off, abandoned my flock, and let that lawyer bully me out of my pulpit.

"Are you *okay*?" Max looks at me above her glasses, one of three pairs she uses for different distances. "Reverend, you're looking a little puny since you got home."

I wave it off, and she continues clicking. "Silver Bells" from a distant radio station wafts into my consciousness. My choices seem clear: hide out in the parsonage till Mim decides man cannot live on gourmet Italian —or work—alone. I stand shakily and take three steps toward the door before I hear her say behind me, "He's in ICU. They might make you wear a mask."

* * *

But they don't—though he's wearing one. Turns out Adrian aspirated part of his breakfast, and his breathing got bad enough to put him on oxygen, along with heavy sedation. With the IV and usual array of tubes and wires encircling him, he doesn't do much talking. I watch his expressive hazel eyes and avoid his ravaged face. Yes, I take advantage of his silence and vent—let God judge me—but his eloquent eyes encourage me to describe my journey through hell and back. *Yes, yes, go on. Then what happened?*

Through nods and shakes and occasional whispers, I ascertain that his partner abandoned him upon learning of the sickness. (I recall Adrian's addiction to one-nighters in New York under the pretext of seeing Broadway plays.) It's after dinner by this time, and I find myself unable to leave. I wonder whether Adrian wishes I would go, but he makes no sign, dozing off every now and then, nurses occasionally coming in to check vitals. They're glad to see a visitor for someone who's had almost none (I asked). When the nurse retreats back behind her glass window, that's when it comes to me what he really needs.

When I stand up, knee joints pop. I've been sitting a long time, not eager to return to the chilly parsonage, regardless of whether fettuccine primavera is steeping on the stove. Thinking I am leaving, his eyes widen.

"Adrian, would it be all right if I held your hand for a while?"

He nods, and I approach the bed. Standing beside him, I lay my hand atop his, the one without the IV. It's dry and chilly but not as icy as I'd imagined. His eyes above the mask gleam and almost glow as he continues to stare. Gently I squeeze, then release, keeping my hand on his. But for all the wires and IV, I would pull the curtain around us and ease into bed with him.

When he sighs, it emboldens me. Leaning forward, I place my face beside his on the pillow, and with my other hand palm his bony shoulder in a lying-down hug, careful not to put pressure on his thin chest. I'm still holding his hand, and when he squeezes my fingers with surprising strength, my mind fills with light. After five or so heartbeats, I pull back a little, pause, then brush his forehead with my lips. It is a kiss I would give a sleeping child. When I stand all the way back up, our eyes meet in agreement: we've said all we need to say, all that *can* be said.

Releasing his hand, I turn and leave. Closing the door to ICU, I know that I will be back tomorrow.

* * *

That night I dream that a balding monk in sackcloth (Friar Tuck?) is leading me through a deep forest, pointing, and saying, "Over there." I know he's pointing out my father's grave, but I see nothing except foliage. On and on we go. Finally, awakening in a sweat, I remember that little chapel in Pittsburgh, the assistant pastor there, and how I followed him into the sanctuary. Eyes dazzled, I couldn't see a thing as Garth took my hand and led me to the altar. When he knelt, I did too. The silence was palpable. The light was gone behind the stained-glass windows. I imagined the snow whirling outside, maybe even beginning to stick. When he spoke, I started.

"O God, hear our cry. With heavy heart, Thomas has come to your house. Give him the blessing he richly deserves as your suffering child—now."

When I thought I felt something touch my bald spot, I opened my eyes. Both of Garth's hands were locked in prayer position beneath his chin. For a moment I saw stars. A golden oval opened inside my mind, and I beheld a female face. Mim? But the features weren't Caucasian; it was Amanda Anthony. Her dark eyes drilled mine, passing judgment on a disappointing world.

Garth's voice filled the sanctuary.

"Raise us, Lord."

And though my arms and legs had become useless stones, I was lifted, weightless as a child.

* * *

And, like that, I resume my hospital ministry.

Mim spends long, silent periods downstairs, doing yoga and meditating, I assume, thinking up new recipes to fuel my inner furnace. While I freeze at the parsonage, my blood always warms at the hospital, where I find myself able to sit with anyone, whether speaking or in silence; Holy Marter or not; atheist or believer; man, woman, or child—and stay fully present.

People stop by the house, and though they stand awkwardly on the porch or in the entryway, they hardly ever come in and sit down. Sometimes they bring casseroles or cakes (the latter we eat, the others disappear, I hope to families that can use them). So far, my wife and I haven't so much as hugged, but I am willing to wait. Something is coming.

And I'm playing Dad's guitar. After my discharge, when I first saw the guitar case lying in the Caddy's back seat, I was furious that someone might've stolen it, that Murphy didn't take it with him (as I thought he, as spouse, should've done), that I'd have to deal with it, like giving some normal decedent's clothes to Goodwill. It took

Mim ten minutes to calm me down, and she finally had to put it in the trunk while I went for coffee. About fifty miles from home, with the Gibson safely hidden from my sight, I realized I'd seen it as a murder weapon, as dangerous as any Fury's razor. Only then was I able to face my insanity and let Dad's guitar revert to wood and steel, a very fine instrument, the piece of him I could save. (His ashes, safe in their urn for now, would soon fly.)

At odd times, I close the door to my study, take the thing out of its case as if it might crumble. Smells of beery back rooms, diesel-reeking buses, sweat-drenched sheets, nicotine, and whiskey rise from the sound hole stronger than a spray of roses, dizzying me for a moment. I cradle it, almost expecting it to hum or sigh, maybe even howl. I strum chords, feel the wood resonate against my chest as if the old box wants to talk. Within two days, I'm playing whole songs, his and mine, finding that it's like riding a bike. Once or twice I consider going to the attic and digging out my Fender or Gretsch, but I don't. The Gibson is fine.

On Christmas Eve, Mim goes out. Special service at the Dharma House, I figure. Ron's leading a candlelight service in Holy Mart's chapel, but I can't face those folks yet. After a while, I go into the study and start playing and singing. When I finally put Dad's axe to bed, I look at the clock, surprised to see it's after midnight. In the living room, Mim is lying on the couch reading, though I hadn't heard her come in. I lean against the doorway.

"Sounds great," she murmurs without looking up.

"Sometimes," I say, "I think about going back out."

Now she does look up, squinting to see me standing outside her small circle of lamplight. "Play live?" The squint becomes a frown. "Why?"

I shrug, though she probably can't see me. "For myself."

"Oh."

She returns to her page, and I turn away.

"Thom?"

I turn back.

"He'd be proud."

It gladdens me for a second. Then I remember the face Dad wore after throwing my harmonica out the bus window. Angry, but fearful too. I've claimed all my life that I never saw him show fear. My own fear canceled his out. Now I see: he was terrified I'd become him.

I go on up to bed and lie there staring at the ceiling with a thousand songs running through my head. And finally sleep.

* * *

The figure bending above me swabs sweat from my forehead. "Hush now," she croons, and I know I must've cried out. I hadn't tumbled drunk from a stage after all. A dream.

When she stands, a single shaft of light leaks between the shades, cutting across her naked chest. I fall back onto the raised pillows. Certain I am still dreaming, I keep my eyes open. I cannot move or speak to save my soul.

"Move over."

Though I weigh as much as several mountains, I manage to shift myself, imagining a puddle on the sheets where I lay trapped by my nightmare—both Judge and Dad were in it, though maybe they'd merged. My wife sits on the edge, then lifts her legs—bare too, I see in the streetlight's aura. Now she's stroking my stomach, light as breath.

"Mim, I— "

She puts her finger to my lips, and I smell her hair. Her finger grazes my chin, skims over my neck, and flutters through my chest hair. I relax a little—difficult since her hand is traveling still lower—and come to some semblance of consciousness at last. Her fingers reach the top of my boxers.

Six years. Heat rises in my chest, thickens like a warm salve, making my nipples taut. Inside the waistband, two fingers stroke the hair. Six years. I feel the flutter as I rouse from hibernation.

"I'm sorry for—" I begin.

Then her mouth is on mine, her breath hot as she lifts her lips, exhales lemon and vanilla, before locking on again, exploring my dry mouth with her tongue tip. My hands find her back; I mold the tightness of her shoulders, then let my fingers do their own tracery to her buttocks. Pulling back, she releases her breath in something like a moan, then straddles my thighs. While I grip each firm cheek, her hands are uncovering, freeing. Her face comes close as she kisses me again, this time lingering, her tongue probing mine in slow circles. Then, pulling back, she looks at me hard in the streetlight glow. I want to look away, close my eyes, but as the seconds pass, her gaze becomes easier to bear. My eyes fill, undam, and run down my face and neck.

I am like the deaf; I do not hear;
like the mute, who cannot speak.

Lifting her hands slowly, she lays her palms flat on my chest. An answering wave rises inside me, radiates. Closing my eyes at last, I see the neural pathways, little glowing interstates all though me, alive and thriving. Commerce, motion, speed, *life.* Then we dock. She begins moving above me on the bed, and my mind shuts off, a flipped switch, as when I sit beside someone's hospital bed. The warmth from my chest spreads south, heading for the gulf of me like a hurricane. I've begun moving with my wife, and her breath quickens.

CHAPTER TWENTY-ONE   265

Days, weeks fall away, years falling from my life. Why did I ever think God is only for the saved and not for the sinner? Why did I miss so many chances to tell my father *you can come home?* My god was small, my fear great.

The bed's afire. Flames sweep the curtains and drapes. In moments the whole house will be consumed. Opening my eyes, I see her eyes and face, lashes, open mouth, tiny scar on her right cheek. The light, white as dawn, opens, takes me, closes.

* * *

While our bodies cool and our breathing slows, I hear it—or rather, feel it enter me. I become totally alert, waiting. I can hear the grandfather clock downstairs ticking, the clicking of the furnace that, moments ago, shut off. I'm in that silent depth from which I arose in the hospital after I sought to kill with my bare hands. The clock keeps ticking, and I can almost see sharp sparks of coldness in the air. Laughter wells up. Is this what my father tried to teach me so long ago: be still and listen?

The giddiness dies in my chest, replaced by sorrow, a large bubble swelling against my lungs. When I make a sound, I imagine an infant in the dark, whimpering in its sleep. (Mim rolls over, undisturbed.)

And I watch particles shift and weave in the half light.

You'll try again.

Whose voice? I hush myself, and eventually, my eyes close on the grainy light-darkness.

* * *

It may be minutes or even hours later.

"I'll take the ring now, Thom."

Without hesitating, I reach beneath my pillow. Sitting up in bed, I see her rise to meet me. Eyes wide, she is heartbreakingly young, the girl I asked to marry me eleven years ago. It's only a little too large for her finger.

"I've heard Him," I say quietly.

"You prayed?"

"Listened, yes."

She waits. I fancy that I can hear the snow falling outside. Eyes closed, I'm seeing Adrian Baldridge, Garth Harmon, Dan Kress at the retreat, Emanuel beside my bed, Dad standing at the iron-grey cemetery. It takes every bit of faith I can muster to speak.

"I want to comfort men."

As I watch her face, her age returns, the webbing at her eye corners restored, the lines beside her mouth reappearing, the corners turned down.

"And I want us to try again."

Waiting for her answer is the longest moment of my life. "Not just for us, but—"

She places a finger on my lips, and my heart seizes. Reaching up, I take her hand and kiss the warm, smooth flesh. Then we sleep at last.

Chapter Twenty-Two

I watch my aging congregation pour into Fellowship Hall: the halt and the lame, the aging and the aged, male and female. Most are still in good enough shape to stand upright, but many are past their prime. Some look me full in the face, as if they're heard rumors of my death and are surprised to find me alive. Others avoid my eyes, slide sideways through the door, melting into the crowd. Many hover at the edge, afraid maybe that proximity to disgrace might cause collateral damage. So far, no deacons. Though I don't expect to see Kenneth Branch, I prepare myself just in case. Here it is, late January, and I haven't seen him since he delivered his ultimatum last month.

Some of the elders, like Mamie Crewes, have arms hooked around elbows of fifty-something offspring who find some reason to stay in a town that still stands despite the absence of an economy. Mamie's daughter Colleen answers my questions while her deaf mom smiles and nods. *Yes, yes, Charlie's fine since his surgery; no, no, Brooke won't be back from college till spring break.* Colleen hasn't been to church since last Easter. Amazing how pastors know these things. (I wince. *Former* pastor.)

Some deacons never forgave me for the failure to attract young families, and I can't blame them. "Without young people, you're dead," old Van Campbell, retired New Pres police chief, had said.

"Maybe we oughta just close up shop and let people stay home and watch TV preachers." I had counted my blessings that none of the other deacons agreed. Or maybe Van's death, during my first year, had killed his idea. It was no secret that Holy Mart, if it didn't attract young families with children, would have to face grim facts some-day soon. What they really needed was . . .

"Hey, Rev, you need a band?"

When I turn toward the voice, I almost don't recognize the young man standing before me in a smart, grey, pinstriped suit with blood-red tie, long blond hair swooped back on his high forehead. He's holding a hard-shell guitar case. Of course. He would play nothing less than a Martin.

"Patrick," I manage to get out, "you made it."

I grasp his shoulders hard. With great forbearance, I resist bury-ing my face in his neck and weeping for joy, so like the young Israel Jones he seems (except he's smiling like a happy third-grader).

"Wouldn't've missed this gig for the world. Where you want me to put my axe?"

I point to the podium at the front of the hall. Mim decorated it earlier with a mixture of twining greenery from pines in our back-yard and a single spray of roses. "I know it's not a funeral," she said when she saw my frown. "But roses seem right somehow." She waved her hand as if to explain. "Your father, he . . ." I hugged her. I don't understand, not rationally, but I know.

Patrick shields his eyes. "Holy Toledo, is that what I think it is?"

He's glimpsed Dad's Gibson, nakedly gleaming in the neon glare, every gash and scar visible. I grin and nod. I'm also notic-ing the stares Patrick is getting. Before the evening is over, he'll be basking in some female attention, if Holy Marters are not too dead to recognize a rock god in their midst.

Sensing someone at my elbow, I turn again and behold my first deacon, unsmiling, his hands clasped awkwardly before him.

"Henry," I say, grasping his hand and pumping for all I'm worth. When I finally let him go, I step back and see his eyes are wet.

"You won't reconsider?" he whispers, discreet as always. For a second I don't get it, until he pats his blazer, and I remember his placing in his inside pocket the letter I'd written the night before last.

So I do reconsider. And I am tempted to stay rooted here, to preach right into retirement, death even, earning my place in the Holy Martyrs Hall of Fame right there alongside my predecessors, iron men all. But Mim and I've decided that, after the memorial service Murphy's organizing in 'Frisco, after dispersing the ashes below the Golden Gate, we're going to Port Townsend, Washington, to help Mim's friend with her new spiritual center (I think fondly of Sacred Space and Garth), desperately in need of child care. Mim's eyes, when she told me, flashed passion for a moment before returning to neutral, but I'd glimpsed her still-kid-friendly soul. And where there are children, there are fathers. Maybe out west I'd find out what "comforting men" means. It is time to be led.

The only death worth dying is the one that makes you live. Dad's words—from "Arc of the Covenant"—carved into my cortex, burned into my bone.

"No, my friend," I say, squeezing Henry's shoulder, "I've got to go."

He stares at the floor until I remove my hand. Finally he looks up.

"I'm not sure how to phrase this, Thomas, so I'll just spit it out." He looks side to side to see if we're being overheard. "Do you need money . . . to get resettled?"

"No, thank you, Henry. God really does provide."

He nods. "Expect miracles, they say."

I hadn't, but just after New Year's, Mr. Arthur Pierce, Chicago attorney, called to inform me Dad left a will for the dispersal of nearly three million dollars. He named me executor, and although the list of inheritors is long, including many names I recognize, from drivers to roadies, to musicians and writers who kept him moving down the road, Mim and I are receiving the largest gift, enough to see us well into our new life. It was a shock to see he hadn't left Murphy a dime, but I thought I knew why. Dad begged his best friend to quit gambling—once, famously, on his knees in front of everyone on the bus (a story Murphy loved to tell)—but I suspect gambling is the one addiction he'll do till death. Dad finally accepted that, but like Moses's God, he giveth and taketh away. I've decided, however, Murphy will get his fair share. If he sticks with Conor and AA, he'll know what to do with it.

"Well." Henry clasps his hands before him.

The veil parts, and I see him for the surrogate father he's been—how could I not have known? Before I can reconsider, I grasp him in a bear hug, not quite getting my arms completely around his girth. And he's returning it.

Watching the gentlest man I've ever known walk away, clearly disappointed with my decision, is almost as hard as awakening to a world without my father in it. It makes me hark back to that day I wandered lost and blind in Pittsburgh, when, in retrospect, I should've seen all the puzzle pieces falling into place. I not only let my father's death happen; I wanted it. Because *he* so obviously wanted it. Now he's gone, and I miss him terribly. I'll forget he's dead for two, maybe three, minutes (say, during a shower, sex, or while reading), then, when it suddenly falls back on me, the weight staggers me like bags of sodden sand. The world's a lot more dangerous without him in it.

I find myself instinctively looking for Mim, although she said she wouldn't appear until later. As the room fills, I survey the swirling sea of my congregation in the neon glare. Later, when Mim arrives, the lighting will be muted, for we agreed *we'd* be in charge of things this time. What we've decided to do and say is too important to get lost in the mindless chitchat that plagues most potlucks.

No, we have nothing to lose tonight and much to gain. Mim's been inscrutable in her Italian Zen way, as if she might be concealing something from me. But that's all right; I have my own surprises. For now, I'm watching the food amass on the folding tables. Nothing stops Holy Marters from any opportunity to clog their arteries. Since the invitation in Sunday's bulletin (and announcement from the pulpit by Ron) said "a celebration of fathers," they've probably assumed this shindig is a wake for my dad. If so, they assume wrong.

Yes, the word is certainly out that the pastor had a very famous father. Maybe that's why some of the younger ones, like Sally White and Rosa Bragg, are here. Buddies since grade school and now in their late thirties and seemingly headed toward spinsterdom, both bank tellers at Miners & Merchants, they just smile when I speak to them (when they attend not only Easter and Christmas but an occasional Sunday here and there, not to exceed six or seven per year). No doubt they've heard the rumors about me and Joanna, about my strange father, and are here to get the scoop. Am I being unkind or simply honest? My heart lifts when Maxine arrives wearing a long fur coat that could've been her grandmother's. Without her glasses, she looks a lot younger, and I imagine her, at seventeen, shrieking "Piece of My Heart," cigarette in one hand, half-empty bottle of Southern Comfort in the other. Tonight she looks like she still might have a couple of choruses in her.

"I haven't seen you around your office, Reverend," she says, leaning toward me, as if we're conspiring.

"It's not mine anymore."

She wrinkles her nose and mouth in her smirky way that means *we know more than they do.* "Not what I heard. I hear they offered you the whole enchilada back." If she leans in any closer, we'll look married. "And I heard Dennis Strickland ate major crow, so Kenny Branch is looking for a new church."

I'm appalled. I say a quick, silent prayer that it's only gossip. As she brushes my cheek with a kiss, Maxine whispers, "Don't give an inch."

Little does she know I'm giving it *all.*

"Thanks for everything, Max."

She looks shocked. "Like what?"

"Damage control while I was on the road."

"Oh, *that.*" She bats it away. "Control is my middle name. As for damage," she giggles. "That used to be my first."

She squeezes my forearm and retreats, giving me up at last.

* * *

The feast lasts over an hour, and Fellowship Hall rings with the sound of voices, like Christmas and New Year rolled into one. Huddling at one end of a long paper-covered table with the two bank tellers and Henry Owens, I stuff myself with potato salad, lime Jell-O, fried chicken, and country fried steak, while contractor Wayne Tabor cracks us up with stories about bathroom remodeling projects gone wrong, critters in the attic, and septic tank debacles. The only thing that would make it better is Mim's presence, but my wife's doings are her own, and though we planned this event together, we never actually said we'd *be* together, at least not the whole time. I respect how much Mim hates the fishbowl, never more than eating in public, smiling till your face screams, and stuffing yourself till your stomach heaves. It isn't Mim's scene, but I hope she'll join me later for my swan song. When the roar dies down at last, she still isn't here. And Ron is talking . . .

"Israel Jones was many things to many people," he is saying, as if this were just another Wednesday night prayer meeting, as indeed maybe it is, even if it is a bitterly cold night in January. "Many Americans considered him the conscience of their generation, the man who asked hard questions of the rulers, though he denied such a designation always, even fled from it. To the generations that came after, he was—he hated this label even worse—a legend. He was both a rigorous sinner and fervent believer to the very end, a man who took the God of Moses and Saint Paul very seriously."

Ron folds his hands at his waist. "I didn't know Mr. Jones personally, but I've been in deep counsel with his son, Reverend Johnson, ever since his father's death. And I've conducted my own research, unbeknownst even to Thomas."

He let it hang in the air.

"I've listened to Mr. Jones's albums." Patrick, sitting across the table, emits a low whistle. Maxine laughs. "Well, a few of them. And I feel I've glimpsed the man's soul. I am most thankful for this opportunity not only to know this unusual man's heart, altered by disease though it was, but also to know my own better. For I believe Israel Jones gave himself to us the same way Jesus did."

I brace myself to hear a sharp intake of breath; I imagine my tablemates hissing behind their hands. Jesus versus a dead rock legend? *Heresy.* But although I listen hard for it—judgment, or at least disapproval—it doesn't come.

I'm enjoying the silence when I realize Ron is staring straight at me. A few heads turn. He must've called my name. After glancing once more toward the door, I rise. My legs are willow boughs, barely carrying my weight. The squeak of my soles on the tile sounds loud; the neon light is an eerie yellow haze. I stand before the ragtag group—wifeless, fatherless—without the rush of anger, alcohol, or ambition.

"Thanks, Ron, and thanks to all of you for coming." Taking a deep breath, I let my gaze rove unseeing. "Reverend Jenkins has told you about Israel Jones, but I want to tell you about Hugh Palmer Johnson."

The faces tipped up at me look a little stunned, except Maxine's. Head cocked to one side, the hint of a grin on her face, she is looking at me the way she often does when I am about to face the deacons. I decide she is my compass.

"My dad would be the first to say he ran out of luck around 1969, after that car accident when he tried to hole up and raise his family, only to be plagued by seekers. So he left home, left a wife and son behind to go back to the road and a life of performing. He had no way of knowing it'd be forever, that he'd become addicted to motion, to homelessness. And if his world had been small with his family under siege, it got even smaller on the road, consisting finally of a closet at the back of a bus, the three- or four-foot space behind a microphone, and an occasional room at the Days Inn."

I lick my lips, which have begun to stick to each other. Why am I doing this? But when I told Mim that I thought they deserved to know the truth about my father, she hadn't said no. When I glance at Max, she is nodding, eyes forward. All right. Israel's last Psalm.

"The legend became a monster, like Frankenstein, created thoughtlessly, then cast out to fend for himself." I stand up straighter, glance toward Dad's Gibson sitting on its stand several feet to the left, along with his Bible and boots. (I never saw the black coat again; I hope with all my heart that somebody burned it.)

"That lasted until Dad had his first heart attack. After that he decided to stand and take whatever God had to dish out. He said,

'I will stand in the fire till God smites me with his sword.' Even though my father sometimes thought that Moses had come off the mountain empty-handed, he believed destiny was unfolding, according to a plan." For a moment they all disappear, and I see red like sun through fabric. My knees weaken, but I do not fall. Things resettle. (Will Mim ever come?)

"Israel Jones's last stand wasn't between him and a cult of self-mutilators, and it certainly wasn't between him and me. It was between him and the God of Moses, the warrior-god he wanted to deliver him with a blazing brand." Sweat pours down my sides. "If he were conscious at the time, he would've seen the blade above him that day on the bus as homecoming at last. And he would've wanted us to see it that way as well."

I feel them settle back in their seats. "And coming home has come to mean something else . . . to me. I've decided I must decline your kind and generous offer to remain as your pastor. I've already delivered to the deacons my letter of resignation, effective immediately."

I stop and scan their faces, avoiding Henry and Maxine. At first, a wave of disappointment rises, but as the moment stretches, it becomes something else—a tingling up my legs, then burning from the gut upward into lungs and throat, primal and sweet, swelling heart, watering eyes, clearing my mind. Is this what people feel, what I've never felt till now, when they hear my father sing: sweet release?

Just when I am about to speak, the door on the opposite wall opens, letting in a sudden burst of cold. All eyes turn toward the interruption. Mim enters, wearing her long skirt with multicolored patches, sequins, and looping embroidery—her gypsy skirt from Morocco—and a long, fringed, teal shawl. If she is cold, she doesn't act like it, locking her eyes on mine as if only we two exist.

Looking neither right nor left, she walks to the first table, strikes a match, and lights the long taper she placed there earlier. Reaching behind me, I switch off the lights, plunging the room into shimmering shadow. We become Christians in the catacombs, communion observers, a darkened arena crowd awaiting an encore. *Is-reel. Is-reel.* The air tightens. Sally and Rosa stand and join my wife. Soon they are moving among the tables in silence, cupping their hands, lighting everyone's candle. Flames flicker with our breath. The only sounds besides the occasional cough are Mim's skirt swishing and the click of Sally's stiletto heels. At last Mim pads softly to my side, turning to face those who've watched her for so many years in the bowl. I clear my throat and dispel our collective enchantment.

"Upstaged as always by my lovely wife."

They laugh politely. Beside me, Mim whispers, "I want to speak." I can't believe it. But her eyes, her whole demeanor, is very calm. She's probably been meditating until only a few minutes ago. I step aside as she adjusts the mic's height. Not till then do I notice she is wearing Grandma's ring.

"As you know," she begins, "this is a celebration of fathers." She stands straighter. "For a short while, my husband was a father . . . and I was a mother." While we wait, the flames bravely hold back the darkness. "I've never thanked all of you publicly for all you tried to do for him, for us."

The flames sway. Not one eye blinks. My heart beats at a good clip, not too fast. Mim sags a bit, and though I go on alert, I remain where I am.

"I'm thanking you now for the help I mostly refused. I thought if I never accepted your help, I didn't have to accept my baby's death. I . . . I couldn't even say my daughter's name." She sags further, grasping the podium's sides, but before I can unglue myself from the floor, chairs squeal and two figures glide toward the front, standing on each side of my wife. Rosa and Sally, the two women I judged earlier.

"Her name was Catherine." Mim takes a breath, looks left, and when her eyes find mine, they burn with every hour she's borne it alone. Somehow I do not look away. Facing forward, she fills the room again with her voice.

"I had a baby girl, and she died. Now I know I've got to give her up to get her back."

They suffer the silence. Stepping back, she might've fallen, but the two women lace their arms through hers and lead her slowly back toward their table, heads high, bride and bridesmaids. I've never felt more married. And though I certainly am not ready, the final act has arrived.

Back behind the mic, I say, "I want to introduce a very special guest who's traveled a long way to be with us tonight."

Patrick is already rising, striding forward.

"Mr. Patrick Stiles was a loyal member of my father's band during his last days—as a matter of fact, the *most* loyal member. Although Dad's manager and the rest of his band deserted him for a while, Patrick never did." We shake hands before he turns to face them. "And Pat's agreed to help me sing my father home." Eyes lowered, Israel Jones's last, best apostle actually blushes.

When I sling the strap over my shoulder, time slows way down. Grasping the Gibson's worn-smooth neck, I feel a hum go through me, like holding a sleeping baby close. I've decided to give Patrick Dad's axe when this is over. He will shake his head, refuse for a moment, before he sees the wisdom. Now the stillness that too rarely arrives during sermons comes over me, and I find myself surrendering.

Catherine. For you.

Pat's Martin is out of the case, and he is quietly strumming. The Gibson answers; we are in tune, at least close enough.

"I'd thought I would play one of my father's songs." Patrick's blue eyes glint in the candle glow, the dimple in his chin way deep. My heart begins to jolt. They were all his sons, the boys who played beside him. "In a different life, I was a musician too—against Dad's better judgment. I see now that he did everything he could to keep me out of the biz. Anyway, this is one of the songs he wrote upon picking up the word. It's called 'My Father's Land.'"

Before my fingers can unlimber, Patrick strum-picks the intro Danny Kirtchner played on the record. When our eyes meet, there is nobody else in the room, and we're in that place that demands as total a commitment as the pulpit. Fingerpicking softly, Patrick waits for me to find my voice. Just as on any given Sunday, I open my mouth to see whether God will give me breath. He does. I sing:

> *When men revile me, hissing behind hands,*
> *When feet stumble and I tread desert lands . . .*
> *When I am left with dregs of days*
> *Ashes and blackness, burnt churches, blazing rage . . .*

I step back from the mic, drenched in sweat. I turn my head to find Patrick hovering at my elbow, strumming quietly, eyes closed. *My father, his father.* I've failed to see so many things, gotten so many wrong. Mouth as dry as ash, I go on, somehow make it to the chorus:

> *My father's land, so vicious with love,*
> *Runs knee-deep with martyrs' blood.*
> *It scourges men with searing blade.*
> *My father's land is the tender brush*
> *Of a babe's lash against bitter cheek.*
> *I will seek the one who never left me,*

Though Him I often sought to flee.
I will seize silver fingers,
And in my death be twice as blessed
As someone who sought only peace and rest.

At this point, Danny played a blistering solo on the record, but Patrick pursues a softer course, playing the melody high up the neck, swooping low for an answering bass lick, and I remember what Dad taught me about the dialogue between high and low, bass and treble, sky and ground. I back off, keep my rhythm solid, giving Patrick a place to stand. Closing his eyes he goes further, much further, flirting with notes not quite inside the scale, risking dissonance, mourning one moment, rejoicing the next, all the time moving his lips to repeat the things his strings are saying.

The room shrinks until only me, Patrick, and Mim are present. And one other. I see him out of the corner of my eye, coattails flapping as he struts and stalks. Young Israel, consumed by uncontainable energy that could only be expended onstage. Mom said that on early tours he was lucky to sleep ten hours in an entire week; she swore he never used drugs in those days, though no one in the press believed it. They are all here: Dad, God, and rock's holiest ghost, every soul in the room declaring the power and the glory, bathed in the blood. Beside me, Patrick whispers, "It's yours, Reverend."

My edifice crumbles. Shaking my head furiously, I take a step backward. My lead playing has always been confined to empty halls and practice rooms; I was always grateful to be able to strum a guitar, write, and sing, leaving the rest to my betters. But Dad's disciple glares at me with blazing eyes, *his* eyes. And though I plead—*I've given enough*—his face is relentless. I know what he and that shadow man want—*everything*. Then I remember what I carry inside my coat.

Reaching inside my jacket, I find the Lee Oskar, dull as a dirty dime till I polished it last night. I knock the harmonica hard against my palm, but it hasn't had any spit in it for a decade and a half. Patrick nods and smiles. When I lay eyes on my flock again, they've become a raucous, blue-jeaned arena crowd. The chant begins deep inside my head. *Is-ree-il. Is-ree-il.* So this is what it feels like to be wrapped in God's armor; this is what *he* felt, night after night. I smile, pitying them. Mim's grin is fierce. *Do it.*

I palm the harp, lift it to my lips, look to heaven, and begin to howl.

Reading & Discussion Questions

1. Snakes are important to many religious traditions. What significance do they seem to have to Israel Jones's life and worldview? Is it fitting or ironic that the novel begins in a snake-handling church?

2. Discuss Thom's possible motives for joining his father's Eternal Tour. Which do you think are the strongest? Do you think Thom himself might have trouble articulating exactly why he's going on the road with his father at this late date?

3. What else is Murphy Kelleher besides a manager to a complicated, stubborn musician? How has Murphy's relationship to Israel changed over the years? To Thom?

4. Both Israel and Thom have "complicated audiences." Are father and son more oppressed than gifted by those they serve? How much of a role do their "congregations" play in the creation and maintenance of each man's identity? Is Thom's life just as circumscribed as his father's?

5. Given Israel's shrunken life, mostly lived in the back of a bus, what seems to be the effect(s) of becoming a myth rather than a man? Using Israel's example, are there any benefits?

6. Who *is* Israel Jones, ultimately? Is he unhinged, even deranged; or sly and manipulative; artist or charlatan; sincerely spiritual or blasphemously cynical? Something else altogether?

7. Are the cutters who follow Israel simply bizarre, or do they offer a critique of American society in general, Christianity in particular? Can you compare them to other cults?

8. Discuss the meaning (and uses) of religion to Israel, to Thom and members of his congregation; to Mim; and to the cutters. What does the novel suggest about the state of religion and/or spirituality in contemporary America?

9. What happens to Thom at the men's retreat? How does it impact his journey, especially in light of subsequent events?

10. How does forgiveness, or lack thereof, impact these characters' lives? Why doesn't Thom do more to save, or at least protect, his father?

11. How do the allusions to classic literature—from Melville to Kafka to Psalms—affect your reading of the novel? Songs versus psalms: how do they compare or differ in Israel's and Thom's lives?

12. What do these characters' lives have to say about fatherhood? Consider not only Israel and Thom but also the relationship of therapist Dan Kress and manager Murphy Kelleher to their sons. What about father surrogate roles, such as Tony Romeo's, Patrick Stiles's and the cutters' relationship to Israel? Thom's relationship to Deacon Henry Owens?

13. What do you think of the novel's women, such as Thom's wife Mim, his mother Emily Sky, his secretary Maxine, Israel's mother, Amanda and Diamond Anthony, Joanna Strickland, and other female parishioners? Discuss similarities as well as differences in Thom's and Israel's relationships with women.

14. During the concluding "celebration of fathers," Thom says, "When I lay eyes on my flock again, they've become a raucous, blue-jeaned arena crowd . . . [and] I smile, pitying them." Why does Thom pity them and what does it say about the meaning of his journey, his life up to this point?

15. What else does music come to mean in this novel besides entertainment or even "universal language"? Do Israel's lyrics, woven throughout the book, "not mean anything," as Thom suggests—or do they provide insight into his character and/or the novel's events?

16. Besides being written by a native West Virginian, does the novel seem particularly Appalachian? How does setting influence the characters and events?

Acknowledgments

Writing a novel is for me a truly collaborative effort. Thus, I have many people to thank for both material and spiritual support.

First and foremost I'd like to thank my wife, Viki Church, for her passionate, positive response to my initial vision—and for reading and critiquing every draft.

Among the first readers of early drafts were members of my writing group at the time, who, while being extremely supportive, made excellent suggestions for improvement: Mark Thaman, Joe Downing, Teri Piatt, and Jeanne Estridge.

Huge kudos also go to later but no less insightful readers, including fellow author and West Virginian Kevin Stewart; old bandmate Freddy Modad; peacenik pal Fred Arment; and writing mentor and friend Bill Vernon, who, in thoughtful, *substantive* comments on almost every page, tried to get the absolute best out of me for the sake of the book.

Much gratitude goes to Myra Crawford and the judges of the annual Hackney Literary Award for an unpublished novel, sponsored by the Morris Hackney family of Birmingham, Alabama, who saw fit to award a draft of this novel first place in 2010. Winning the award kept alive my hope to find the perfect publisher. Also, many thanks to the *Birmingham Arts Journal*, which, subsequent to my winning the Hackney Award, published an excerpt of Chapter One in Volume 8, Issue 2.

Thank you, Hilary Attfield, Abby Freeland, Than Saffel, Jason Gosnell, and the entire staff at West Virginia University Press, for their professionalism and expertise on my behalf. Being published in my native state, at my alma mater, is a true homecoming and a great honor. And to Lee Abbott, who generously gave me the critique of a lifetime. You got it, Lee. Completely.

Any small musical knowledge I possess comes mostly from my days playing rock and roll with musicians whose enormous talents dwarf mine. Also, I read a lot of excellent rock biography and memoir, including Bob Dylan's *Chronicles: Volume One*; Paul Williams's *Bob Dylan, Performing Artist* (Early Years: 1960–1973, and The Middle Years: 1974–1986); Clinton Heylin's *Bob Dylan: Behind the Shades Revisited*; and Jimmy McDonough's *Shakey: Neil Young's Biography*, to name a few whose work immersed me in the world of rock's finest practitioners.

For medical expertise, I'm indebted to *Dr. Dean Ornish's Program for Reversing Heart Disease* and to my friend Eugene Ellis, longtime Duke Hospital nurse, who corrected a couple of medical lapses. Now I hope I've got my esophagus in the right place.

Namaste to my perennial spirit guides: Thomas Merton, Kathleen Norris, Henry David Thoreau, Wendell Berry, David of Psalms, and Jesus of the New Testament. Also, may the force forever be with Tom Verdon, Eric McLellan, and Ken Simon, whose transformative men's retreats of the early 1990s allowed us to blast through walls and build anew.

And finally, to all my fellow rockers from southern West Virginia, with whom I lost my innocence and found something like religion in the wild world of the 1960s and '70s: Keep on rockin'.

About the Author

Princeton, West Virginia, native Ed Davis taught writing and humanities courses at Sinclair Community College in Dayton, Ohio, for thirty-five years before retiring in 2011. He has also taught both fiction and poetry at the Antioch Writers' Workshop and is the author of the novels *I Was So Much Older Then* (Disc-Us Books, 2001) and *The Measure of Everything* (Plain View Press, 2005), four poetry chapbooks, and many published stories and poems in anthologies and journals. His full-length poetry collection *Time of the Light* was released in November 2013 from Main Street Rag Press.

Reborn after seeing the Beatles on *The Ed Sullivan Show* in 1964, Davis soon picked up a bass guitar and never looked back, playing with, first, The King's English, a mainly Rolling Stones cover band, later becoming lead singer and bassist for the Visions, a group specializing in the Ventures' guitar sound. His musical peak occurred in 1973, when he played with the Christian rock group Faith during spring break in Fort Lauderdale, Florida, after which he traded in his Hofner for a Martin D-35 acoustic and has been strumming in his living room ever since.

Today he lives with his wife and cats in the bucolic village of Yellow Springs, Ohio, where he bikes, hikes, volunteers with Tecumseh Land Trust, and blogs mainly on literary topics. Please visit him at www.davised.com.